CONTAINMENT

Timothy Todd
Ephesians 6:12

CONTAINMENT

The Beacon Trilogy
Book 1

Timothy Todd

TATE PUBLISHING
AND ENTERPRISES, LLC

Containment
Copyright © 2013 by Timothy Todd. All rights reserved.

No part of this publication may be reproduced, stored in a retrieval system or transmitted in any way by any means, electronic, mechanical, photocopy, recording or otherwise without the prior permission of the author except as provided by USA copyright law.

The opinions expressed by the author are not necessarily those of Tate Publishing, LLC.

Published by Tate Publishing & Enterprises, LLC
127 E. Trade Center Terrace | Mustang, Oklahoma 73064 USA
1.888.361.9473 | www.tatepublishing.com

Tate Publishing is committed to excellence in the publishing industry. The company reflects the philosophy established by the founders, based on Psalm 68:11,
"The Lord gave the word and great was the company of those who published it."

Book design copyright © 2013 by Tate Publishing, LLC. All rights reserved.
Cover design by Anne Gatillo
Interior design by Mary Jean Archival

Published in the United States of America
ISBN: 978-1-62854-139-7
Fiction / Science Fiction
13.10.18

ACKNOWLEDGEMENTS

I would like to first and foremost thank God. He is the inspiration behind this story and those I hope to follow. I am merely a pencil in the hand of the Creator. Next I am honored to thank my friends and family. They have stood by me and believed in me even on days when I lacked such courage and faith. I am humbled and grateful to have you in my life. By name I must mention Bonnie (my mom), Richard (my dad), Jeff, Jon and Ryan (my brothers). First among my friends I must thank my girlfriend Katie, you are very near and dear to my heart. Also I am delighted to thank my friends Chris and Ian. By each one of you I have been blessed. Finally, but in a position of great esteem, I thank everyone who takes the time to read this work. I hope you have as much fun reading it as I did writing it.

CONTENTS

Prelude 9
Odiria 15
Ribus 19
Valdria 29
Theban 39
The General 43
Cyra 52
Brunick 64
CJ Dreams 76
Impact 93
Fallout 99
Feldag Pouncers 102
Repose 107
The Task 113
Journey's Beginning 116
The Hollow 120
Drilgon Prairie 122
Dark Wood Lodge 129
Deserted Lands 135
Zykor 141
Serendipity 147
The Ship 153
Restorations 157

Darknov Purge Base	161
Phytis	168
The Mission	172
Contact	175
Flight from the EE-SP	183
The Search	188
The Place of Skulls	193
Temptation	198
Barren Lands of Bergda	204
Zxyers Mountain	210
Conflict over Gu	216
Resupply	219
Bomb	227
The Deepest Hollow	230
Leap of Faith	237
Devious Device	240
Dark Mind	243
In the Crater	255
Lexicon of Serendipity	259

PRELUDE

The deeper you cut, the sooner they die. This was the motto of Queen Odiria, the great and terrifying ruler of Toria Vilorious. It was the motto she used in her rise to power; many had been cut deep. She was feared by the multitudes, and her rule was challenged by a few. Her decenters were all paid off, or she paid someone to make them "disappear." One living in Toria Vilorious lived by her rules, or they didn't live at all. It was for this queen that Ribus was now risking his life. Ribus was one of the queen's most trusted and reliable *errand boys*. He was, first and foremost, an assassin that was a wizard with a sniper rifle, then a thug, gambler, gangster, and a lowlife of the city—a regular jack of all trades at all of these occupations learned by living the shady side. To succeed on his task meant a life of luxury, failure... well... that wasn't an option. He would sooner put his pistol in his mouth and rearrange his brains than try to explain his failure to the queen. It would save her the trouble of pulling the trigger herself.

Ribus flew around a corner in a luxury hovercraft with one of the queen's lackeys named Judka running the back machine gun turret. Forty rival thugs from the local Vilkra gang were hot on his trail and crammed into ten modified hover sleepers. The sleepers were sleek hover cars that levitated mere inches from the ground and contained four enraged gangsters apiece hanging out the side windows shooting at Ribus in his plush speeder. Ribus had long lost his shields on his car, and he was now in a tight spot.

In the front seat sat a precious cargo; not Ribus, nobody particularly cared that he lived, but rather they cared about the crystal he had just stolen from the Vilkra. As far as he knew, it was just an alien artifact that landed planet side three planetary rotations back; as far as the Vilkra knew, it could fetch a hefty price on the black market. Only the queen of Toria Vilorious suspected the actual purpose of the crystal, but she wouldn't tell anybody why she wanted it. All Ribus knew was that if he failed to retrieve the crystal as ordered, there wouldn't be enough of him left to do a DNA scan by the time the queen's brutes finished with him.

He banked sideways around a sharp corner leading to a back alley and gunned the motor in effort to lose the Vilkra, who boiled with rage at having lost their prize. The side of the craft sparked against the buildings in the underworld of the city. All the buildings were built close together to allow maximum population in minimal space. One of the sleepers attempted to follow but didn't quite make the corner; the wrecked vehicle got wedged in the alleyway. The crashed, smoldering sleeper prevented any other sleepers from following that way, but they would soon find another way around. In any case, it gave Ribus time to think. *Yes of course!* thought Ribus, *Industrial Way!*

It was a large freeway with busy traffic even at that late hour, and it was the perfect place to lose the gangsters that hounded him.

Ribus soon rounded another corner and slipped onto the large, sublevel highway. A bullet passed through the side window and punctured the front glass announcing that the other nine sleepers had picked his trail back up. More bullets perforated his hover vehicle. Ribus heard Judka yell in pain as one such bullet nicked his brow. Judka returned fire with enraged fervency. The fresh barrage of bullets launched by Ribus's coconspirator ripped into one of the sleepers. The Vilkra craft pulled sideways as the dead driver slumped on the steer stick. The vehicle, with no living occupants, swerved into an oncoming gas tanker. It exploded upon impact, and the tanker immediately followed suit. A huge fireball spewed forth from the crash destroying three other sleepers. *Five down, five to go*, Ribus thought.

The Vilkra returned fire. Blood spattered the windshield in front of Ribus as the queen's lackey took a shot to the right shoulder. Ribus could hear Judka sharply suck in his breath in pain. Judka, with the use of only half his body, tried to continue to use the gun he was stationed on, but a disheartening click told him that it was out of ammo. He wasn't going to give up so easily though. Judka still had a few options available; he grabbed an explosive charge that was attached to his belt and primed it. He dropped the charge onto the roadway as Ribus weaved in and out of traffic. The first charge bounced in an odd way and exploded near a bus of workers returning home from the graveyard shift. The bus swayed as the front hover apparatuses disintegrated, the vehicle then slid to a halt while the sleepers skirted by. The second charge Judka threw bounced high off the road and went through the glass of a pedestrian vehicle. The explosion gutted the car and sent debris from the vehicle spraying down the rain drenched highway.

Judka muttered under his breath, "Third time's a charm," as he primed his last charge, and this time, threw it at the closest sleeper. The charge missed the first three cars, but it hit the front of the forth and detonated. The sleeper that was hit rapidly lost velocity, and the other sleeper behind it collided with the smoldering Vilkra vessel. "Two birds with one stone!" Judka exclaimed to Ribus. "I got…" Judka didn't finish his last thought because a bullet to the brain cut him short. Judka's lifeless form slouched forward and fell out of the back of Ribus's sleeper. His lifeless corpse tumbled down the busy freeway like a rag doll. This terrible event only earned a shrug from Ribus who had never been too impressed with Judka.

The other Vilkra were not messing around. They had just seen seven crafts full of their fellows get disabled or dismembered, and the night was growing long. Now, it was time to wrap things up. The bullets they were firing now were aimed with ever-increasing precision. Ribus ducked low in his seat as bullets ripped through his car. The shots shattered the front windshield. Rain streamed into his face and blurred his vision. Ribus knew an off-ramp was nearby. Light from oncoming traffic mixed with the water in his eyes made it even more difficult to see, but when he saw what looked to be a sign pointing to the off ramp, Ribus cut across the other lane of traffic, barely missing an oncoming industrial hovertrain. More sparks sprayed off the front corner of the, once, plush craft as he scrapped a guard rail, but he made it to a part of the city that had police drones.

The three sleepers tried to follow, two were successful in making the ramp, but the third was wiped out in a burst of debris as a hover train careened through it. Ribus cruised down a main artery, dodging traffic as he traveled down the sidewalk, but occasionally, he took out a bystander. He looked to the pistol he had on his hip and thought if he could actually take out eight gangsters in a firefight. He frowned, one assassin versus eight didn't figure well when the math was done. A warning light flashed on the dash—his back engine was out. He didn't need the light to tell him though, the sound of the back portion of the craft scrapping on the ground was a sure fire sign Ribus's life was about to get worse, or end altogether.

His craft pulled sideways in the street in a shower of sparks, and an oncoming car clipped his front end, causing his craft to roll over and over in the street. Ribus was thrown out the already shattered front glass and landed in a nearby trash heap. The two remaining sleepers slowed to a halt, and eight Vilkra got out of their sleek, black mobiles. The gun-toting mobsters looked even more insidious in the pale, red lights of their vehicles. The streets emptied of any pedestrians, anybody out at that late hour retreated into a nearby pub to avoid what came next. One of the gang members stooped to the ground and picked up the crystal that Ribus had endured so much to get.

It must have been thrown from the car in the wreck! Ribus thought. He swore under his breath. The eight gangsters peppered the car they imagined Ribus to be in with gunfire to make sure he was dead. They then approached. They didn't know he wasn't in it, but soon they would. Ribus began to debate whether Trilumina, the rumored God of Ephesia, was a myth or not. If Trilumina was real, Ribus tried to guess if he would hear a petition from a sinner like Ribus. He figured it couldn't hurt to ask for some help, and so Ribus muttered a prayer for assistance in his perilous position: "I definitely don't deserve any mercy from you, oh mighty Trilumina, but now is as good a time as any for some divine intervention."

A gangster stooped to look into the overturned car. The man yelled some profanity and stood up. He told the other gangsters to look around, but they never got the chance.

"Freeze!" a robotic voice ordered. From Ribus's vantage point in the trash heap, he breathed a sigh of relief. Four police drones had made it to the scene. "Police" was a loose term; they were more robotic enforcers of the queen's will. There were factories on the planet of Solbia that produced police drones, but there were no prisons, in other words—if one did something that was severe enough to attract a drone's attention, it was severe enough to kill the perpetrator.

Rather than freezing, the gangsters opened fire on the drones; the gangsters knew how the system worked. One of the bots dropped instantly in the gunfire, but the other three opened fire with Gatling laser cannons. The gangsters took cover behind whatever they could, but it was to little or no avail. A brief firefight ensued, but the gangsters, one sleeper, and three of the four drones ended up scraped by the conclusion of it. Ribus limped out of the trash heap. He walked toward the gangster that had picked up the crystal, but he found, to his dismay, that the remaining bot had just placed the dark blue, quartz-like crystal into an internal vault that only the queen and her people had access to. Ribus swore once again as the object of his mission disappeared into the darkness of the vault. The drone then spoke to Ribus in a drear, mechanical tone: "The queen needs to talk to you."

"I am not Ribus. The person you are looking for ran down that alleyway!" Ribus exclaimed in response. He knew what came next: the bot would examine his face to gauge whether Ribus was telling the truth. The drone stepped closer and began scanning to confirm Ribus's claim. As it began cross-referencing Ribus's face against the known people archives of Toria, Ribus, with wicked speed, drew his pistol and blasted the drone in the face. It dropped to the ground with a loud clank in a heap of metal. Ribus didn't even try the vault in the drone's chest; he knew that it no longer mattered. The queen had dubbed this night a failure, and Ribus was to be held responsible. He quickly grabbed some weapons and ammo from the dead gangsters and climbed into the remaining Vilkra sleeper. Ribus then drove into the night. He had to escape the city—he was now a fugitive of the queen.

ODIRIA

Queen Odiria moodily stormed into her chambers and sat down at her plush wood desk. Her desk, which overlooked the city of Toria Vilorious, was situated in the tallest tower in the city, which naturally Odiria took for herself at the end of her rise to power. The tower was called Delduna, but most of the citizens called it "Cursed." In her ascension to the throne, a lot of blood, sweat, and tears had been put into her campaign (mainly blood), but naturally, none of these fluids stemmed from her. The blood, gallons of blood, came from those she used to get to her position of power and from those who opposed her terrible crusade. Her story was the regular tale of the underdog with a twist. She started out as a prostitute scrapping dirt at the bottom of the slums of Toria Vilorious, but she had advantages: freakish attractiveness and an eerily enchanting charisma. She could influence and manipulate people through her sensuality as though they had no free will of their own. She had wavy, silky, long, black hair complemented by a perfect face—these facets coupled with the body of a goddess and an uncanny knowledge of people's weaknesses allowed her to bend people to her will by promising them their wildest dreams. Often, all they inherited was sorrow when her hollow promises dissolved like sand slipping through one's fingers. Once she manipulated people to the zenith of their potential, she then eliminated them. Her philosophy was simple: dead people don't talk. At the age of eighteen, she was a prostitute; at the age of twenty-one, she was married to a royal who was running for the position of king of Toria Vilorious. When he was mysteriously and indeed, unanimously elected… …he then disappeared, and Toria Vilorious had a new queen. Any successors to the kingship also vanished without a trace, or suddenly became exceedingly wealthy and dropped from the running. For years, this trend had continued, and by the time, the police in the city got scent of all that was foul in the upper workings, the police department was dissolved by order of the queen and replaced by the queen's loyal and conscienceless drones.

For years, the queen's rule was uncontested, and her dictatorship seemed as though it would last as long as she did. As long as nobody complained, the already high body count following her tyrannical itinerary would not rise. Her rule had gone unchallenged for years now, but circumstances had changed recently with the arrival of a Purge fleet in the Solbian system. The Purge didn't appreciate dictators, and they had the firepower to tell Odiria that she would be fair, or she would be dead. This put her out of sorts and thus explained why she sat at her desk with rage festering in her breast.

Odiria rested her pistol on the solid wood of the desk and eyed her advisors coolly. Under her gaze, they straightened up and sharply drew in breath. The look on her face and the fact that she had her high-caliber weapon placed for all to see was testament that they needed to give a good advice, or she would end them.

"The Purge has set up a small base on the skirts of the region of Toria… They don't appreciate the way I run my city, but they have enough weaponry to force my resignation… Have I ever been forced to do anything before?" she asked of her advisers.

"No, my queen," they said in unison.

"What am I to do then? I refuse to resign, but I refuse to die at their hands. How can I live through my refusals?" she asked.

"Why did they come?" one of the advisors inquired. He was a counselor that was fresh to the council due to the fact he was filling the place of the last consultant that had displeased Odiria. He was an elderly gentleman that was wise and, fortunately, had what could be called some favor with the queen. In other words, he hadn't given reason for her to dislike him. The consultant was fresh, but knew that if they didn't venture a solution, she would grow angry. When she grew angry, the results weren't good for the advisors.

"My sources say that an alien artifact landed on the outskirts of the city. The Purge tracked it here. It seems to be some sort of beacon. They want to destroy the device because it is rumored to be a harbinger of death. Why do you ask? Does this have anything to do with my current circumstance?" the queen eyed the gentleman suspiciously. He looked down from her gaze.

"Perhaps they fear the origin of the device?" he queried.

"…it would seem they have a certain disdain for the creatures that made it, yes… What are you getting at?" she had good intuition and could tell that his guidance was levelheaded.

"If they fear them, they must have a reason. Perhaps the aliens are more powerful than the Purge. Perhaps they aren't aliens at all, but rather it is from a human faction with a superior army to that of the Purge. If this is true," the gentleman said as he stroked his beard, "maybe we could get the said device and summon the potential allies," he replied.

"What is to say they will strike a bargain with us at all?" another advisor interjected. Odiria picked up the pistol and put a third eye in the forehead of the advisor.

"Don't interrupt!" she gently said as the body fell to the floor. "He had a good point though." She gestured to the corpse. "…what is to say they will strike a bargain with me?" she asked of the elderly gentleman that had ventured the idea of joining with the foreigners.

"What is to say they *won't* ally with one of such wealth as you? It would certainly expand their bank account if they took care of the Purge for you. Even if they aren't friendly, the Purge would surely rush to fight them, and once the victorious faction had been weakened from the fight, you could finish whatever side won in their debilitated state," he shrugged innocently.

"That's evil, conniving, and twisted! It's exactly my style! Excellent, we shall retrieve the artifact and summon our army," she smiled smoothly. She then turned to one of her top officials and told him to get somebody to remove the body of the deceased advisor and to give Ribus the mission of getting the artifact wherever it may be.

The councilors were then dismissed. Before the gentleman who suggested the plan left, the queen held up her hand: "Sir, may I know the name of my wise councilor?"

The elderly gentleman with a wizened face turned and replied: "Saezyn."

"Thank you for your insight, Saezyn," she smiled mischievously.

"Don't thank me until you get my bill," he grinned and walked from the palace. His mission was complete, if all went according to plan, the queen's reign would be at an end very soon. Saezyn walked down the hall until he was out of earshot and whispered: "The soul that sins shall surely die, and you, oh queen, have sinned a lot."

RIBUS

Ribus hadn't slept much in the past two weeks and had long ditched the sleeper he had stolen from the Vilkra. He had spent the last few days avoiding the queen's drones. Also, anybody that looked like they had connections with the Vilkra—he avoided like the plague. The only difference was the plague didn't kill anywhere near as quickly as the enemies he had made lately. He had to get out of the city of Toria soon and go to the edge of the world, or a different world altogether. In the sublevels of the city, he had a price placed on his head big enough to buy a city block, and in the main city, no price was placed on his head, but any drones that saw him would shoot him on sight. During the day, he traveled from building to building via skyways (glass bridges between buildings), but at night, he hid in obscure corners and disguised himself as a homeless vagrant. This coupled with the fact that he hadn't shaved in a while allowed him to pass mere feet away from Vilkra gangsters unnoticed.

On the far side of the city, there was a sky-bus platform for refugees leaving the city. A sky-bus was exactly what it sounded like: a large flying transport for people that wanted a cheap method of travel. The sky-bus platform with the most lax security was past the impoverished part of Toria Vilorious, known by all as the "Old City." It was where Toria originally began and was really called Toria Bondervous, but everybody just called it the Old City. The center of commerce had since migrated from where Toria began, and now, this part of the city was on the fringe of the newer portion of the bustling metropolis. The Old City was not a nice place; they were the slums of the slums. In other words, Ribus, in his current bum attire, would fit in perfectly. This thought comforted him, but he was weary of the other fact that he knew about the Old City. In his shady line of work, rumor had reached him that a large branch of the Vilkra gang resided in the Old City. Doubtlessly, they used the abandoned skyscrapers and cheap rent to grow "crops," manufacture weapons, and in general, add to their long list of moral offences. It was easy for them to do these activities in the old city where the queen cared little for the occupants, and her drones seldom patrolled.

Ribus stopped in front of a half-open, rusty gate in the middle of the night. Dull, flickering lights above the street revealed the lock that used to hold it fast was long dismantled. It could be spied broken on the ground in a small pile of garbage nearby. This gate marked the divider between the thriving parts of the city from the Old City. Ribus hesitated as he thought of what lay on the other side, but he quickly ducked behind a pile of refuse as he saw lights round a nearby corner. From his refuge, he saw a sleeper approach. The craft stopped in front of the gate, and a Vilkra thug got out of the sleeper. The man toting a high-powered laser rifle opened the gate. It drew back slowly with an eerie creak and allowed his fellow gangsters passage. The sleeper glided through leaving the man behind to guard the gate.

Ribus saw all of this from his hiding place and under his breath, cursed his luck when he saw that the Vilkra member was left. Ribus needed to go through, and he had long discarded his guns because sensors placed intermittently throughout the city would go off upon detecting his armaments and thus, draw unwanted attention. For a while, the man stood with his hands brandishing his lethal weapon in an intimidating pose, but he soon grew bored at the lacking eventfulness of the twilight and soon reached in his pocket to pull a pipe. The thug dressed in a leather trench slung his weapon over his shoulder and fiddled with a laser lighter. After a few unsuccessful attempts, the pipe lit, and the man puffed on it until it glowed gently in the low light and illuminated the stern face of the criminal.

Ribus sat in his secret place, waiting for his chance to eliminate the guard, but little was happening. He even debated just sleeping in the trash heap and moving to another gate tomorrow, but as Ribus toyed with these thoughts, the necessary distraction occurred. About a dozen Purge military vessels roared over where Ribus slumped in the trash. The guard looked up at them as well. They were flying into the heart of Toria. A short while later, explosions coming from a midair conflict between the Purge ships and the queen's drone shuttles caused the guard to momentarily abandon his post as he tried to get a better view of the action. He chuckled as he saw several of the police drones get blown from the sky, but the snicker was the last air that passed his lips. For as he abandoned his post, Ribus saw that the Vilkra had walked past his hiding place and indeed had his back to Ribus. He did not hesitate to sneak behind the thug and snap his neck as casually as he would button a shirt.

After Ribus finished hiding the body in trash and swapping clothes with the Vilkra, he took one last glance at where the explosions had originated from. Fires from ships that had crashed in the city could be seen as distant blotches of red in the night-darkened city scape, but no sound of conflict could be heard. *The queen's drones must have stopped whatever the Purge's quest was*, thought Ribus. He then primed the laser rifle and walked into the Old City.

He walked for a few minutes past the decaying city buildings and sporadic hobos who shied away from Ribus in his borrowed gangster attire. He pulled the trench coat tighter about him as rain poured forth from the leaden skies. Occasionally, Ribus would pass another Vilkra who he would greet with a head nod, but otherwise, nobody bothered with him or even acknowledged his presence. It was five miles to the other side of the Old City where the sky-bus platform lay. Ribus thought he may have a good shot of making it disguised as a Vilkra.

Half through the city, he wandered near to what was, by far, the tallest building in the Old City: the Biogen building. The 130-story building, once, was a place used to grow replacement organs for the sick, but now, it was used for a different kind of biology. It was used to grow Spikeradon, known in the streets as the "thorns of Ordam" (TO for short). The extract from this flammable plant would give people a great high, but it often became horrendously addictive and life-threatening. Ribus had had close friends that had been murdered at the hands of this drug. They were murdered because part of the Vilkra advertising program for their product was to give hapless bystanders "free samples" of the drug by injecting it in them against their will. The result was the people would sell *all* that they had to feed the addiction they couldn't kick. A slight odor of the drug hung in the air that told that the rumors of the drug operation Ribus had heard were indeed true. The building had in recent times been retrofitted with pipes that dispensed toxic gases from the drug manufacturing facility. Ribus walked inconspicuously in front of the glass doors of the otherwise surprisingly plush building. If not for the pipes, it would have looked like a rose in a pile of manure; all around the Biogen, the other buildings had broken out glass, and all the lights were out, but the Biogen building stood in pristine condition with full power. Drug money allowed for certain luxuries, no doubt. As Ribus passed, a Vilkra thug guarding the door whistled and motioned for Ribus to come near. Ribus did as he was bidden.

"Hey, you!" the thug exclaimed. "Don't you know we have a shipment tonight?"

"Yes, of course," Ribus replied. I was just clearing my head of the stink of the TO."

"You're new here, aren't you?" the thug chuckled.

"You could say that," Ribus replied.

"Yet you look oddly familiar…" the thug stared harder at Ribus's face.

"No doubt it was when I was here last shipment," Ribus said calmly. Inside, his heart raced. If he was found out, he would surely have to fight against impossible odds for his life.

"Must be, you better suck it up and get back to work, or the boss man will use your rigor mortis corpse as a stir stick for the gook they concoct in there," the thug replied and motioned over his shoulder at the entrance of the Biogen building.

"Bosses these days! They think they know everything!" Ribus exclaimed.

"Ain't that the truth!" the man replied as Ribus walked through the sleek glass doors of the Biogen building.

Ribus soon found his way to the first basement floor of the skyscraper. A large machine with a pipe that rose out of the center was producing phials of what Ribus knew to be TO in narcotic form. These phials came out on a conveyor belt and dropped into boxes. Several tables also stood nearby that had some serious weaponry placed on it for the Vilkra to use in case the queen's drones tried to impede their goals. Threescore of Vilkra thugs were gearing up with weapons and taking crates of these small flasks and putting them into the trunks of the sleepers waiting to go out. They were going to "hit the town" tonight, which meant several dozen hapless souls were going to against their will be injected with that which would ruin their life. Fueling the addiction would cost them their money, their friends, their job and eventually—their life when they overdosed or got killed in the cruel withdraws. Ribus examined the machine: the large pipe ran up through the ceiling near the central elevator shaft. From where he stood, he couldn't know for sure, but Ribus had a strong suspicion the pipe went to every floor in the building.

What Ribus did know is that the pipe was full of the TO, which was highly flammable.

As he thought of what this terrible substance would do to the populace of Toria Vilorious, and what it had done to those he knew… suddenly, escaping the Old City wasn't priority—but rather bringing this accursed facility down and dishing out long overdue retribution for his lost friends.

"Are you just going to stand there?! We need a driver for a shipment. The man scheduled to be here must have wandered off, so you will have to do," a thug grunted.

"Of course… Let me gear up. I feel naked without a good pistol at my side or rather two good pistols at my side." Ribus smiled sinisterly as he put his rifle down and picked up two beautiful, short-barreled, silenced assassin's pistols. He quickly strapped them on and got into the sleeper with three other criminals equipped with rifles. He pushed forward on the steer stick and silently floated up a ramp out of the underground garage.

"Where to?" Ribus asked.

"Upper city, our goal is to get some upper-class addicted. They have more money to fuel the addiction," the thug in the passenger seat grinned morbidly.

Ribus, after driving a few blocks, soon went around a corner to a secluded alleyway. He slowed to a halt and got out of the car.

"Why are we stopping?" one of the thugs yelled.

"Keep your guns holstered boys! I just gotta empty my clip, if you know what I mean." Ribus gave a wink and turned around like he was going to go take a leak.

"Seriously! What do you think you're doing? We got a job to do! I'm going to report you to the boss for this!" exclaimed the Vilkra in the passenger seat.

Ribus turned unexpectedly with only one gun drawn, and before any of the thugs could get their guns up to meet him, a bullet had pierced each of the three thugs' skulls in the *dead* center of their foreheads.

"You can make your report to the boss in the Abyss when he meets you there," Ribus muttered darkly. He then went into the car and programmed the navigation to drive the drug-laden sleeper into the large machine in the basement of the Biogen building. The craft stole silently out of the alleyway and cruised to its final destination. Ribus walked calmly out of the alley and counted down the time in his head until showtime. As the count was nearing zero, he heard yells echoing down the empty streets coming from the Biogen building, and then, a loud explosion that shook the ground and rattled the glass panels of the surrounding buildings. Ribus turned to see the explosion run up the Biogen building as the pipe in the middle exploded. The fire that blew out from the building level by level started in the basement and raced its way to the top. The firestorm consumed the giant, gutting floor after floor with rapid efficiency. Shattered glass and flaming debris that spewed out from the building in all directions rained from the night sky. A gentle grin passed over Ribus's lips—his friends had been avenged.

He walked quietly for the next few minutes and slipped into the crowds of people that had congregated to watch the building burn. Among the bystanders, a local biker gang had ventured out of their pub to spectate. An eerie sound quickened Ribus's pace: the building's supports were melting in the heat. Ribus looked over his shoulder and saw that the building was tilting in his direction!

Ribus took a quick glance at his surroundings and realized his only chance of a rapid escape was to hijack one of the biker gang's hover bikes. They were sleek, elongated crafts that had open sides; however, they did possess a roof that aerodynamically encompassed where the rider would lay in a forward position on the swift craft. Under normal circumstances, he wouldn't dream in his worst nightmares to take a biker gang's bike—it was suicide. The gang, specifically in this case, the Zykor Dragons, would very slowly fillet Ribus alive when they caught him. There was no if about it. They loved their grudges as much as they loved their bikes, so they would not stop until they had found the thief. These thoughts passed through his mind's eye, especially the skinning alive part, in a nanosecond, but the increasing sound of strain in the burning skeleton of the Biogen building had a better argument. With everybody looking at the precariously, tilting remnants of the Biogen building, Ribus mounted a beautiful, blue Zykor bike and gunned the throttle. The gyrator in the front engine spun momentarily until the turbine motor belched out hot fumes, and the bike rocketed down the street. He could barely hear enraged Zykors swearing over the noise of the engine. He soon faintly heard the sound of other bikes rumbling on. In his rearview mirror, Ribus saw the headlights of seven other bikes pursuing. He pulled one of his pistols with his right hand while he kept his left hand on the accelerator. Ribus fired at his pursuers. To his delight, he observed two of the craft veer suddenly and crash into nearby buildings. One craft exploded and took a third Zykor with it.

Ribus turned back from watching the destruction his volley had caused just in time to see a building blocking his path. He veered for the glass store front of the building and rampaged through the abandoned habitation, leaving in his wake, fragmented glass and strewn wreckage. Soon, his four remaining pursuers followed suit and came out of the building in a spray of shattered glass.

"Why does this always happen to me? This is the second time this month…" Ribus muttered under his breath. Flashes in his rearview mirror caused him to look up. The flashes he observed were gunshots from his pursuers. They loved their bikes, but they would rather destroy one of their own vehicles than let somebody get away in one. Fortunately, most of the shots went wide or ricocheted off the body of Ribus's bike. Luck of an unusual kind was on Ribus's side despite the incoming fire. In the mirror, he observed that the Biogen building in its fire-gutted state had lost its fight against gravity and began to fall perfectly in line with

Ribus and those who hunted him. He waited until the last possible second and veered down a side alleyway. By the time the noise of the falling building was louder than the biker engines, the Zykor in pursuit realized their peril, and it was too late for all but one of them. The remaining bikers finally realized that the Biogen was almost literally right on top of them and tried to branch down alleys, but the burning building crushed them quickly and painlessly. The only pursuer left scarcely cleared the top of the falling building and would have been able to continue hunting Ribus, but a piece of debris clipped her bike and immobilized it. Her craft slowed to a halt, but its rider was in one piece. The Zykor biker babe outfitted in leather clothes that accented her figure nicely (but not sleazily) stepped out of her smoldering bike.

"I'll get you!!! I swear it! You are mine!" she yelled over the sound of burning buildings and falling wreckage. The red glow of destruction in the backdrop of her as she hollered these words made her look all the more menacing. She fired one shot after the thief, but he was out of range. She then slung her semi-automatic shotgun that fired explosive rounds over her shoulder and set off in the general direction of the one who stole her bike.

Ribus, of course, saw or heard none of this. He was long gone into the night. He wasn't far from the sky-bus platform. He ditched the bike a half mile from his destination and walked the rest of the way. He soon arrived at the station and began to climb the steps that led to his one chance at not being avenged by all those he had wronged in the last few days. It was slightly run-down with smudged glass and garbage littering the first floors, but it looked better than the rest of Old City. He looked at the schedule when he reached the main platform and saw that the next sky-bus wouldn't reach the platform for another two hours. He bought a ticket from an electronic booth and slid the cardstock ticket into his trench coat pocket. There was nothing to do but wait. Ribus sat on a bench that had its back to the wall and checked both his pistols. The criminal fed a fresh clip into each of them, and upon hearing the satisfying click of the weapons' bolts sliding back, Ribus relaxed only slightly where he sat.

The assassin sat in the glass-walled station, passing the minutes by watching, as little by little, the station filled up with a small crowd of people. It surprised him that so many wanted out of the city at that time of night. A gleam of light out over top of Toria made him think perhaps it was closer to morning than he had originally thought. It resembled a sunrise, but upon a quick glance at his watch, Ribus realized something was wrong. Orgasoli wouldn't shine down upon Toria Vilorious for another four hours! The sky was burning! Ribus watched in wonder as the flames spread across the sky. He soon realized that the reason for the inflamed sky was that dozens of large ships were entering the atmosphere. Ribus stared in horror as the ships began to fire sinister bolts of purple-black energy down upon the city. Buildings began to catch fire. He saw hundreds of ships flying toward the enemy threat. Ribus realized the mass of ships were the queen's drone shuttles racing toward the hostile vessels. They too were being hit by the alien force. Odd, dark-bluish-colored pods rained down from the large ships suddenly and covered the city.

Ribus, not knowing what was going on or what else to do, decided to stick with his first plan: wait for the sky-bus and escape the city. He now only had a half hour until it arrived at the station. The battle progressed, and more people began to flood into the station. As he contemplated the situation, a woman who was clearly a Zykor biker sat down next to him. The crowds of people must have masked her presence until it was too late to dodge her. Her leather clothes and an obviously modified shotgun were testaments to her occupation. Ribus soon realized an alien invasion might be the least of his worries.

VALDRIA

Valdria sat back in a booth of a run-down bar called Pilfering Pete's in the middle of the Old City. It was the haunt of the local Zykor Dragon biker gang. The Zykor had the motto of "ride fast and shoot faster." All Zykor were constantly armed with highly illegal weapons to the point that even Vilkra thought twice before messing with them. Valdria sloppily took a gulp at her beer and slammed it down roughly on the tabletop. She interrupted her swig to add to a poorly told joke that a biker named Steter had just missed the punch line. He had had too many to drink, but nobody cared. Steter would talk a lot and slaughter jokes when he was sloshed and that, combined with his stuttering, was often more funny than the jokes themselves. His nickname was Stutter—in honor of his occasional stammer brought on by his inebriation.

"No, it was. What's the difference between a Vilkra and a bucket of dirt?" she corrected.

"What is the difference!" another biker yelled out joyously.

Several joined in answering the often-told joke: "The Bucket!!!" Then a loud laughing ensued, and another round of drinks were called for. The Zykor had no love for the Vilkra. Before another joke could be told, a loud explosion echoed throughout Old City. The windows shook, and someone dropped their beer which shattered upon impact with the burgundy tile floor.

"What was that?" Valdria asked with a startled look on her face.

"Sorry, I just burped," Stutter slurred.

Several of the Zykor laughed at his joke and his garbled speech.

"That's the funniest thing you've said all night, Stutter," Valdria replied, and she clapped him on the back.

The bikers weren't staying in the bar to continue telling jokes though; they were migrating into the streets to see what caused such a blast. Valdria helped to support Stutter as they walked out of Pilfering Pete's double-hinged doors to join the crowd of people who had flocked. Half of a smoldering Vilkra sleeper was buried in the side of a nearby building. Burning debris and shattered glass fell from the sky and littered the streets, but as soon as one spied the devastated Biogen skyscraper, the shards were forgotten. The crowd stared on in awe. Nobody rushed to help or see if anybody had survived the blast; they knew it was the Vilkra HQ. Several bikers and people who shared the Zykor's disdain for the Vilkra yelled above the roar of the fire and falling ruination: "It's about time somebody burned those wretches out of house and home!"

Valdria stood in silence. Like most people in the city, she had known somebody or known of somebody who had fallen to the vile schemes of the Vilkra, but she wasn't the type to glory excessively at the misfortunes of the sinister gang. She simply smiled and watched the burning fruits of their labor.

"I've seen enough, I'm going to…" Valdria turned around as soon as she heard the very distinct sound of her hover bike. It had just turned on, and she wasn't anywhere near her metallic steed. The twin gyro engine blared for a second before her bike took off into the night. It was her life's work—painted ghost blue with phantom flames streaming off of a skull. A very uncouth word flew out of Valdria's mouth, and in a second, she had mounted Steter's dark red bike and took up pursuit. Steter's bike was painted with a flaming Pyrian falcon covering the body of the vehicle. The headlights of the bike were the fiery eyes of the lethal bird. Six other Zykors revved on their bikes as well and joined the chase.

Valdria, by drifting out of the line of fire, scarcely dodged shots coming from the thief, but several of her fellow bikers weren't so lucky. She looked back and saw one of the bikes behind her had fire streaming out of the front engine compartment. In the second backward glance, she saw another bike crash and explode. The fireball that radiated from the explosion disabled the nearest bike which skidded to a halt in a shower of sparks. The rider rolled off of the bike and failed to get up again. Valdria lamented the fate of her gang members, but she knew that they would want her to catch the person responsible. Vengeance: that was the Zykor way.

Valdria followed her prey through a long-abandoned building. She tucked her arms close to her so that she didn't catch herself on any of the sporadic crates or chairs that lingered in the condemned, decrepit structure. She struck an empty crate with the front of her bike, the box, in turn, exploded into splinters and chunks of wood. Soon, Valdria, leading the vengeful posse, emerged on the other side.

"Enough of this!" Valdria exclaimed as she unslung her weapon from her shoulder with a skillful shrug. All Zykor had a weapon that they favored; Valdria's specialty was a semi-automatic shotgun that fired explosive shots. She opened fire, but most of her rounds went wide. Not enough of the munitions were impacting with the stolen bike to disable it. Broken glass from the back window was all the award she was granted for her efforts. The other members also opened fire only to see similar results.

Movement in the corner of Valdria's eye, and an odd rushing noise caught her attention. She looked at her rear view mirror to see the shocking sight of the burning frame of the Biogen falling rapidly on her position. She veered quickly and merely dodged the top needle of the building, but debris that burst out from the impact of the building's descent peppered the bike she rode. Valdria quickly slowed to halt; the readings on her power gauge suddenly fell through the floor. She quickly dismounted the bike to look and to see what was wrong. Upon brief evaluation, it was apparent the bike was finished: molting metal shards from the building had burned into the craft's engine compartment. The bike was now scrap metal. She turned in time to see the fiend responsible fleeing down a side alley.

"I'll get you!!! I swear it! You are mine!" she yelled after the retreating thief over the sound of burning buildings and falling wreckage. In anger, she futilely fired her shotgun one last time after the antagonist before turning to look behind her for any trace of her fellow gang members… none. They were dead… all of them. Behind her she could see where Fourth Avenue and Pilfering Pete's used to be—now, it looked like hell. All that stayed too long to watch the building burn surely were crushed when its burned-out mass crashed to the ground. Her biker family was among those destroyed; a hot tear slid down her cheek. She quickly wiped the tear away; grieving had to wait until retribution was served in full.

Valdria, who had cunning instincts, imagined the mostly likely place the perpetrator would go in effort to escape Toria Vilorious would be the sky-bus platform. Upon this thought, she slung back her weapon of choice and set off on foot following the main street through Old City. This street led almost directly to the platform. Her mission was to fulfill the way of the Zykor.

Vengeance.

An hour later, Valdria's already lousy night was about to get worse. She was over three-quarters of the way to the platform when she noticed a different color in the monochromatic shadows in the metropolis's night scape. The color came from the entrance of an abandoned alleyway off the main street. Gleaming, blue paint on an unidentified object shined in the dull glow of a street light. The object was situated beyond a dumpster. Upon closer look, Valdria, to her pleasure, realized it was her bike. She promptly mounted and began to cruise toward the station. She was not on her bullet-perforated but still beautiful craft two minutes when a drone shuttle came out of nowhere. Over a loud speaker, the drone pilot issued some ludicrous order resembling "Stop," which Valdria promptly ignored. Instead of stopping, and most definitely getting shot for possession of an illegal weapon, she veered into an abandoned warehouse for cover. She quickly hid behind some crates and turned off the engine. Out of a half-broken window, she spied the drone craft that was shaped much like the torso of a dragonfly. It was a versatile vehicle that usually flew with one drone occupant as a pilot and occasionally, a cargo hold full of ten more. The drone shuttle, also called a drone descender, was equipped with Gatling laser cannons and missiles, but the reason for their moniker is that a portion of the back would split into six sections and become legs. Once descenders landed, they became six-legged mech walkers.

Valdria hoped it would get bored and leave when she didn't surface, but tonight, luck of a different kind favored her. She saw the craft land in the warehouse and deploy its six metallic limbs. The main cockpit elevated into the position of a head on the Mech and the laser cannons that were mounted as the Mech's arms swiveled throughout the room searching for a target. The lethal armaments moved like antennas scanning for information. Escape with the descender in the confines of the warehouse was almost impossible, the Gatling guns had an extremely high yield when they strafed. Valdria saw only one solution to her predicament. She revved the engine of her craft, jammed the throttle to floor and let the riderless hover bike fly at the Mech. Lasers perforated her bike, but momentum carried it to the desired destination. The wrecked bike hit the descender and knocked half the legs out from underneath the drone vehicle, causing it to fall sideways. The Mech collapsed to the ground in a loud cacophony.

Valdria quickly ran around the craft being sure to steer clear of its line of fire. Upon skirting the downed foe, she walked over to the cockpit and fired her shotgun twice: first, the glass; second, the drone pilot. With the Mech defunct and the pilot's head in more pieces than an expert jigsaw puzzle, Valdria continued walking to the sky-bus platform.

※

When she made it to the platform, it was moderately busy much to her frustration. The hustle and bustle of the late hour would make finding the culprit difficult. She quickly reached the climax of the stairs and momentarily leant against a pillar to catch her breath. Since the action in the warehouse, Valdria was without any form of rapid transportation and was marginally winded from her multi-mile trek through the bowels of Old City. Her brow perspired ever so slightly. She quickly regained her composure; upon doing so, she noticed a group of five no-goods in a dimly lit part of the station. The gang eyed her lecherously. They were a gang of long misguided youths on the cusp of a dismal adulthood. The *men* slowly began to drift toward her, weaving in and out of the occasional passerby. She could tell by the wild look in their eyes that they were tripping on Spikeradon. When they got close enough to see the whites of her eyes, she unslung her shotgun and leveled it with the lead member's head. The intoxicated fools turned on their heels and ran out of the station. The wisest move they had made in their silly, little lives.

A murmur passed through the station. Valdria thought it was because of her threat towards the druggies, but she soon realized it was for a different reason. The people in the room were looking out of the weather-dulled glass ceiling of the sky-bus stop. The reason was clear: a large force of alien warships had arrived and was bombarding the city. The queen's drones were vainly retaliating. Whoever the enemy was, their technology was far superior. Navy-black pods were soon ejected from the large alien carriers. These pods fell upon the city in a gloomy deluge. Passengers in the station stared intensely with mouths open at this sudden shock; any prior plans were forgotten in the face of the cruel onslaught. Valdria could understand their astonishment, but she soon diverted her gaze, this attack on the city made her business more pressing. She knew not how long she had to live, but she was determined that she would make sure that the fiend that stole her bike would pay before she passed on. Alien forces would not deny her her quarry.

Valdria searched among the citizens who watched the sky like it was the opening night for a long-awaited movie. None of them seemed like they stole her bike, and she had no way to tell for sure even if one of them had. Maybe vengeance wasn't possible after all.

The fool might have gone to another location altogether, she thought to herself as she walked through the people and looked them over. The more time passed in her search, the harder it got because as the battle raged over the city, more people began to flood into the sky-bus station. The tone was one of panic or silent awe. Valdria was getting peeved at her apparent lack of success; the stressful aura wasn't helping either. She was about to yell in rage above the tension thick din of the room when she spotted an anomaly: a man that appeared calm.

She soon sat down next to the one person who seemed relaxed in the face of approaching oblivion. He was dressed in a leather trench coat, complemented with dark skin, dark hair, handsome face, and a few-day-old beard, and he seemed to possess an inscrutable self-assuredness. He startled only slightly when she sat next to him.

"It's going to the Abyss out there…" he stated detachedly.

"It is… why don't you seem to care?" Valdria replied. She was trying to read this guy. Perhaps he was the one who jacked her bike, but he was a tough read.

"Perhaps, I think this city deserves to go to the Abyss…" He turned and looked her in the eyes. They stared for a moment; measuring one another. He continued: "Most of it anyway."

"Do you deserve to?" she gave a slight grin.

"More than most… I think I have finally gotten tired of it… I need to get away," he grinned at first but finished his sentiment with a tired frown.

"May I know your name?" she asked.

"I guess it doesn't matter anymore. See that wanted holo-display panel over on that pillar?" He pointed to a screen that showed a wanted picture of a man named Ribus.

"Yes."

"I'm Ribus. I had a bit of a debacle with the Vilkra, and they want me dead. Are you going to turn me in?" he grinned.

"It depends," she smirked back. She was only toying with him; she was not in a frame to smile genuinely. The only emotion in her heart was hate.

"May I know your name?" Ribus asked.

"Valdria," she replied. Her voice had a fierce edge to it.

"Fire and ice…" Ribus muttered more to himself than to Valdria.

"What?" she probed.

"Oh… just my first impression of you: fire and ice. You look like a woman of passion, but also, you look like you are a cool mistress… somebody not to cross," he explained.

"Do you seek to flatter or deride me?" she smiled slightly. It was a more genuine smile than before.

"Neither. Both flattery or derision may provoke you. If my assumption of your profession is correct, then both may be fatal mistakes."

"What is my profession?" she asked.

"By your weapon, your clothes, and that tattoo of the dragon crushing a skull in its jaws on your neck, I would presume you are a Zykor dragon," he replied observantly.

"You have a good ability to measure people. What of you? What did you do before you fell out with the Vilkra?" She still couldn't see past his wall.

"I was an assassin before I stole an alien artifact from the Vilkra…" He paused for a moment and stared out the window. He looked as though a lightbulb had turned on in his head. It was the first glimpse Valdria had over his wall—Ribus had an idea why the city was being attacked. "The Vilkra didn't appreciate that, maybe the aliens didn't like it either…" he said and finished in a mutter.

"Why did you steal it?" she asked hoping to get a better feel for him.

"My! Aren't you curious? Perhaps we should take turns with the questions?" he countered.

"Okay, fine, shoot."

"Are you taking the next shuttle out of the city?"

"I am," she replied.

"Why not ride your bike out of the city? I hear that a Zykor's enamor for their bikes is legendary…" he enquired.

She paused before she responded, "…engine trouble. My turn… Did you hear that the Biogen building was destroyed tonight?" She hoped to get him to admit to being near to the building. If he slipped and made that information known, she could, perhaps, trick him into revealing more information or slipping in another way.

"I heard that Spikeradon is rather flammable" was his reply. It revealed nothing. Valdria swore inside. Ribus always seemed to be one step ahead of her, but in her gut, she suspected that he was the one she was searching for, but he continually knew what to say to feign innocence.

"How did the building get destroyed?" he asked.

"Fire, but you already knew that…" She looked at him suspiciously. His previous sentence basically revealed he knew it caught fire.

"Did I?" he replied.

"It's my turn to ask the question! How did you know the building went up in an inferno?" She tightened her grip on her shotgun.

"I didn't say I knew how it was destroyed… I just suspected an accident with the harvesting equipment. A fire mixed with the "thorns of Ordam" would cause a big mess real fast. You seem on edge, is there something on your mind?" he asked calmly. His placid response diffused Valdria to some extent. It at least bought Ribus more time on the countdown.

"Somebody stole my bike tonight and killed some of my fellow gang members... I suspect it was you... All your answers are evasive which makes me suspect you all the more... My question for you now is if you were the son of dirt that did such an idiotic thing, would you own to it if asked directly, or would you lie like the pond scum I suspect you to be?"

Ribus kept his cool and stroked his short beard before he responded: "If I did do it and admitted the deed you would surely scatter my brains across the station with your boom stick there, but if I didn't and said 'no,' you would still probably kill me because you already suspect me of the misdeed. My question for you is how could I convince you of my innocence if indeed I am?"

She studied him for a second before she replied with a question: "Answer me this, how come you have paint flecks the same color as my bike in your hair?"

The com pronounced that the sky-bus was docking, but the announcement wasn't necessary due to the sound of the large craft roaring overhead proclaiming its presence.

After the sound of the sky-bus had subsided, he replied, "Is that the best you can do? Of course I don't have blue flecks in my hair! Even an amateur would clean themselves after..." He stopped. She had done it. He had slipped and said the previously non-stated color of the bike. They both knew it. She grinned and began to raise her shotgun, but he was faster. He drew one of his pistols in the speed of a blink and shot the weapon out of her hand. The shotgun clattered across the tile floor, and Ribus disappeared into the now huge crowd of terror-stricken people shoving to get aboard the enormous, multilevel Sky-bus.

THEBAN

The drones belonging to the queen broke down the door of Theban's workshop. They pushed him (none to gently) onto a shuttle craft and took him to the queen. He didn't bother putting up a fight; he was one of a rare breed of people that took no pleasure in destruction but rather delighted in building and restoring anything and everything. Theban was a bear of a man: short and covered in hair except on his head and outfitted with a welding visor that he never took off. He also possessed advanced tools that were constantly on his person. Overalls that smelt of metal shards and oil covered his round belly. He was muscular from long days and nights of work. Though short in stature, he had an intense face that could unnerve those who didn't know his warm nature. The drones took him to Delduna tower in the middle of the city. He soon found himself in Queen Odiria's high-ceilinged, gaudy chambers. She swiveled on her chair the moment he was escorted in. She looked down at him from where she sat behind her desk.

"Theban! Good to see you," she exclaimed warmly. Of course, she was putting on a show—she wasn't a kind person.

"I wish I could say the same," he whispered under his breath. "Oh, my queen, how may I be of service?" he said loud enough for her to hear.

"Your skill as a craftsman is renowned, and I have admired the work you have done for me before. I find your masterpieces to be excellent. Once more, I have a project for you," she replied.

"I will be glad to build it, but why have I been removed from my shop?" He didn't even feign that he was happy about his abduction. Fortunately, when one is as skilled as Theban was, one could get annoyed at the queen without being blasted in the head.

"It is a secret project. I need you to build it here. All you need will be supplied at your word," she replied.

"Fair enough… What is it I need to build?"

That conversation took place two weeks ago. Theban was currently putting the final touches on the project he had been given: an amplifier. The night he was captured, a strange crystal was also brought in. He was tasked with building an amplifier that would broadcast the odd energy pulses that stemmed from the crystal. Though he was finishing up the device tonight, it had been successfully transmitting since last week. He was currently just making it look more attractive to gaze at. Its ascetical appeal was necessary because the queen insisted on having the device built into her chambers.

Theban wouldn't be released until the queen was done with him, so until then, he was a prisoner in the most plush containment facility on Solbia. It was nice, but any place where one is held against their will is still a prison no matter how luxurious. He preferred the metallic smell of his shop that had varying alloys littering the shelves, and metal shavings coating the floor like thick dust. Oh, how he missed that place… his place. Theban eyed the door: two guards with high-powered rifles prevented escape. The guards were as tough as bricks and as quick as the tip of a whip. Theban sighed and polished a piece of metal for the tenth time. He was waiting for the queen to check over his work and allow his release; somehow, he knew she would "forget." In the shiny pewter, Theban caught an odd glint coming from behind him, which he turned to see. He looked out the large window of the room at the night sky. Sporadic explosions from rockets and muzzle flashes of heavy machine guns were soon apparent. Theban used his modified welding visor to zoom in. He could faintly make out a task force of several military craft streaking towards Delduna tower. He had recently heard rumor that the Purge had established a military base on Solbia a few weeks ago, so he presumed these craft to be theirs. He hoped they would make it and maybe, overthrow the queen, but they were meeting heavy flak supplied by drone shuttles. The Purge craft tore through the drone resistance like tissue paper, but occasionally, a Purge infiltrator would drop after sustaining incredible damage and crash into the city below. There were only half a dozen incoming vessels present when Theban realized they were coming up on the tower, and they were coming fast.

Theban took cover behind an oversized couch made from the crimson silver hide of a very rare sheep called Creeb. The guards at the door identified the oncoming craft and rushed to defensive positions in the room, in case things got messy. They did. Bullets peppered into the room and took out one guard. Following the barrage of munitions, a precisely aimed rocket flared through the night sky and in a spray of glass, streaked into the room. The rocket hit the amplifier and blew it, along with a good deal of the room, to bits. The concussion from the blast tore through the place with breathtaking force that momentarily caused static to flash across the digital display of Theban's welding visor. A moment later, other rockets splashed into the building with preplanned precision. In the shock of the moment, Theban was glued to where he hid behind the couch. This terror that froze him where he crouched may have been what saved his life, for as he ducked, the remaining guard in the room shot a well-aimed barrage at the starboard engine on one of the approaching Purge craft. The bullets found their mark, and the engine burst into flames. The craft in that moment lost all control and began spinning in a ghastly circle. In an instant, the Purge infiltrator bashed out the remaining glass of the huge window in the queen's chambers and slid across the floor. It screeched to a halt in a corner of the room.

Theban peeked over the couch; the Purge ship had barely missed where he cowered. Upon a cautious inspection of the war-torn room, he realized that both guards were dead. One had been shot so many times that he mirrored a bucket full of holes, and most of his innards weren't in anymore. The other guard was hit by the ship that crashed in the room, and his condition wasn't much better than his fellow.

Upon seeing this, Theban knew he was free to go as he pleased, provided he could get out of the building. If he got caught, he might not live too long… Before Theban could concoct a slapdash plan, a metal upon metal scrapping noise disrupted his thoughts. It came from behind him…

THE GENERAL

"What!!!???" Drask exclaimed. General Drask was one of the most skilled and loyal Paladins in the entire Purge. He would be higher in ranking in the Purge core, but his devotion to duty and his love of the fight kept him in positions he could see the action. Usually, he loved being on the front, but today, he wasn't so sure. He was placed in the Darknov region on Solbia to monitor potential Armada activity, but his sensor outpost was under-equipped to take on any serious foes. If he saw any action, Drask would most likely have to retreat, and that was not his style. His bald head turned to face the corporal at the control panel that had just addressed him. The General, as he was called by all, stared relentlessly at the corporal who was all too familiar with the unyielding gaze. The young, muscular jock of a private named Baatric was fresh out of base camp and was barely twenty. He continued his readings from the terminal were he sat.

"The sensors in the quadrant west of the Mussolbia Nebula are picking up Armada energy signatures. It's likely the signal coming from the Delduna tower caught their attention," Baatric replied. The young man didn't like doing terminal work; he joined the Purge to shoot stuff. His obsession for guns was so great that most of his fellow soldiers called him "Trigger."

"How dumb can they be!" The General exclaimed. It was more of a statement than a question. "Don't they know the Defected

Armada is pure evil?! If that signal stays on, the Armada will be all over Solbia and its capital Toria Vilorious in no time!"

"Is there anything we can do about it?" Linia asked. She specialized as a field nurse and spent her recreational time as a racing pilot. She preferred to renew life as opposed to fighting, but if needed, she could lay down some gunfire along with the best. Linia was tall, blonde, and beautiful inside and out. Her heart was for helping those in need, and she was well-respected for it.

"Of course, we can," the General replied. He softened his tone because only few people had the heart or lack thereof to yell anything at Linia.

"What we gonna do, General? Are we gonna get to finally shoot some stuff on this drear world?" Trigger asked. His face lit up. He had been doing menial tasks on this base positioned on the fringe of Toria Vilorious for weeks now, but it seemed years for the young green horn.

"Yes, we finally are… Send a report of our findings to the Purge. Request permission for an operation to take out the signal originating from Delduna tower and request a fleet in case all that can go wrong does go wrong," Drask ordered. His command was greeted with a swift salute and smile from Trigger.

"What's the word from the commander?" Linia yelled over the roar coming from the engines of the Purge infiltrator that she sat in. An infiltrator was a multipurpose Purge craft not unlike a helicopter in layout, but it had turbines instead of a prop.

"As you know, we have orders to take out the amplifier. The commander of the Purge has also given word that a fleet will be joining us in a few hours to defend the world of Solbia from the Armada," the General replied.

"Pah!! We can take em' solo, General, me an' you!" Trigger exclaimed from where he sat behind a heavy turret.

"I like your spunk soldier, but when you have seen the Armada for your first time, you will be glad for the backup! We aren't going up against them though, well, at least not yet. Let's hope that we take out the amplifier before they come to the city," the General replied. He was positioned at the turret opposite Trigger. Linia sat between them in the crew carrying partition of the vessel with a rifle in her hands.

"Pilot, how long until we reach the city?" General Drask asked as he watched the faint outline of farmsteads drift by below them in still serenity.

"ETA, two minutes, General," the pilot replied over the com from the cockpit.

The General looked over his task force one last time as their destination loomed: eleven other Purge infiltrators flew with them in a phalanx formation. Each infiltrator had one pilot, two gunners, and a spare Paladin just in case. If all went well, they would destroy the amplifier before the queen deployed her defenses. They weren't that lucky though. The pilot interrupted the General's thoughts to say, "We're going in hot! Get ready for some heavy flak!"

Both the General and Trigger cocked the heavy machine gun turrets they were stationed at and began to focus on hitting any bogey that presented itself. The long shape of an enemy shuttle that was comparable to a dragonfly's thorax soon presented itself.

"Going loud!" Trigger yelled above the engines as he pulled the trigger on the machine gun and unloaded incendiary rounds into the target. The hot, white shells of infiltrators cut into the drone shuttles and quickly ripped them into flaming pieces. The large smithereens of decimated craft dropped from the sky and fell into the dim cityscape below. The shuttles exchanged rounds with twin, rapid-fire Gatling laser cannons making for an intense firefight. If the Purge infiltrators were not better armored on the front, they surely would have had a tough time breaking the ranks of the enemy shuttles. The queen also had heavy turrets placed on some of the taller buildings as well, which made the Purge's perilous mission into the heart of the city extra spicy.

The Purge was outnumbered three to one, and the flak was heavy, but doubtlessly, the queen's drones were not ready for the Purge. Drask and his force hit fast and hard… so fast that few of the ubiquitously scattered lasers found the hulls of the infiltrators, but every now and then, a Purge craft that had sustained terrible amounts of damage would drop from the phalanx formation and crash or make an emergency landing in the city below.

"Deploy rockets!" the General ordered over the roar of his machine gun.

Purge missiles with enemy-tracking technology locked onto the drone craft and blew them into oblivion. As for the many drones the Purge destroyed, there always seemed to be another to take its place, and now, the enemy was flanking from behind. A nearby Purge craft took too much damage and tore to pieces violently as its systems overloaded. Fragments from the ally craft clanked off the hull of Drask's infiltrator as it flew through the plume of debris. The lights on in the Delduna tower before them acted as a beacon guiding them to their destination.

"We are almost to the Delduna tower… We need to make it to the amplifier! Trigger, cover our backs!" the General ordered.

"My pleasure!" Trigger responded. He gave a wink to Linia who had an obvious look of concern on her face as she braced against the explosions of the occasional flack impacts. He then swiveled the gun on its tripod mount as he rammed the bolt back to prime a fresh belt of ammo. He was now facing behind the craft and had a clear shot at the drones following after them. In the Solbian night, Trigger could see the luminescent glow of the cockpits and engines of the drone vehicles. Obviously, he aimed his gun at these weak places. Trigger laughed gleefully when he saw that he had split open the head of one of the drone pilots of a nearby shuttle, it tore into the upper levels of a nearby building with very little damage otherwise sustained. It was one of the seldom few vessels that took little damage because upon the targeting of the next vessel, Trigger learned that if the engines were hit, the drone crafts would explode in a rather large boom, so he changed his targeting strategy. Under his vigilant gunmanship, the flanking drones were forced to back away or be slaughtered quickly and efficiently.

"Do you have the amplifier signal homed in?" the General asked.

"Nearly there… yes! Just got it! Shall I fire?" replied the pilot.

"Fire now!!" cried the General as he peppered the room containing the amplifier. His volley took out a guard he saw running through the room.

The pilot flipped a switch, and a single rocket streaked ahead of Drask's infiltrator and broke through the glass of the Delduna skyscraper that now towered intimidatingly above them. The missile belched forth a fiery explosion that cast shattered glass out of the wrecked room into the otherwise still night.

"Signal is down, mission successful!" the pilot exclaimed.

"Let's go home!" Linia gasped thankfully.

An unnervingly near explosion shook the craft. "I'm afraid, sweet miss, that that won't be possible, we just lost engine two," the General replied. He was clutching his hand over his forehead to a freshly received wound from shrapnel that blew out of the devastated engine two.

"Brace yourselves!!! We're going down!!" the pilot announced.

The infiltrator began to lose altitude as it went down in a sickening circle. It slammed into what little glass was left in the room that once contained the amplifier. The craft screeched to a halt and smoldered next to the pile of debris it had snowplowed when it ripped through the chamber. They had landed.

"Is everyone ok?" Linia managed through a gasp of dusty air.

"I'm fine," Trigger coughed.

"General?" Linia asked.

"I'm alright, a little banged up, but I've been worse," he replied. It was true; there were few generals in the Purge core that hadn't been wounded severely. A gash to the forehead was little more than a paper cut in comparison to some of the General's previous wounds.

"What about the pilot?" Trigger asked.

Linia peered over the seat in the cockpit and held her hand to the man's neck to check for a pulse.

She turned back and frowned. "Nothing."

"Too bad, he was a good man, a good pilot… He saved our lives by landing where he did. He took the oath of the Purge and meant it… he would be proud to go this way," the General said. The oath of the Purge was "I vow to live right, fight forever, protect the innocent, and give all that I have for the good of the Purge." The pilot fulfilled it to the letter.

Linia soon saw to the General's wounded forehead with her medical expertise. The cut from the shrapnel was superficial, and a bandage soaked in a cleansing and healing agent was quickly and skillfully applied to his wound.

"Let's get outta here!" Trigger said with enthusiasm. As soon as everyone had their weapons ready, Trigger tried the door. The side door of the craft screeched as its bent metal form scrapped in its track, but with some effort, it opened enough for the Paladins to vacate the craft.

"Trigger, you take point, Linia and I will take up the rear. Our goal is to get to…" the General trailed off the second he saw a bald, round man wearing a visor come out from behind a pile of rubble. The General leveled his rifle with the man's head just in case he wasn't as innocent as he appeared. The man held up his hands in surrender.

"Don't shoot! I'm on your side!" the man cried nervously.

"Identify and explain yourself!" the General ordered. He lowered his weapon until it pointed at the floor.

"I'm Theban. I was taken captive by the queen to build the amplifier...I...was hoping you could help me escape...." Theban finished in a mutter.

"It could be a trick!" Trigger expressed with a hint of disdain.

"No, he is an honest man. I can tell by his face (at least what I can see of it). He is probably one of the few decent people in this city, and if I am right, he could be a great asset. I have been on this world for a short time, but rumors of Theban's skill with tools are the stuff of legends," the General replied. He turned to Theban. "You can come with us as long as you do what we say and know that if you doing anything funny, I will put two eyes in the back of your head faster than you can say 'oops,' okay?"

"Absolutely! Thank you so much, and I won't do anything to cross you!" Theban said with tremendous gratitude.

"What's the plan, General?" Linia asked.

"First, get out of the building and then get out of the city. Are you familiar with the layout of this building, Theban?"

"Yeah, the best way out is to go up to the roof... there is a bay where shuttles are docked. The bottom floors are full of security guards and drones," he replied.

"How can we get to the top floor?" Linia asked.

"Elevator?" Theban suggested.

"How do we know he isn't leading us to a trap?" Trigger exclaimed exasperatedly.

"You have a lot to learn about judging a person's nature, Trigger. Shut your face! That is an order," the General replied to Trigger's paranoia. "Theban, where are the elevators?"

"Just outside those doors, they are likely to be guarded, so be careful," he replied.

The General motioned for the small group to follow Trigger out of the room. Quickly and stealthily, they skirted to the door exiting the room, which they silently opened. Trigger looked both ways.

"All clear," he whispered.

The group jogged to the elevator doors a few yards away. Theban tried the door. Nothing happened.

"It's in lockdown," Theban whispered. Trigger muttered an unprofessional phrase under his breath. The General smacked him in the head. It was against the code of the Purge to swear.

"Should we take the stairs?" Linia quizzed.

"Won't be necessary," Theban replied. He took a tool out of his overalls and grabbed a piece of debris off the ground. He quickly scanned the door lock to the elevators and then put the piece of metal in a slot on the scanner. The scanner buzzed quietly for a second before it ejected the piece of metal. It had used a laser to cut a key out of the random scrap. Theban plugged the makeshift key into the keyhole in the panel to the left of the elevator doors. Upon a turn of the key, the doors slid open, and they stepped inside.

"He is handy, isn't he?" Linia smiled.

The gold doors slid noiselessly before they clamped together with a gentle thud. The elevator began climbing rapidly to the roof of Delduna tower.

"Trigger, Linia?" the General said.

"Yes, General?" they replied in unison.

"If anything tries to impede us on the roof, it has to go. Understood?" the General stated solemnly.

They gave a nod just as the elevator slowed to a halt, and the doors slid open quietly. The Paladins bolted out of the shaft with guns at the ready. Five drones that were on patrol in the hangar bay didn't have time to react. The Paladins had rifles scoped in on the heads of the bots before they could face them, and two bullets a piece impacted with their metallic crania in a shower of sparks that dropped the bots to the floor. After a swift scan of the landing bay, Drask gave the "all clear," and Theban got out of the elevator.

"Cover our tracks," the General nodded to Trigger.

Trigger gave a nod back and dropped a grenade in the elevator and closed the doors. A moment later, a muffled thud impacted with the doors, and a high-pitched sheik emanated from the shaft as the destroyed elevator fell unchecked to the basement of Delduna tower. It would prevent anybody from easily following.

A moment later, Theban seamlessly hacked open a dull, grey-colored, inconspicuous shuttle craft belonging to a ventilation company.

"Let's go," Theban said in a hurried whisper.

The Paladins piled into the craft. Linia took the controls and nonchalantly flew away from the tower.

"General, we only have enough power to get us to the edge of the city... Where should we go?" Linia asked after a quick glance at the gauges.

"To the sky-bus platform on the edge of Old City is where I would go," Theban interjected. "It has low security, and poor people the queen doesn't care about go on the sky-bus to get out of the city."

"Sounds like a plan. Make for that platform Linia," the General ordered.

CYRA

There were no schools in Toria Vilorious. Most people gained the knowledge they needed for making a life in Toria off a program called Nexgen. It was a database that had people answer questions on tests for varying topics. Once one passed the test for one level, they would move on to the next. The computer would search for aptitudes and fine tune the tests people took to suit their gifts. Once people reached an acceptable level, they were ordered to start working in the field they excelled at most; if they didn't like where they were placed, well, that was just too bad because nobody messed with the queen's education system without suffering severe consequences.

It would be more accurate to say nobody messed with the system except for Cyra. Short blue hair topped the young girl of sixteen, and a "no nonsense" attitude put into her nubile form made Cyra the definition of a firecracker. Thick makeup on her face gave her an older appearance that matched her sixteen-going-on-twenty-five spirit. Nobody told Cyra what to do; she had the rough-around-the-edges persona that came from growing up on the streets. She was smart too. She hacked the Nexgen system at the age of eight and deleted her records from the database. As far as the Nexgen User Interface program was concerned, Cyra didn't exist. She, as a young teen, spent her time doing more lucrative activities such as hacking computer databases for the highest bidder or bypassing security systems on expensive hover cars, which she promptly taught herself how to drive. Now, she was older and seldom went on crime sprees. When she was a child, people would let her by with her crimes, but the justice system for adults was a bit strict for her tastes. The judicial system being a jurorless trial and often a bullet to the forehead in the queen's execution chambers; this was the cause of her behavioral reformation. Cyra knew no car was worth taking that chance.

Other reasons had prevented Cyra from swiping and hacking lately; she was mourning the death of her mother. Cyra's mom was the only person she had been close to. Her dad had gone off to who knows where years ago, and honestly, Cyra didn't care. Cyra and her mom, however, had been through thick and thin, and now, she was gone—struck down two weeks ago by a thug who was being chased by the Vilkra. The hover car hit too hard for Cyra's mom to make it. Cyra was at her dead-end job as a custodian for a large corporation when it happened… The same dead-end job she was walking to as she thought about the last few weeks. Life seemed so empty without her mom—so hollow.

"What is this life about? Why am I here? Is it just to feel pain? To hurt?" she suddenly burst out, as emotions of sorrow and sadness refused to be contained anymore.

"I have heard rumors of a loving creator… Trilumina… Are you there? I thought you were supposed to be all powerful! I thought you were crafting everything together for good! That's what I've heard anyway… What were you doing when my mother was plastered? Don't you care?" she yelled. She stood still in the shadows of the dark alleyway for a moment. Tears streamed down her cheeks that she quickly wiped away.

Soon, Cyra regained her composure and walked out of the alleyway. She was two blocks from work when she spied a Vilkra sleeper passing her by on the street. It slowed to a halt a few yards in front of her. Two thugs got out. Cyra knew this could be trouble—the Vilkra's "advertising policy" for their "products" was not unknown to her.

"Hey, miss! We have something for you to try!" one of the Vilkra said to her when she got within earshot.

"What might that be?" she asked, but she kept walking.

"Have you heard of Spikeradon? It will rock your world!" the other guy smiled.

"So I have heard. I hear it can kill pain and small dogs too," she smiled. It was a halfhearted smile. She was simply trying to diffuse the situation.

"Funny! Stacker, we have a comedian here! Let's give her something to laugh about," one thug said to the other.

She went to run past the big, heavy-built thug named Stacker, but he anticipated her movements and grabbed her arms. She soon was in a restrained position, and the other thug produced a vial from his coat and a syringe. Cyra struggled in vain against the Vilkra holding her tightly. The other thug approached and drew some of the drug out of the vial.

"I said I don't want your drug! Let me go!" she yelled and struggled for all she was worth, but Stacker was a strong guy, and Cyra at 5'3" barely weighed 120.

The other thug wrapped a cord around her arm to make a vein bulge. He was trying to get the needle in, but she was putting up a fight, and it made his attempts fail. She knew she couldn't keep the fight up forever though. Cyra had heard the horror stories of what Spikeradon did to people, and she knew she already had enough troubles without being hooked on a destructive drug. She was shrieking now and cursing the thugs and the mothers that spawned them when her salvation came. Overhead, explosions echoed in the night, and flashes in the sky from a conflict between the queen's drones and the Purge distracted the thug with the needle long enough for Cyra to kick him with all her might in the groin. The thug dropped to the ground and balled into the fetal position. The other thug named Stacker motioned toward the car. The sleeper's door opened, and another Vilkra began to emerge.

Out of the night sky dropped a rocket from the skirmish above them—the stray projectile hit the Vilkra sleeper. The car blew off the ground and twisted debris scattered everywhere. The thug that was in the process of exiting the vehicle was blown through a nearby storefront. Cyra, much to her surprise, found that she was no longer being restrained by anybody, and when she turned around, the reason became apparent: Stacker had been standing with much of his back toward the car when it exploded. The debris from said explosion hit him much like a ghastly-sized shotgun shell.

Cyra saw the thug she had kicked in the testicles trying to get up. She doubted that fate would smile on her twice, so she did what any street-savvy teen would do. She grabbed the syringe and stabbed the thug in the neck and injected well over the safe dosage into the Vilkra. The man coughed and gagged for a second, and then his body went into horrible convulsions before he stopped moving altogether. She then turned from the scene of carnage and ran the rest of the way to work with fear and adrenaline coursing through her veins.

Cyra quickly slid her security clearance card through the slot when she arrived at the door to the high-rise building she worked at. The door hissed open and shut tight the moment she entered. She hated the place. Not just the work, but the city. Toria Vilorious once seemed promising to Cyra, but now, it had robbed all that she had: her mom, her joy and sense of purpose. This combined with almost getting mugged by the Vilkra… It was too much. She needed to get away, but where would she go?

She walked across the plush interior of the building; fancy architecture, glass desks, and random artwork that cost more than she was worth to the company was on display in the lobby. The elevator opened automatically at her approach. She sat down with her back against the wall of the cramped room of the elevator. There, in her solitude, she wept.

"If you are real, Trilumina, please grant me a way out. I can't do this anymore. Help me! If you are real!" she cried out with her body shaking. The stress of the last few days coupled with the events of the night had finally broke through her tough exterior, and now, her internal, bottled-up emotions flowed freely in the confines of the small room where nobody would see her cry. Her thick makeup that usually made her look more mature was gone, and it was plain to see she was a simple teen who was alone and scared in a city that couldn't care less about her.

The elevators opened at her floor. Cyra looked around and realized something wasn't right. She sniffed back any tears that might have tried to come out—curiosity replaced sorrow. The lights flickered, but mostly, the room was dark with broken glass scattered across the carpet. Cyra soon discovered the cause of the damage to her floor: a downed drone shuttle had crashed into the building. *It must have been shot down in the fighting earlier tonight*, she thought.

Several computer desks were tipped over, and wrecked office equipment littered the ground nearest to where the ship had crashed. The craft she knew to be nicknamed a descender was completely still. She slowly and cautiously advanced. When it continued to remain motionless, she approached the cockpit. Through the shattered glass, Cyra saw a drone slumping in the pilot chair that had half its head lying in its lap. The other half of the face still dangled from a wire connected to its neck. The bullet that had disabled the robot had also put a blackened hole through the headrest, but the ship looked to be in working order. Cyra, avoiding the random debris, walked around the descender and checked for damage to the engines. She didn't spy any obvious trauma to the hull, so she went back to the cockpit. She unbuckled the drone, and with much effort, Cyra pushed the robot corpse from the seat. It thumped to the floor of the cockpit. Once the seat was cleared, Cyra had more than enough room to pilot the ship, if only it would start.

She examined the buttons and gauges for a moment and checked over the health meter of the ship. The readout said the hull integrity was at 82 percent of optimum, and power levels were at 75 percent. That was more than acceptable. She pushed the power button, and then the gauges glowed brighter, the front lights on the ship lit up the room, and the engines rumbled on gradually. Cyra's heart beat faster—this might be the way of escape she had asked for!

She glanced once again at the readouts displaying data for the ship. One such readout told that one of the slide doors on the craft was partially open and could affect the aerodynamics of the descender. Cyra soon found a button that she thought would close the door. She was mistaken, the doors opened wide when the switch was hit, and the ten drone patrol bots contained in the passenger bay hummed to life. They exited the ship and began to look around.

Cyra slumped low in her seat so the drones wouldn't see her. She scanned the control panel before her, desperately in search of how to take flight. An information banner glided across the bottom of the screen directly in front of Cyra. It said "Hold top button on control stick to engage engines." Cyra followed the direction, and to her delight, the ship began to levitate and the side doors automatically clamped shut. The drones took no notice of this because they figured they were being dropped off to search the building. The shuttle scrapped the ceiling in its levitation and tiles that fell clattered to the floor. Cyra initially struggled to get the ship to fly at the right height, but she was a quick study and soon had the hang of it. She spun the ship 180 degrees in the confines of the building to turn around. When she did so, the tail portion of the descender knocked five of the drones out of the window. This was good because those drones fell to their destruction over a hundred feet below onto parked hover cars, but it was bad because the other five then perceived the shuttle as a threat. They opened fire, but Cyra was well on her way out of the damaged high-rise building.

"Freedom!" Cyra laughed joyously as she flew away. Blue lasers streaked past her, but she soon was out of range. Cool night air flowed through the broken glass of the cockpit and caressed her face as she smiled. Cyra was right—she was free!

Cyra was nearing the Old City when her freedom met its first obstacle: her shuttle had been flagged by the drones that saw her escape, so any available units were searching for her. Luckily and unbeknownst to her, the majority of the drone descenders were dealing with the Purge infiltrators, but that didn't mean all of the drones were occupied.

She tapped a beat to a catchy tune on the dash of the shuttle. It was from a local club she often visited and was probably the only place she would miss when she left. As she made her way out of the new city, a flash of light below caught her attention. A second later, her vehicle lurched as the flak from a turret stationed on a skyscraper hit the side of the descender. She went into a series of evasive maneuvers to avoid the next bout incoming, but once she made it out of range, she realized the damage had been done. The initial impact had damaged a power regulator, and her reserve power was being sapped by the wound. She only had two minutes of flying time or less left.

"No! No! No! No!" she exclaimed to herself. "I need out of this cursed city!"

Cyra at that moment began to do that which she did best: think. She knew that she needed to fly lower in case the reserves didn't last as long as she had quickly calculated in her head that they would, and then she scanned through a map on the ships internal database in effort to locate another method out of the city. The map soon revealed the location of the sky-bus stop in Old City.

"That will do," she smiled to herself and adjusted her course to make it as close to the platform as was safe before her craft crashed. With mere seconds to spare before the ship would drop like a rock out of the sky, she came to a halt on the top of a ten-story, condemned apartment building several blocks away from the Biogen skyscraper, and a few miles from the sky-bus platform. She grabbed a pistol off the dismembered drone pilot on the floor of the cockpit before she climbed out of the descender. Cyra wasn't fond of guns, but a brief look around the shabby structures of Old City told her that the pistol would more likely than not be a good thing to have on her person. She checked the clip. It was full. She cocked the gun and let the bolt slide back with a reassuring clink. The gun, maybe, was the one possession she had that would prevent terrible events from happening to her. Before she gained the courage to brave going through the unexplored passages of the building she stood upon, she realized that she needed something to help her navigate. Cyra had grown up in the newly built part of Toria, so she had knowledge of those streets, but in Old City, she was an outsider.

Cyra rummaged around in the cockpit for a moment until she had discovered what she was looking for: parts to a navigation panel. She popped the screen from the control console to the ship, stripped some wires from the computer and salvaged a battery and data processor from the dead drone. She quickly combined these components, downloaded a readout of the city from the ship's database, and fifteen minutes later, she had built her own digital map of Old City. With a digital display of the city in one hand, and a pistol in the other, Cyra shot the rusty lock off the cellar-like doors which lead into the building. The double doors creaked open on rusty hinges to reveal a dark maw. She took a step forward and lingered nervously in the penumbra between the darkness of the building and the gentle radiance of the city lights. She then took a breath of air and set forth to brave the darkness.

———※※※———

Fortunately, the gun she had swiped from the drone pilot was equipped with a flashlight. This made navigating the stairs of the building easier, but the shadows casted by abandoned boxes and rusty pipes combined to make murky menaces that showed themselves in the corner of Cyra's eyes. She quickly turned to look upon these dark threats, but the light chased them away.

"Jumping at shadows," Cyra laughed to herself.

A colossal explosion erupted without warning and shook the building Cyra stood in to its foundations. The once boarded-up windows were blown out, both the glass and boards in the sudden burst. She barely kept her feet in the severe quaking, and the sounds of loose boards and other debris falling could be heard throughout the decrepit apartment building. Out the freshly unblocked windows, Cyra quickly identified the cause of the terrifying tempest: the Biogen building was an inferno from top to bottom. She smiled to herself; the Vilkra had gotten their just deserts at last.

She had dropped both the gun and the improvised navigation device she had made in her fright from the unexpected blast. It wasn't hard to relocate her dropped items though, the red light coming from the nearby inferno allowed for much improved visibility. With hands shaking, she picked up the gun and map contraption. The map had disconnected from its power source, but after a quick reattachment of a wire, it was back on track. With the light of the fire shining through the broken out windows, Cyra soon made her way down the remaining flights of stairs to street level.

The front door of the building was shut tight with a bar that was welded into place, so Cyra took the butt of the pistol and broke out the remaining glass of a nearby shattered window. She straddled the window sill and soon had dropped a short way to the street below. A quick glance at the navigation panel revealed the name of the road she stood upon was Fourth Avenue. It was almost a straight shot down the road upon which she stood until Cyra would make it to the sky-bus platform. Crowds had gathered in the time it took her to reach street level and were gawking at the flaming corpse of the Biogen building. Cyra just hoped that nobody would notice her, and that the rest of her night could pass by with more ennui and less excitement. This wish did not come true.

As she strode a short ways down the street, a panicked murmur arose from the distant crowd. Cyra turned to see the building listing in her direction. With the way her night had been going, Cyra didn't trust gravity to keep the building erect. She wasn't sure if she was out of the range of the building should it fall, but she imagined even the concussion caused by several thousand tons of molting steel hitting the pavement could cause lethal damage. She looked again. The edifice was at an even more perilous angle! Cyra had to think and think fast! *Where should I go!* she thought.

Cyra looked around and saw a stripped car, a half-broken down crate, and a metal dumpster next to the car. She ran past the crate, climbed on top of the car, opened the dumpster and hurtled herself into it. The lid clanked shut enclosing her world in darkness. There she sat listening while she tried to calm herself and ignore the odor of refuse that encompassed her.

Time seemed to slow in the dumpster, to the point Cyra debated poking her head out to check if the building was actually as close to falling as she had originally suspected. The sound of gunshots and a loud rushing noise that turned to a terrible ruckus ceased the thoughts of looking outside. Before Cyra could debate the origins of the gunshots, a force went through the dumpster and slammed her back into some trash bags. The energy wave that hit the dumpster made Cyra feel like she was getting pulled apart molecule by molecule, but a moment later, all was relatively quiet save for a gentle roar in the background. She waited for a few more moments just to be sure nothing else would happen before she dared to crack the lid open a tad. Dull redness and heat seeped into the crack when she finally dared to lift the cover.

Cyra opened the dumpster wider and poked her head out to look around. Fiery debris was strewn over the ground, but from where she sat in the dumpster, it didn't look too bad, so she climbed all the way out of the dumpster. When she looked around upon getting out, she noted her hiding place had been moved several feet from the impact of the tower falling. Cyra was surprised at how little damage was around her; she thought this until she exited the alleyway. Outside the alley, Fourth Avenue was completely destroyed. It was in shambles before the building fell, afterwards— well, it looked as though it had been bombed twice. The building that Cyra was in just a few moments before was half of what it used to be and on fire, but everything between that apartment building and where the Biogen building used to be was reduced to flaming rubble. Ash was in the air, and occasionally, the clink of smoking debris hitting the ground could be heard, but the thick hot air would cause one to choke if endured for too long. A few burning frames belonging to hover bikes dotted the remains, and nearer than she would have liked, a Zykor biker chick was glaring down a nearby alleyway. Her wrecked bike was a few feet from where she stood. The woman who was garbed in attractive, figure-complementing leather fired a round from her shotgun down the alleyway that she scowled upon. The woman yelled, "I'll get you! I swear it! You are mine!"

Cyra didn't know who the woman was, but she didn't seem like one who would be wise to cross, so Cyra quickly decided it would be better not to linger. She kept low and continued on her trek to the platform. Fortunately, the biker continued down the alley she had initially fired down; this allowed Cyra to take the more direct and, hopefully, safer route to the platform.

Roughly two hours had passed by the time Cyra made it to the base of the steps of the sky-bus stop. Then Cyra noticed some light shining in the distance over the newer portion of Toria. She glanced at her makeshift navigation device at the clock in the corner of the screen: 4:13. Orgasoli wouldn't be in the sky for another four hours! She looked again. Large, sharp-angled ships were in the sky above the city and the brightness in the firmament was from the fire streaming off the hulls of the ominous vessels as they entered the atmosphere. At least two dozen of these large ships were taking up positions above the city so they could besiege Toria.

If Cyra had any doubts about leaving the city, they were in that moment entirely dissipated. Taking flight was the only option, and through all the crazy events of the night, she had ended up at the safest way of escape. The sky-bus platform of Old City was the farthest point away from the attacking, alien ships. Cyra ran up the steps of the station and hoped the sky-bus would get her away from imminent doom.

BRUNICK

Brunick, a thirty-year-old mechanical wiz, cruised down Fourth Avenue in an old, classic hover truck with a flaming paint job on the front. He had fiery, short, red hair that matched the graphics of the truck, dirty hands, and a young face. His duster, which doubled as a shop coat, covered his muscle-bulging arms that were a side-effect from working on hover cars. The man was an expert and, indeed, a mechanic that had a surreptitious operation in a small farming town outside the city. It was a straight shot out of Old City if one traveled on Fourth Avenue. The man would reach the gates of Old City in about two hours, and past those, in the distance, he spied the golden silhouette of his destination: the Biogen building. The radio was cranked up to a catchy electronic/classic hybrid type of music called Melodium. The infectious tune had him bobbing his head and tapping the dashboard to the beat. Brunick was in an especially jovial mood because today, he would get paid for services rendered to the Vilkra.

Brunick's "services" were to build the modified sleepers that the Vilkra drove; these sleepers had technology that would blind the city sensors for a half-mile radius around where the cars hovered. This allowed the Vilkra to smuggle/use drugs and firearms without being seen by the sensors. The only way the queen would get wise of the Vilkra's illegal operation was if a drone saw the Vilkra's operations themselves. This wasn't *usually* a problem because the Vilkra had other people that knew the patrol routes of the drones, but it was Brunick's advanced operations that allowed the Vilkra to stoop to the bottom of the barrel time after time. He was one of the main men of the corporation, and though he didn't directly touch any of the money-making operations of the drug and weapons trade, he was well-paid.

The song changed on the radio, and Brunick switched from tapping the dash to snapping his fingers. Upon the instance of one of these finger snaps, a flash of red light rent the night-vista before him. It only took Brunick a moment to realize what had happened: the Biogen building that once stood dozens of floors above its surrounds like a beacon in the night had been morphed drastically from a towering, illuminated skyscraper to a great, flaming column. Brunick swore, but the beat of the music drowned out his curse word. Before he could do anything else in response to the destruction of his employer's headquarters, his truck lurched as it slammed into an unbeknownst object that proclaimed the impact with a dull thud. Brunick, as he looked down from the destroyed Biogen building, momentarily saw the outline of a man in the blink of an eye before he was sucked under the truck.

Brunick quickly pulled to the side of the lonely freeway and slowed to a halt. He got out of his truck and looked for the man he hit. Amazingly, the man was already walking toward Brunick. He drew in breath in surprise as he saw the older fellow walk toward him. He gasped because the man, minus his agedness, looked perfectly well, no wounds could be spied on him when he should be dead.

"Sir, could you give me a ride to the city?" the older gent asked calmly.

"Are you ok? Are you hurt?" Brunick asked hurriedly out of concern for the man's safety.

"I'm fine. Can you give me a ride?"

"Of course! Are you sure you are fine? You should be dead! I hit you at eighty miles per hour!" Brunick replied.

"I knew I would be fine before I stepped in front of your truck," replied the man.

"You…did that on purpose?" Brunick looked on in wonderment.

"Yes, of course! I needed a ride, and nobody stops for people anymore, which is wise, but I do need a ride, so how about getting back on the road?"

"Sure, but you were coming from the city, why do you need to go back?" Brunick asked.

"I had a meeting to go to out here. The meeting is over so now I have business in a location I have yet to be told, but I need to go there wherever it is, so how about us getting back on the road?" the codger pressed.

"All right! All right! What's the hurry?" Brunick exclaimed.

"You'll see."

The man sat calmly in the passenger seat of Brunick's truck as they neared the city. The destruction of the tower had been forgotten momentarily, as Brunick was consumed with curiosity about this man that should be dead, but Brunick would only chance brief glances at his mysterious passenger that sat silently or replied only with brief responses when questioned.

"Who will tell you where you need to go once we get into the city?" Brunick asked.

"The One who always tells me where to go."

"Who?" Brunick asked.

"Trilumina," stoically replied the man.

"Of all the nuts in the barrel." Brunick muttered under his breath.

"Don't you believe in Trilumina? Why not?" the elderly man quizzed.

"What proof is there of an omnipotent, ubiquitous being? It's not like I can walk outside and see Trilumina!" Brunick snapped disbelievingly.

"Do you believe in the wind?" the man replied.

"Of course! What does that have to do with anything?"

"You can't see the wind, but you can see and feel the effects of it, so you know that it is there. It is the same with Trilumina. You cannot see him, but you can see the universe, the galaxy which he built, and the goodness he places in the hearts of those who trust and obey him. You can't see Trilumina, but you can see the works of his hands." The man stared at Brunick with intent eyes as though he was drilling in his point.

Brunick hadn't really thought of it that way before and didn't like the way the conversation was going so he tried a diversion.

"Who were you supposed to meet all the way back there on Fourth Avenue?"

"You." The man gave a smile.

The rest of the distance in transit to Old City passed in silence. They made it to the billboard-sized electronic sign that would have said "Welcome to Toria Bondervous," but it was dirty, aged, and the backlighting blinked. As the truck hovered past, the light flickered its last, and sparks showered down as the bulb shorted out. A drear, red glow replaced the blackness that usually occupied the urban scape of the Old City. The origin of the crimson pallor revealed itself as Brunick rounded a curve in the road: the Biogen tower had fallen into the city below. Brunick had expected to see this as soon as he spied the building explode nearly two hours ago, but what he didn't expect to see was the terrible carnage that was now prevalent in the debris field. Besides the fiery rubble and red plume of smoke coming from blocks of this newly created wasteland, an intense battle between drones and the remnant of the Vilkra was occurring. Lasers, bullets and missiles streaked back and forth between the opposing factions, and Brunick sighed as he saw one of the sleepers he had built get destroyed by an errant rocket. The Vilkra and the drones had been attracted to the zone of destruction. The Vilkra were out for blood, and the drones were out to teach the lesson that destroying the property of the queen was unacceptable, so naturally, they began punishing one another.

Brunick slowed to a halt in the shadow of a building a block away from the carnage and shrugged. "I guess I'm unemployed as of right now. I've got nothing better to do, where do you need to go?"

"We," replied the codger.

"We what?" Brunick countered.

"*We*, not just I, need to go to the sky-bus stop," replied the weird one.

"Did your Trilumina tell you that?" Brunick quizzed tersely.

"You wouldn't believe me if he had. I do need to go there though, you can stay here at your peril, but I have work to do and information to gather," the codger replied in a tone that was terse as well.

"It will be a while because I got to take a detour. Fourth Avenue is gone, and much of the Old City is wrecked as well. I'll have to go through Toria Vilorious," Brunick said. He half-hoped the man would offer to get out and walk.

"Fine, I've got time."

A stray laser from the nearby battle hit near Brunick's truck and prompted him to start on his way speedily.

Brunick's old-school truck cruised past the sign saying "Welcome to Toria Vilorious, the City of Odiria's splendor." It was a bright sign and perfectly maintained. The old man in the passenger seat gave a dry cackle laugh as they passed the sign.

"What is so funny?" Brunick asked.

"The sign, the queen, this city will all get what it deserves tonight. It's not really funny, but the queen's narcissism is so great I can't help but laugh at her folly," the man replied.

"I doubt that this city could get destroyed tonight, there is only four hours until morning, but as for the queen's egoism, *that* I can agree with!" Brunick replied.

"You don't believe that a city the size of Toria Vilorious can be destroyed in a night? Look at the sky." the old man responded.

Just as Brunick looked up at the midnight sky, it burst forth with a bright flurry of crimson, auburn color that chased the night away from the rent firmament. Soon, twoscore of large, sharp-angled ships were poking out of the fiery cavity.

"What are they?" Brunick mumbled in awe.

"The defective Armada, they have come to do what they always do." the old man replied.

"What is that?" Brunick turned and looked at the odd man.

"Destroy." As the man said the word, one of the ships had flown down so that it was only a few hundred yards above the Delduna tower, and it began firing dark purple bolts of energy that bent in odd arcs and cut into the city below. Fire began to spread, and debris began to fall from above.

Brunick had heard of the defective Armada before, but he thought that they were a myth just as much as Trilumina was, but now that he saw them, he didn't doubt anymore.

"What should we do?" Brunick said with a tone of anxiety as he tried to avoid falling debris while he sped through the city and weaved in and out of the wreckage.

"Keep on this road and drive into the under levels of the city at the next off-ramp. That will prevent us from being hit by the bolts of darkness, but we must be careful of the drop pods. They could cause difficulties. Whatever you do, stay close to me. Trilumina will keep me safe, and if you stick close, he may spare you as well," the man replied.

More of the alien ships had bridged the atmosphere and were opening fire. The first large craft that had initiated the attack opened its dark underbelly. Shadow, blue pods began to descend upon the city from the opening—like the first few rain drops that fall just before a terrible tempest unleashes its full fury. Brunick gunned the throttle and made for the nearest ramp that descended into the sewers of the city.

"Why could those drop pods cause difficulties?" Brunick asked as the sign indicating the ramp he was making for approached.

"It is better that you don't know, but I will tell you anyway. They spawn terrible creature-like machines. If they dwell in a place too long, anything near them undergoes a sickly metamorphosis," the man replied.

A pod struck a few hundred yards in front of the truck and exploded into shards of black-blue crystals and drops of dark silver fluid. The explosion sounded like a one-ton chandelier dropping from a skyscraper and shattering into the ground with a chest-thumping blast. The dark silver, mercurial substance splattered out of the pods and moved across the ground like water spewing from a tipped-over bucket. The substance glided across the ground and covered a bystander who cowered beside an overturned car. When the substance glided past the person, only a metallic shell casting a perfect image of what once was human was left—the man had been turned to a statue. Brunick quickly hovered past the disturbing scene and descended into the bowels of Toria.

"You were right. I really didn't need to know or see that. I think I just vomited in my mouth," Brunick expressed distraughtly.

They hovered quickly through a tunnel that ran under the main streets next to the foundations of the skyscrappers and the huge, rotten Festra River. If Brunick wasn't in survival mode, he would have commented on the tremendous stink of the river, but since more pressing matters were on his mind, he focused solely on keeping himself alive and avoiding the numerous hobos and occasional dog-sized rats (which the hobos were known to eat) that resided in the clandestine sewers of Toria.

At first, the going was relatively smooth with only the occasional thump from hitting a rat that was slow to flee from the rapidly moving hover truck, but as the bombardment of the alien vessels drearily hanging above the city increased, more pods dropped into the city, and several happened to break through the metropolitan streets. These pods splashed into the Festra River or imbedded in the foundations of the skyscrappers. The pods that hit the river frightened the rats and other filthy creatures that resided in the depths of scum and drove them onto the sublevel road. In the cones of light that emanated from the front headlights on the truck, Brunick could spy hundreds of screeching rodents in exodus of the river. Soon, Brunick was plowing into scores of the creatures or barely dodging the odd hobo. The vermin would get pulled under or thrown over the hood of the vehicle. Brunick muttered terrible profanities proportional to how much the situation degraded.

"Enough of this!" Brunick yelled as he pushed a button on the dash. Out of the back of his truck, a heavy, rotary laser turret reared its armament like a deadly cobra ready to strike. The turret automatically targeted hostile entities that got too close. Bright blue lasers illuminated the wide tunnel as the high-powered cannon hissed forth its scorching munitions. Through the chaos that seemed never ending, Brunick's traveling companion sat perfectly calm in the passenger seat with his eyes closed. Without opening his eyes the man spoke: "Before we round the next bend, program the turret to target the middle of the torso of the hostile soldiers. The dark fluid that overwhelmed the person we saw earlier today is actually made up of billions of little robots called mechamites. These creatures are powered by the crystals that they travel with. They will take any metal they can find and make more of themselves. They then will fabricate terrible devices out of their own vile multitude with shards of crystal at their core acting as a brain. If their crystal core is breached, they will fall."

Brunick risked taking his eyes off his driving to throw a brief look at the man. When he spied the man that was so peacefully yet seriously sitting there, he shook his head and decided to do as he was bidden. Mere moments after the command to target the center of hostiles was programmed, they rounded a bend in the sewers only to come upon a terrible scene of mayhem. Dismal light from the burning buildings filtered in from above. The orange glow seeped in through massive rifts in the street that used to conceal the sewers; drop pods and heavy munitions had ripped the streets to shreds to the point that many hover vehicles had dropped into the sewers. Brunick skillfully dodged the ruination, but he couldn't help notice that gallons of the mercurial substance, also known as mechamites, were oozing into the sewer with the torrential rain that also fell. He tried not to think of this, but soon, he could no longer ignore it. The substance had leached into wrecked cars, light posts, dumpsters, and any other metal thing, and twisted the objects into sickly humanoid robots. Had Brunick failed to adjust the targeting on his turret, the guns would have targeted the heads of the metallic entities. That would have been fruitless because the brains which were the shards that came from the broken pods were stored in the center of the bots not their heads.

The lasers continued to hiss out of the turret in the back of the truck. It strafed left and right, cutting hostiles into pieces in a flurry of blue death. Brunick's passenger finally opened his eyes.

"Take the next ramp out of the sewers and cut through the center of Toria. If we stay in the sewers, we will be killed. The mechamites have streamed into the depths of the city. They are cutting into the foundations, and soon, the city will literally fall, so we must risk going in the open. If we stay in the sewers, it will take us too long to reach the sky-bus, and the city will come down upon us," the eccentric man said.

Brunick didn't bother arguing, he was clearly out of his element in this city that was falling apart, and whether the man who was sitting eerily calm in his passenger seat was a man of Trilumina or not, Brunick did not want to chance not listening to one who might have divine protection. He soon came upon the desired ramp; with a sharp jerk of the control stick, the vehicle glided into the exit passageway. Paint scraped on the side of the tunnel, sparks flickered in the dim light of the shaft, and an Armada bot that was too sluggish to avoid Brunick's custom truck shattered into metallic dust as Brunick turned onto the ramp leading to the main street level. Fortunately, upon arrival of the upper level of the street, they found the center of the city was in relatively good condition.

"Why is this place not wrecked? It's in the center of the assault!" Brunick exclaimed.

"Tactics," the man replied.

"How do you mean?" Brunick replied shortly as he jerked the control stick to avoid a pod that splashed into the street mere feet away. Crystal shards that radiated from the splintering pod imbedded into the side of the truck.

"The Armada is mainly attacking the perimeter to prevent people from escaping. Once they have completed a perimeter around Toria Vilorious, they will encroach in upon the center of the city and systematically destroy everything and everyone. Evil is very clever in its methods of destroying the souls of man," the revelatory man replied; a look of sorrow shown momentarily on the mystic's face.

"Will it make any difference if we make it to the sky-bus stop then?" Brunick vented.

"Yes, I have been privy to the knowledge that the Armada is more interested in Toria Vilorious than they are in the Old City. I don't know exactly why, but I suspect that it is that they are more interested in the people of this part of the city. Perhaps, they think they can easily snatch the people of the slums when they have finished here."

"Whether you are right or not, I think I would prefer to believe we still stand a chance."

A nearby hover car in front of them, fleeing in the same direction, in that moment, was hit by a dark bolt from one of the Armada capital ships and was instantly turned to fiery shrapnel. A random expletive exploded out of Brunick's mouth as he merely dodged what used to be the main engine block of the decimated vehicle. Once Brunick straightened the truck back up from his near miss, he pushed his craft to its limits. The engines roared, and the truck blurred through the deteriorating city.

The metropolis flew by with Brunick experiencing dozens more close calls while his odd gentleman of a passenger calmly watched the remaining drones of the queen put up a futile fight. It had been less than a half an hour since the Armada had arrived, and already, the city was beyond repair.

Not a moment too soon, Brunick slammed trough a rusty gate that represented the divider between Toria Vilorious and Toria Bondervous (the new and Old City). Just as Brunick's passenger had indicated, the fighting was less here. The Armada capital ships were forming a ghastly halo around Toria Vilorious, but they were focusing their fire on the inside of their devious circle.

Less than an hour after Brunick had met with the man on Fouth Avenue they cruised to a halt in front of the sky-bus station. The old man kicked open his door which had been jammed shut by the shards that had perforated his side of the truck earlier. The man stretched and yarned slightly. Brunick got out of the truck and stared at the man in awe.

"I don't think I would have made it out of that alive if it wasn't for you! Who are you?" Brunick asked in bewilderment.

"Nope, you wouldn't have survived that if Trilumina wasn't protecting us, and my name is Saezyn. I am a prophet of Trilumina, and you should thank *him* not me for your miserable life," Saezyn replied. The eccentric and indeed mysterious prophet then climbed into the back of the truck that was scarcely holding together after the hell it had been through, and Saezyn grabbed the back turret. With a little effort, he managed to disconnect it from its plinth.

"What are you doing?" Brunick asked.

"Oh, you can go inside and get our tickets. I'll take care of this," replied the mystic. He then stood a little ways away and held down the trigger and peppered his side of the truck.

"Whoa man! What are you doing! Hasn't my truck been hit enough?" Brunick exclaimed, but Saezyn didn't stop shooting until the truck was burning.

"Containment. It had been hit too much. Just one of those crystals with mechamites on it is enough to gradually turn this truck into one of those Armada bots that we drove through moments ago. Luckily, we got here before the mechamites had made too many more of themselves. Don't look so down, it was just a truck anyway. Let's go inside, the sky-bus will be here soon," Saezyn replied merrily.

Brunick stood aghast looking at the rubble of the truck he had put hours into throughout his life. Saezyn stooped to the ground and picked up a handful of mechamites that had been deactivated when the crystals were destroyed. Saezyn let them pass through his fingers like sand.

"It was either that"—he motioned toward the burning vehicle—"or this," finished Saezyn as he dropped the rest of the mites on the ground. He then handed the turret to Brunick: "You'll need this. Come on, let's get inside," Saezyn said warmly. They both turned and walked up the stairs leading to the station.

CJ DREAMS

CJ Dreams sat tranquilly on her living room couch leaning against her husband; his arms wrapped warmly around her. Xyles (her husband) was a reserved data scrounger: the more educated type that had brains but lacked bronze and courage for that matter. His ghost white skin contrasted sharply with his dark black hair. He was rather dull in appearance. CJ was the opposite. She had blonde hair with streaks of red which gave her a fiery mane of hair that complemented her vibrant personality perfectly. It was this odd anomaly in her hair that she was named after, the red and yellow was the origins for Carmine Jasmine or CJ for short. She was beautiful like a flower but came on like a scorching tempest in her zest for life. CJ and Xyles were the definition of the phrase "opposites attract." One could call it fire (CJ) and dust (Xyles) if they wanted.

"I really don't think that is a good idea. We have an apartment here, and we both have decent jobs and a steady income," Xyles replied to CJ's plea she had ventured while they cuddled on the couch.

"You have a decent job!" CJ pulled away from where she leant on her husband. "I have to endure dozens of men ogling at me on a daily basis. Sure, exotic dancers are paid well, but it comes at a high cost to personal comfort. I'm tired of being an object to whoever the queen is trying to distract while she manipulates them. I'm tired of being held up in the Delduna tower for as long as Odiria needs me to woo her guests. I'm tired of that plush prison. I'm just tired, Xyles. My sense of decency has been violated time and time again by what I have to see and that which I have done. I never wanted this, that stupid Nexgen computer selected me for that duty when it noted my unusual hair coloring and exemplary physical proportions for what the queen wanted in her harem. She has us wear a veil over our face! Do you know why?! Because the queen's clients aren't supposed to view us as people but rather as desire inciting entities. Let us leave this place! We could go far away and live our own lives and do what we want to do! We have enough money now," CJ petitioned once again.

Xyles stood up and began to pace. He was a wuss of a man. "Honey, we can't leave! Where would we go? I don't think it would go quite as well as you think it would," he replied spinelessly.

"We don't know unless we try. Come on! For once in your life, do something adventurous," CJ pressed.

"I don't think so sweetie," he replied after a pause.

"You don't think so! What you aren't thinking about is your wife! You aren't thinking of anything past yourself! You should stand up for me, protect me! But you're hiding in your comfortable data processing job while I suffer under an insidious queen! Don't you care?" CJ yelled.

"Of course, I do!" he replied defensively.

"Then show that you do!" CJ screamed. She stood up and paced toward the door.

"Honey, where are you going?" Xyles asked.

"Don't honey me, you spineless bag of fluff! It looks like I'm going to stay in this wretched city." She reached the button to open the door. She slid on a leather coat, grabbed her large purse that almost could double as a tent, and turned to look back at Xyles as the door slid open. Her neck-length, gold crimson hair danced about as she faced him, "I'm going for a walk to catch some air," she replied in a much cooler tone.

"When will you be back?" he questioned in a subdued manner.

"I don't know… Eventually… Perhaps." She walked out of the door and it slid shut behind her.

―――

CJ walked alone. Angry. Wanting more—but wanting Xyles to want more too. He was so apathetic to her situation, and his lack of gall to stand up for her was just plain pathetic. *Why couldn't he gather up enough testosterone to man up and get out of his plush life to do the right thing*, she thought. She felt like screaming but instead, kicked a rusty lock across the rain-drenched streets. It panged into an open metal gate that clanged with the impact as the energy reverberated through the metal bars. She was so lost and frustrated in her thoughts that she had reached the very edge of Old City. CJ had walked the two miles from where her apartment positioned in the new part of the city in Toria Vilorious to Old City in a haste fueled by her anger toward Xyles.

CJ looked at the wide-open gate leading toward Old City, she knew it led to the most dangerous part of the metropolis, but she certainly wasn't afraid. She only checked her fast pace momentarily before she strode past the timeworn gates onto the weather-torn streets of Toria Bondervous.

―――

The deeper CJ plunged into the dim, dull-shaded realm of Old City, the more her anger-induced courage began to subside, and the more she began debating returning home. As she thought of going back, she thought of Xyles and his lack of compassion for her, this recharged her anger and increased her resolve to face the dark of the city she now explored. The rain had increased, and her wet hair now clung to her skin. A nearby streetlamp illuminated thousands of streaks made by falling rain which was supplied by the torrential downpour that had broken free from its cloudy prison far above. This same cloudburst drove CJ under the cover of a nearby broken out storefront. Fortunately, the place was abandoned, and no hobos or criminals occupied her hiding place.

She waited for the liquescent surge to subside, but it seemed to go on and on.

CJ sat on an old chair behind the broken glass storefront. A look around the room revealed this place might have been a barber shop or dentist but now no more. *Its original glory has faded. It's not the only run down thing that has lost much of its former glory... My relationship with Xyles is as in as bad shape or worse than this dump. Why do things have to break down? Why is life so hard? Where did it all go wrong?* she thought. Xyles was originally married to somebody else, but CJ used her arts as an exotic dancer to seduce him and to take him from his wife. It had made CJ happy at the time, but now that he wasn't really there for her, it could be said she had buyer's remorse. Moister brimmed in her eyes until a duet of tears slid down her cheeks. Anger had given way to mourning at choices made. Xyles had seemed so nice when she met him two years ago at Frenzy, the local club; it seemed an eternity since then. He wasn't nice, he was weak or selfish. Whatever Xyles was, she could see it now after the emotions of love had faded with the time and perpetual acts of carelessness toward her. She was blinded by her love for him, or perhaps lust, but now, where excitement once abounded, only sorrow remained. She wiped away her liquid sorrows and sniffled. The rain had let up, but only on the outside; inside, the monsoon of emotions continued. She decided not to linger in the place anymore, she would go home and go to bed and hope and pray to Trilumina that Xyles would have a change of heart. CJ then, for the first time in years, lifted up her circumstances to Trilumina. Perhaps if she uttered a prayer sooner, she would not have had to scrape the bottom of the barrel of desperation, but she made her decisions and would have to drink the cup she poured for herself.

CJ walked out of the run-down shop with going home as her main objective, but before she had slowly walked too far; a nearby commotion drew her attention. She heard a whole bunch of people yelling of what faintly sounded like "Stop!" CJ rounded a corner nearest to the din. From where she peaked around the building, she spied the tremendous Biogen building; a Vilkra sleeper was racing towards the skyscraper, and Vilkra were peppering it with gunfire trying to get it to stop. The vehicle disappeared into the basement of the structure. For an eerie moment, time slowed, and an unearthly silence reigned supreme, disturbed only by the distinct impact of rain on the streets and the sound of water running into drainage culverts. Quiet gave way to utter chaos a moment later—fire ripped through the building going from the bottom up, and debris showered out of the devastated form of the edifice.

CJ knew she had stayed in Old City too long. She turned to run from the scene but was too late. A random object (the back of an office chair) that was thrown from the building impacted with CJ's cranium. Blackness overtook her world, and she dropped to the street unconscious.

Through hazy vision, CJ glanced at her watch. She blinked a couple of times to clear away the blur that clouded her eyes. It was 3:59, the middle of the night. She was cold, wet, and laying in the middle of a side walk which happened to be the heart of immediate peril. A crimson orange glow emanated from around where she lay. A dull roar of something burning sounded in the background, and occasional explosions complemented by the staccato sound of laser fire could be heard. The blasts of laser fire were far nearer than she would have liked, but nearer, she heard the hydraulic, pressurized movement of something large and robotic. Soon, the "something" entered her peripheral: it was a drone. The metallic minion looked down at CJ, she stared back. The bot that was in defensive mode began to point its laser rifle at CJ. She tried to climb to her feet to avoid the barrel. Suddenly, the sound of a laser resonated in CJ's ears. For a moment, she looked herself over, thinking that the drone had fired at her, but the drone hadn't fired, it had been shot. CJ looked up in time to see the drone's laser-blackened head fall from its shoulders to the ground with the rest of its body following suit. The drone had been shot by a Vilkra gangster. In that moment, CJ had time to briefly glance around and make sense of things. The dull glow that surrounded her was from the collapsed, fire-consumed form of the Biogen building. Its gutted carcass had toppled while she lay unconscious. Also, in the few hours she was passed out, drones had gathered to investigate the destruction of the building; the remaining Vilkra had come seeking vengeance against whoever destroyed their building. When they saw the drones, the Vilkra assumed they were to blame just as the drones imagined the Vilkra were at fault. Now, CJ was up to speed and realized that the battle between these two corrupt forces wasn't over— a laser that shot out a streetlight above her head announced that CJ was in the thick of the zenith of said battle. Shattered glass rained down onto her head. CJ ducked for cover behind an overturned sleeper.

After a few moments had passed, she scanned her surrounds. The fighting was happening down the street near the destroyed buildings by the Biogen, but it was also happening behind her. She was cut off! All around her, drones of the queen and Vilkra gangsters were exchanging fire. A well-aimed drone rocket streaked a few feet to the left of CJ and hit one of the mobster's cars. The subsequent explosion engulfed the passenger quarters of the sleeper in flames and blew the doors off. The nearby gangsters were disoriented or destroyed in the metal and glass shrapnel that came from the disintegration of their car. CJ took this opportunity to run past the gangsters. She stooped momentarily to pick up a rifle and a pistol off a dead thug. She wasn't fond of guns, but she was not at all averse to doing what was necessary to stay alive. Around the next bend in the street, CJ hoped to see a clear shot to new Toria, but instead, she only saw two dozen drones coming straight at her. The automatons began to fire at CJ. She quickly dropped behind a burning dumpster. She peered through a crack between the wall and the dumpster to see if they were still approaching, and they were—but not for long. A Vilkra hover tank came sideways around an alley corner at high speeds and rammed into the advancing drones. In a flurry of sparks and severed drone appendages, over half of the minions were decimated. The rest took up defensive positions. A brief firefight ensued that the drones lost, but CJ didn't stay to watch and have the tank turn its attention to her. She ran to her salvation: an abandoned Vilkra sleeper in a nearby alley. She ran over to it with her rifle at the ready, but when she made it to the craft, much to her relief, nobody came to kill her. CJ opened the door—it was unlocked. She quickly closed and locked it after her. She tried the on button. Then the car hummed to life, and a screen glowed in the center of the dash. It was a navigation panel that to CJ's delight, showed the positions of any hot spots in the city. The bad news was that she could not get back to her house via any of the major arteries, but the good news was there was a clear shot to the sky-bus station.

"Yes! I can go home via the sky-bus platform. It can drop me off at one of the stations in the new part of the city!" she exclaimed out loud. CJ turned the car on to leave the alleyway. She gunned the motor; in her haste to leave, she ran into a solitary drone that passed the entry to the street she was on. The hapless robot was severed messily into two, and CJ was away into the night.

It was 4:10 when CJ had made it to the station. She ran up the stairs quickly, just in case she was followed. She slipped the weapons she had scrounged earlier into her oversized purse which looked more like a luggage item. She kept her hand in her purse with her hand clasping the pistol. With her guard up, and weapons discretely at the ready, CJ slipped into the crowd of people that had gathered at the bus station

About the time she had bought her ticket and found a bench to sit down on, she noticed something very peculiar out the glass ceiling of the bus station: the sky was glowing like a lantern in the night, and dark shadows were seeping out of the gapping, orange oval in the sky. A murmur of dismay ran through the crowding station. CJ watched, horror-stricken, like the rest as the alien craft opened fire and bombarded the city with dark munitions and atypical bombs. She pried her gaze away from the scene of carnage long enough to grab her mobile communicator. She called her house and frantically hoped Xyles would pick up. Her communicator played an annoying tone as CJ waited for Xyles to answer.

"CJ! Where have you been?" Xyles answered frantically on the other end of the line.

"There is no time to explain now! Get out of the apartment and meet me at the sky-bus station in Old City! We need to get out of the city! Some gigantic ships are attacking!!" she replied even more frantically.

"The queen's drones will take care of them. We have a good home here. I'm not leaving," he replied sternly.

"'We had a good home here'—it's going to get destroyed! I'm sorry for anything mean I may have said to you, Xyles, but now isn't the time to go through that! You need to come meet me while you still can! If the queen's drones defeat whatever this is, then we can discuss moving back later, but for now, let us go to safety!" CJ pleaded.

"I'll be fine—wait…" The sound of glass breaking in the apartment sounded over the connection. CJ heard Xyles murmur to himself: "What is that? It looks like mercury." The link was relatively silent for a few moments. CJ listened intently. Then she heard Xyles yell: "It's moving… Wait no! It's after me!" For the next few moments, she heard the sound of him breathing heavily as he ran, but soon, she heard him cry out in pain, as whatever had invaded the apartment, caught up with him. The link then was cut off in static, leaving only Xyles's last pained utterances echoing through CJ's mind.

CJ dropped her phone to the ground and shook her head as she wept and said over and over "Poor fool, poor fool."

The com in the station heralded that the sky-bus was docking. The announcement was complemented by the sound of the bus engines roaring overhead, and shortly after, the docking clamps locking the vessel into place. CJ reached to pick up her communicator from where she dropped it, but a stampede of passengers pushing and shoving to get in line stepped upon her device. Among the crowd, she noted a blue-haired teen with a pistol on her hip; she, specifically, was the person who accidently broke the device. The young woman gave CJ an apologetic look before she was swept away with the crowd. CJ's focus was soon distracted from this girl when a biker chick yelled very loudly "You Spag! You back trodden bilge water! Spawn of a Nemen Toad!" at a man in a trench coat who disappeared into the crowd. She also made a solemn oath that she was going to "put him in the ground." The biker then picked up her shotgun. She fired it at the ceiling, and as the shattered glass of the skylight fell onto the people below, she yelled, "Move it!" The crowd noted a menacing look in her eye, and a path formed so she could follow after the thug in black. CJ could faintly see him running down a long glass hall that led to the sky-bus. The sky-bus could be dimly made out in large lights that illuminated the docking yard. It was a tri-level monolith that could ferry over two thousand passengers. It had large engines in its rear portion and large fins sticking out of the top and bottom of the craft. It, in many regards, resembled a colossal shark. On the side of the craft, the service number PSD-891 was scribed. Underneath the official designation, the name *Double Edge* was written as the title of the transport.

CJ joined the back part of the mob and continued watching the spectacle. The biker was running down the hallway too, but the man had already disappeared into the large craft. He could hide almost anywhere in the massive behemoth of a ship. Before the dangerous woman was half down the glass gangway, three people equipped with machine guns and grey battle armor ran after the woman, yelling what sounded like "Stop" after her. The woman and the soldiers (CJ assumed they were the rumored Paladins that had recently entered the Solbian system) disappeared into the bus. The crowd of people pressed onto the boardwalk after the armed fellows. Security went into protocols when somebody passed a checkout without a ticket. The doors tried to close and deny people access to the plank leading to the sky-bus, but a man wearing a black duster that contrasted sharply with his fiery, red hair stepped forward with a rather large laser repeater and blew down the doors. CJ, in the crowd of passengers, was rushed forward in the mayhem and soon found herself inside the large transport.

On the floor of the bus, spent casings lay on the ground, and holes perforated the walls and seats of the first level, but the only people that could be seen besides the mob that had just rushed in were the Paladins. The biker and the shady man were out of sight. CJ walked past a younger soldier as he reported to his battle-scarred yet still handsome, older superior: "They are hiding somewhere on the transport, sir."

The gruff general gave a grunt and replied, "Do a search, they could hurt the passengers if we don't find them."

CJ climbed down some stairs leading to the bottom floor of the craft. She sat in a seat near to where the escape pods were positioned. Her seat was next to a stubby man wearing a visor and overalls. The man extended a hand and gently touched CJ.

"Hey, miss, I noticed your eyes are red— like you have been crying. Is there anything I could do to help?" the man said.

CJ wiped her eyes and replied, "I don't think so. Maybe we could just talk about insignificant things like a normal day and pretend the world isn't ending—and that my husband didn't just die."

"I see. I'm sorry. Well…" He paused for a prolonged while, and the part of his face that wasn't covered by a visor looked uncomfortable before he continued. "My name is Theban. I'm a craftsman. I build intricate things, but I must give my honest non-flattering opinion: you are more beautiful than the sum of all the things that I have made."

"Why, thank you, Theban." CJ smiled. "My name is CJ Dreams. Your kind words mean more than you can know."

"I must correct my previous statement. I have not seen anything as beautiful as a woman such as you when you smile." He lifted up his visor to reveal his eyes and show that he was indeed in earnest. His words were in the same tone as a father comforting his daughter, for indeed, Theban was older than CJ by some years. He just wanted to comfort a soul in mourning.

She smiled pleasantly. "What about you, kind sir? What sort of things do you craft?"

"Oh, just trinkets really, some jewelry, some motorized. Anything and everything really." He shrugged and adjusted his visor.

"How did I get so fortunate to have your company tonight? What brought you here?" CJ quarried.

"I had a building assignment from the queen that went bad." He paused and shook his head. "It went very bad. I hate building for that spoiled, evil harpy. Fortunately, some Paladins saved me from a rather tricky predicament," he replied.

"Were they the Paladins I saw earlier when I got on the bus?" she asked in return.

"The very same."

"It just goes to show you that we are all connected in some way. I, too, worked as a… well… I worked for the queen and detested every minute of it. I think that is pretty common ground in Toria though," she replied. She laughed with half her heart.

"It is, indeed," chimed in the voice of a stranger. The voice belonged to an enigmatic older man wearing robes. He had recently sat down across the center aisle.

"I apologize for my interruption and eavesdropping. My name is Saezyn. When people speak of their disdain for Queen Odiria, I can't help myself. My family and she have a history," Saezyn explained.

"More than understandable. My name is CJ, and my new acquaintance here is Theban," CJ replied from across the aisle.

"CJ… Carmine Jasmine?" the gentleman supposed.

"Why, yes it is! How did you know!" was her stunned reply.

"The same way that I know the sky-bus we are on needs to take off now! Great is our immediate peril!" Saezyn replied. He then stood up, gave a noble bow to CJ, and rushed up the stairs in great haste.

"What was that about?" Theban asked.

"I don't know. Let's find out!" replied CJ as she got out of her seat and followed after the odd gentleman.

When CJ and Theban reached the summit of the stairs, they found Saezyn talking to the three Paladins. Also among them was the man with the heavy repeater. The Paladins must have stopped him to see why he was so armed.

"Why do we need to take off? What is the problem?" asked the Paladin general.

"We need to take off now!" Saezyn replied in a creepily calm voice.

"I agree with you completely, but we have no choice. It's a computer-automated system, and we don't have a technician. We are just going to have to wait until the scheduled time," the Purge general furrowed his brow in frustration as he expressed his thoughts.

"The Armada is approaching as we speak! If we don't get off the ground soon, we will never get off the ground at all," Saezyn stated grimly.

"I saw what the Armada can do. We *need* to get away from this damned city!" exclaimed Brunick who was the man with the repeater and fiery, red hair. His hair seemed to increase in redness as its owner got more excited.

"Is there nothing we can do, sir?" interjected the tall, blonde female soldier in a melodious voice.

"Not likely," muttered the other soldier who was obviously a newer addition to the Purge.

Out of nowhere, a teenage girl strode forward and nervously interrupted: "I couldn't help overhear your conversation. My name is Cyra, and I may be of some use to you."

CJ recognized her as the same blue-haired girl that had stepped on her communicator.

"How so?" the General quizzed.

"I am an expert hacker. I have been splicing into systems since I was five. I even broke into Nexgen and removed myself from the system. The queen doesn't even know I exist." She blushed slightly.

"Smart girl," Theban whispered to CJ.

"That is quite the resume! You'll do nicely, and I don't think we can afford to put our hope elsewhere with the time we have left!" the General exclaimed.

Moments later, CJ, Theban, Saezyn, and the Paladins were all in the bridge of the *Double Edge* watching Cyra work her magic. Brunick also stood in the room with his repeater at the ready near the door; he had one eye glued on the entrance to the room and one eye watching Cyra do what she did best. She had the system hacked in fifteen seconds, and the computer feeding out of her hand in another ten. A literal minute after Cyra had popped open the control panel in the bridge of the craft, it had been hacked and was running through the take-off sequence.

"How did you do that?" the young recruit they called Trigger asked.

"I've hacked security systems on military craft. This was child's play," she replied.

"You may want to take a mental note of that, General," Trigger nudged the General.

"Oh, don't you worry, it's been noted," the General replied.

Cyra sat down at the captain's chair of the *Double Edge* and took the helm.

"Have you ever flown one of these before?" the beautiful, blonde Paladin named Linia asked.

"Nope! It's my first time!" Cyra smiled a coy but confident grin.

The bridge had other seats as well. Upon the revelation of Cyra's lack of flying experience, the seats soon became occupied by those who were listening. Everybody buckled their seatbelts and watched as Cyra toggled varying controls. She pushed a button, and then the docking clamps released with a gentle clank. The engines roared as Cyra gunned the throttle. The *Double Edge*, with a streak of blue glow from its propulsion system, pierced the night sky as it soared freely away from the scene of carnage wrought by the Armada, but the entire might of the Armada was not entirely engrossed by the destruction they were causing. A solitary cruiser was attacking some of the farmlands surrounding Toria Vilorious, but as soon as the *Double Edge* passed by it, the craft began to alter its course.

"Enemy craft adjusting for intercept," Linia said as she stared nervously at a monitor on the bridge.

"Can you make this go faster?" Trigger pressed. He looked at Cyra skeptically.

"Negative," she replied.

Trigger stepped closer to one of the screens displaying a basic cross section of the Armada vessel nearing them. "What are those lights beginning to glow on the side of the craft?"

"Pods," Saezyn interjected.

"Cyra, do we have any weapons on this ship?" the General asked.

"Again, negative, but if it is going to hit us with pods, we still have a chance."

"What chance do we have if we can't shoot back!" Trigger exclaimed.

"Wait and see." Cyra almost whispered in reply as she focused on what she was about to attempt.

"Enemy pod has been launched! In moments, we will be in dire straits," the General stated with an anxious edge to his voice.

"One moment. One moment." muttered Cyra as she watched the pod grow ever closer. "Now!" Cyra suddenly burst out as she pushed a button. The others in the room watched in amazement as an escape pod from the *Double Edge* was ejected and intercepted the incoming pod. Both destroyed pods fell out of the sky in a shower of debris.

"Excellent timing!" Theban shouted gleefully.

"Stunning," the General muttered under his breath.

"Don't get too excited just yet. If the scan of the enemy vessel is correct, they still have two more pods," Cyra replied.

"You're right! Two more pods in bound!" CJ yelled louder than she had intended, but the intensity of the moment got the best of her.

Cyra didn't say anything; she just glanced at her instrument panels and mumbled half-calculated equations under her breath. The second her mumbling stopped, she fired two more escape pods at the approaching Armada projectiles. Both escape pods successfully found their targets. The occupants of the bridge cheered. CJ stopped in the middle of a hoorah when she noted a ghastly statistic on a nearby screen; it was the velocity of the Armada ship, and it was higher than the velocity of the *Double Edge*. Cyra wasn't cheering either, she had long been aware of the fact they couldn't outrun the fiend.

"They are going to catch us, aren't they?" CJ stated dejectedly.

"Yes, get on the com and tell the passengers to buckle up," Cyra nodded to CJ.

CJ grabbed a microphone on the dash and pushed the com button: "All passengers, we are being engaged by an Armada craft. Find your seats and buckle up."

CJ looked at a monitor that showed the various passenger bays on the vessel. She swore under her breath. The passengers in a state of panic ran to the escape pods and ejected from the *Double Edge*. In moments, the only people on the sky-bus were the people on the bridge. CJ glanced at another screen, and her heart broke. The escape pods that had just ejected could be seen falling behind the ship, and the Armada cruiser in pursuit of the *Double Edge* was systematically shooting each one with a sinister bolt of dark purple energy. No occupant could possibly survive—each pod blew into chunks upon impact with the bent dark energy.

"Well, that went well," Brunick frowned.

"All damned to die for their fear," the General muttered. He sighed and looked at the ceiling.

"And we're next!" Trigger bawled.

"Not if I can help it. We are going to be passing by the Myzex mountain range in a few moments, and we have one escape pod left," Cyra stated calmly.

"So we're going to eject when we are near to the mountains and hope we don't kill ourselves on the rocks?" Theban asked.

"No, we are going to fly low and stay on the ship," Cyra started.

"And eject the pod and send a message saying we are abandoning the ship and hope the Armada hears our message and follows after the pod!" CJ finished excitedly.

"Yup, that's the goal," Cyra replied.

"What if they don't take the bait?" the General pointed out. Several bolts from the enemy cruiser hit the back engine compartments as these dismal sentiments were expressed. A screen showing engine power output levels and health began flashing red.

"We very well could die," Saezyn stated grimly. Trigger swallowed hard. Cyra at that point sent the abandon ship message on all open frequencies and ejected the pod just as they soared yards above the first mountain peak in the approaching mountain range. The pod was blocked by the mountain range so the enemy cruiser couldn't target it. The Armada craft adjusted its course to hunt down the last pod.

"It worked!" Linia exclaimed.

"Sorta, the reason they aren't following us because we have all but lost our engines. We are going down!" Cyra explained glumly.

The bottom of the *Double Edge* roughly scrapped over a jutting mountain peak with an unnerving screech caused by fragmenting rocks and the metal that was ripped off the craft. The *Double Edge* was going to crash. The crew strained against the turbulence, prayed for mercy and braced for impact.

IMPACT

The *Double Edge* barely missed the other murky, jagged peaks in the Myzex mountain range, but there was no way it was going to miss hitting the great Dekdir forest of the planet of Solbia. The craft dropped altitude as though gravity was playing favorites with the ship. The *Double Edge* cut first into trees, then into underbrush and, finally, into the soft dirt of the forest floor. It cut a long trough, as momentum used the ship as a futuristic plow before the *Double Edge* finally came to a steaming halt partially submerged in a small marshland. The bottom level had been ripped off and left strewn in chunks in the wake of the crash. As for the crew: one could only hope they were in better shape than the fractured hull of the *Double Edge*.

CJ opened her eyes a while later; she was still in her seat. The others were as well, but CJ knew that though the enemy cruiser had broken pursuit, they were still in a perilous position. The monitors on the bridge that weren't displaying static or lying broken on the floor in the midst of shattered glass and branches were displaying all that was wrong with the ship; there was more wrong than what was right. In a brief squint around the room, CJ could see that the others were alive as well. It was a bit hazy to see much of anything through the iterating warning lights and the sporadic shafts of morning light that leaked through holes in the ship. She unbuckled her seat belt, and as she went to stand up, the General helped her.

"You okay?" he asked.

"I'm fine. Just minor cuts from the glass. How is everybody else?" CJ replied.

"They are a bit shaken up with minor cuts too, but it seems Trilumina smiled on our prayers this day." He turned and looked out a shattered window at the debris trail behind the *Double Edge*. Twisted metal that was left in the massive gash in the forest glinted in the morning twilight. He continued with his tone aghast: "We should have died!"

"There is time for that yet," Cyra interrupted.

"Why? What do you mean?" Theban asked. He stood up from his seat and brushed off some wreckage from his overalls.

Cyra pointed to one of the few remaining functioning screens. "The engines are obliterated, but the generators that supplied the power to said engines were not knocked out. In fact, they still aren't down," Cyra said from where she still remained—in the captain's chair.

"What does that mean?" Linia asked. She was bandaging a mild laceration on Trigger's side.

"It means this place is going to go blow!" Trigger replied as he winced through Linia dabbing the wound with a sterilizing agent.

"Are we all able to move?" the General asked.

"Yep, let's get out of here!" Trigger bellowed.

The occupants of the bridge, hastened by warning alarms, climbed out of one of the broken windows on the bridge and slid down the curved surface of the *Double Edge* to the shallow swamp below. It took them only a few moments to skirt to the edge of the marshland where they took refuge under one of the wings that was braced against a large boulder. The wing had been ripped off the craft when it touched down. Much to their surprise, they found that two people were already under the chosen place of asylum. CJ recognized them instantly as the man in the dark trench coat and the female biker that was pursuing him, but what she couldn't understand was that the man was taking care of the unconscious woman. He was patting a wound she had on her forehead.

"Hurry up and crouch down here with me! The ship is going to blow!" the man exclaimed. The General and his two troops looked at the man warily; the man had on his person two pistols and the shotgun originally possessed by the biker.

"Oh, don't worry, I mean no harm. If I wanted you dead, I would have killed you already," the man said.

"I doubt that," Trigger snorted.

In response, the man didn't even look up from gently mopping the brow of the biker as he pulled his gun, shot a two-foot-long monarch cricket off a nearby frond and holstered his pistol afore any of the Paladins could raise their weapons. Before any other verbal interchange could be ventured, the smoldering form of the Double Edge began to groan under the stress of the extreme power buildup. Everybody at that point took shelter with the gunslinger beneath the wing. Their flight was not a moment too soon because the craft immediately experienced a ship-wide system failure, and then the generator blew. Fire raced through the *Double Edge* gutting her corpse and spilling more wreckage throughout the small bog it had come to rest in.

"That was close," Theban muttered as he looked at the debris that was still falling from the sky. Theban, being the craftsman that he was, realized how much work was just senselessly wrecked before his eyes when the ship tore itself to pieces under extreme stress. He couldn't help but stop and stare, as a sudden wave of sorrow hit his chest. The destruction of the ship reminded him that all he had ever built and all those who he had built for had been destroyed a mere few hours before the crash.

Nobody commented on Theban's utterance though, they were already staring at the man who was taking care of the girl that had initially tried to explode his head like a melush melon.

"I gotta ask. Wasn't she trying to kill you?" CJ said finally breaking the awkward silence.

"With a vengeance," he mumbled as he looked down kindly at her face.

"Then, why are… you love her, don't you?" CJ couldn't hide the surprise in her voice.

"I can't explain it, but I do. More than I have loved anything in a long time. In an odd way, this woman who wanted to take my life—actually saved it. I can't explain it," The gunslinger wandered off in thought.

"I can explain it, you're insane," Trigger murmured under his breath.

"Who are you exactly?" the General asked.

"He is Ribus! A.k.a. pond scum incarnate!" the woman who was lying on the ground shrieked. She had awaken from her head wound, and she was upright and at Ribus's throat before anybody knew what was going on. Fortunately for Ribus, Linia and Trigger rushed to grab the biker's arms and hold her back.

"You killed my gang! I will cut out your spleen and feed it to you!" she screamed.

"It looks like she loves him too," Brunick whispered to Trigger. Both chuckled.

"I also saved your life twice," Ribus countered calmly.

"When you blew up the Biogen building or was it when you summoned the aliens to destroy the city?" she spat.

"You blew up the Biogen building!" Brunick burst out at the revelation.

"I did blow up the Biogen building, but I only retrieved an alien artifact for the queen. She probably summoned those monstrosities. As for me saving you, I saved you a moment ago when I hauled your unconscious body out of the sky-bus. I don't expect your thanks, but I did do you a favor," Ribus replied in his defense.

"When was the second time?" Linia asked sweetly.

"When I blew up the Biogen building, I also stole Valdria's bike." Ribus motioned to the biker chick as he continued. "She didn't like that at all, so she took up pursuit. Had she stayed behind with her fellow bikers, the building would have fallen on her and killed her with the rest of her gang. As for the bikers I killed, I did that in self-defense."

The biker who everyone now knew to be named Valdria sat silently, but she glared fiercely at Ribus.

"I can't believe you are the one who blew up my employers!" Brunick suddenly grew silent as the others looked at him disdainfully. He had forgotten in the heat of the recent revelations that the Vilkra were not popular people.

"You're a Vilkra?" Ribus glared at him. Even the General who had only lived a few months on Solbia cocked his high-powered rifle. Word of the Vilkra's ill deeds had spread far and wide.

"No, I'm not. I make equipments for them. Like their sleepers and such," Brunick knew he had to tread very carefully.

"What is the *and such*?" Cyra asked coldly. Her encounter with the Vilkra earlier the previous night did not cause her to look fondly on Brunick.

He looked at the angry faces staring him down, and he knew that even with the heavy repeater he held, he couldn't defend himself against all his adversaries when they were so armed. Had Brunick tried to explain his way out of the hole he had dug, the others would surely have buried him in it, but Theban saved him with a sudden outpouring of guilt. Since blame had started being assigned, Theban felt he must confess his part in the night's events.

"The queen didn't summon the monsters! It was me. It was all me! I'm so sorry! I built an amplifier that caused that cursed crystal's signal to be broadcast widely. She made me do it! I didn't want too, and I didn't know so much trouble would come from it!" Theban suddenly burst forth. Everybody turned and looked at him.

"No, it wasn't your fault, Theban. It was mine," Saezyn said firmly to shake the man out of his guilty conscience.

"What do you mean? How are you so sure?" the General asked.

"I told the queen to summon the Armada!"

FALLOUT

Everybody looked at him with aghast expressions upon their faces. This man who they suspected to be a prophet had just taken responsibility for the annihilation of millions of people.

"Why? Did you know that the crystal would bring the Armada?" CJ managed through the shock.

"I did."

"You wanted to destroy the city?" the General asked in utter bewilderment.

"Yes, allow me to explain. For centuries, my family, the Seldocs, have been a family of prophets. In that time, we have gone into the city and pleaded with the rulers and the people of Toria to turn from their lusts, their hate of Trilumina, and their greed—but to no avail. Many a time, we also interceded with Trilumina to not wipe the city from Ephesia like the stain that it was, but time went on, and my family was killed at the hands of those they were sent to save. Three days ago, I sent my son—who was the only other Seldoc left besides me, but he was killed like the rest… like my wife some time ago as well. I loved my son, and they rejected him and thus signed the edict against their lives. That day, Trilumina told me to go pronounce judgment against the grand city of Toria Vilorious, and so I went. I tricked the queen into using the crystal to summon what she thought would be new allies against the Purge, but I knew that the Armada would come, not the allies she expected, and the city would be destroyed." A sterile look was plastered across Saezyn's brow, but it only went so far to hide the pain at losing his son and hurt caused by the hardness of the hearts in the people of Toria Vilorious.

Everybody present was subdued at Saezyn Seldoc's tale. Nobody knew what to say. In that moment, many realized that the sins that Toria was destroyed for existed in themselves, and this softened the mood significantly.

"What can we do now? Are we under Trilumina's curse too? Has he prolonged our judgment?" CJ asked.

"No, he has granted you a second chance," Saezyn stated solemnly.

"What can we do then? What should we do?" Valdria asked, breaking her silence.

"The hardest thing that can be asked of each of you now, knowing what you know about one another: Forgive. Yes, let go of the need for vengeance toward the wrongs that have been done to you."

"That's a tall order, don't you think?" Ribus asked. He was still scowling at Brunick. Not so deep down, Ribus hoped he had gotten rid of all the Vilkra and their associates when the Biogen tower blew.

"I agree! Trusting certain people among us seems hard and to be frank—stupid," Cyra stated. She frowned at Brunick. The fear of being injected with Spikeradon revisited her when one who helped the Vilkra stood in her midst.

"I said forgive. Nobody said anything about trusting. Well, at least not at this point. Also, in answer to your question, Ribus: yes, it is a tall order, but showing mercy is required, since Trilumina himself spared all of your lives! Remember this when you are inclined to grumble against one another: Trilumina is merciful to those who show mercy, and he will judge others by the scale they use for their fellow man," Saezyn replied. He stared deeply at each of the people until they averted from his gaze. He then continued: "You may not always be in each other's company, but for now, I have been told to travel with you and to keep you together."

"Why? Why should we believe you?" Trigger quizzed.

"You should believe me because I am an instrument of Trilumina. I represent the Great One, and to be dishonest would give reason for Trilumina to punish me for my lies. Also, if you leave the group, you will surely die," Saezyn replied.

"What if we don't believe you?" Ribus ventured.

"I know I am hated, and I don't pretend like I don't deserve it, but I traveled with Saezyn last night, and all that he said and predicted was true. He told me before the Armada came that Toria would fall last night, and it has. Also, I have lived outside of the city for a long time and know that dark creatures dwell in the wild, so even if Trilumina didn't strike any deserters down, chances are, the elements or creatures would," Brunick boldly proclaimed.

"He is right! Let us join together and work toward forgetting our pasts and our grudges. Let us move forth and start a new life!" CJ encouraged.

"That is easy for you to say, the Zykor dragons were my family, and now, they are dead! What family have you lost," Valdria vented.

"I lost my husband a few hours ago to the hands of the Armada, and my heart is weeping inside my chest still, but I must move on despite my pain, or my past will become a prison of sorrow and ruin what chance I have for a new life," CJ replied. Valdria's facial features softened significantly, and she looked at CJ apologetically.

"CJ is right! Let us join together and venture forth in hopes of discovering whatever the future may hold! Let Toria and the lives that we lived there pass on! Now is a chance to create something new and beautiful," Theban exclaimed full of gusto.

The group looked at one another doubtfully, but at a scowl from Saezyn, they set out together in the opposite direction of Toria Vilorious. They were leaving the past behind them.

FELDAG POUNCERS

Not long after the ragtag group of survivors left the tall fronds and murky pools of the swamp where the *Double Edge* came to rest, they found themselves in the thick of the Dekdir forest. Saezyn knew the lands well and guided them along an all but lost path. Though it was morning, the thick foliage above filtered the light and painted their surrounds light green and dimmed the light, so visibility was reduced. Everywhere, tigond trees soared above them only to have their true heights masked by the canopy. The trees had large, triangular palm leafs that directed rainwater toward the base of the tree. Though amazing to behold, the tigond trees were not the most captivating plants to witness; the most unusual plants were what looked to be buds as tall as a two-story building. These were scattered amongst the boughs of the monolithic tigond.

"Buldalusia! I heard my dad talk about them, but I had never seen them before," Brunick muttered in awe.

"Is that the name of the trees?" CJ asked.

"No, that's the name of the large, bulbous things we are walking near. The trees are tigond trees," Linia answered.

"I learned these things from my dad. How do you know about them?" Brunick asked Linia. "You who have only been on Solbia a short time." He was surprised to hear someone with little, firsthand knowledge of the planet Solbia to know about some of its secrets.

"I am a medic, as you may well know by some of the markings upon my uniform, but I also use biological methods of healing as well, so I have a grasp of the biology of many of the worlds under Purge control—and even some not under its authority," she replied.

"Did you learn of the dangers of the buldalusia bulb plant?" Brunick asked. It was one of the first times he cracked a smile since the others had learned of his involvement with the Vilkra. They weren't being too warm to him, currently, but Linia didn't hold grudges easy, so she continued talking even when she noted a couple of distasteful glances thrown her way as she continued the conversation.

"I haven't. What are the dangers?" she countered.

"Feldag pouncers nest among them. According to myth, they lay their eggs inside them. When the eggs hatch, they eat the innards of the plant until there are too many feldags inside. Then they burst forth and seek warm-blooded creatures. The word is they have the appearance of a flea crossed with a wolf, and they can jump thirty yards in a leap. That's the rumor though," Brunick replied.

Trigger clutched his rifle tighter, and Theban muttered, "He certainly knows how to get on a person's good side, don't he?"

"Brunick, how confirmed is this myth?" the General asked. He didn't like surprises, so if these feldag pouncers were real, he would want a heads up.

"The only other thing I know is if they are real, they are rare, and that they reside in buldalusia bulbs that are a sick brown color," replied the mechanic.

"You mean like that one." Trigger pointed toward a slightly smaller bulb that had all the decay you would expect to see exhibited by one full of parasites. Everybody cocked their weapons at this point, and CJ gave Theban the rifle she had scrounged the night before so he could be equipped with something to defend himself with.

Ribus turned and looked at Valdria; she frowned at him. He walked closer to her, stared her square in the eye with a stern look, and unslung the shotgun from his shoulder. She returned the hard stare, but much to everyone's amazement, he still gave the gun back to her—knowing full well her aptitude at pulling the trigger. She took the gun and looked almost as bewildered as the rest. Ribus gave her a nod and then turned his back: the ultimate sign of trust, considering the circumstances. No words were said by anyone, but the significance of what had happened was not lost upon anybody. If Valdria wanted him dead, he had just given her all the means to do so. She cocked the gun and raised it till it was pointed at the back of his head, but she didn't pull the trigger. She put the safety on and slung it around her shoulder. A communal sigh of relief was breathed by all. If a tough Zykor dragon biker could forgive, perhaps they all could.

But time to contemplate such things was not allowed because much to everyone's dread, the sickened Buldalusia plant before them began to move. Everybody held their weapons at the ready, even Theban, who was not accustomed to fighting.

"What shall we do?" Theban asked.

"Shoot every mother's son of em' that rears its spag maggot face," the General replied.

They didn't have to wait long to start shooting the "spag maggots," for indeed, out of a hole in the base of the bulb, a creature began to emerge. A cat-sized feldag presented itself. The monster had all facets of ugliness combined together in perfect measure: ragged fur, a double set of spider-like jaws, three gleaming yellow eyes, and glistening, large, grasshopper-like legs. It gave an intense, high-pitched, insectiod shriek and leapt out of the maw from whence it first emerged. It didn't get far from its hole before Ribus—in his lightning speed—put a bullet in its middle eye. The dead beast propelled by its former velocity smashed into a bulb behind them, laid on the ground, and bled out of its fatal wound.

Though the fiend was first out of the hole and first to die, it certainly wouldn't be the last to rouse from its festering den.

More were soon to follow—a lot more. CJ and the group joined together alternating fire at the hole and killing the fiends as they came. The interchanging fire allowed time for the band to reload. Dozens of the creatures were slaughtered in minutes, but the stream seemed endless, and it wouldn't be long before the Paladins and the others would run out of ammo.

"Wait, you guys!" Brunick yelled when there was a break in the flow of creatures. "Let me handle this."

He stepped forward, and his gun roared as he unloaded a relentless volley of laser fire from his heavy repeater. Soon, the bodies of the creatures were blocking their exit of the bulb, but Brunick didn't stop. He kept shooting until the corpse pile caught on fire. The fire quickly spread to the dried-out, rotten, old buldalusia that the feldags lived in. Soon, the den was ablaze, and for a few moments, shrieks emanated from the ghastly bonfire, but soon, the roar of the flames drowned out the parasites' screams. Brunick spat into the fire, put his repeater over his shoulder, and grimly exclaimed: "Die, you damnable spag crickets!"

The General clapped him on the back, and even Ribus gave him a nod that wordlessly said: "You're all right."

The group watched the spectacle of the feldag roast for a few moments before the stink of the smoke drove them on in their pilgrimage through the Dekdir forest. They came upon many beautiful plants and flowers of iridescent blues, greens, and other colors that made one want to weep at the beauty and cry out with joy. Evening began to fall as the trek commenced, and ever so slowly, they began to respect one another even if they didn't exactly like each other. In the twilight, the beauty of the woods was magnified as the plants showed brightly in the contrast provided by the low light. The buldalusia even revealed their secrets. At night, the healthy bulbs would open up and reveal that they were one massive multi-tier flower. Each tier was smaller than the one below and another shade of luminescent blue. The base was dark, but the plant progressed in increasingly lighter shades as one gazed gapingly at each level of the huge plants. The plant seemed to return to the evening the light that it had absorbed during the day and act as nightlights for the group to traverse by.

"Why did you help the Vilkra? You don't seem like their kind of sleaze," CJ suddenly asked as the group beheld the beauty of Trilumina's handiwork.

"It paid well, and nobody else would hire me since I wasn't in the Nexgen system. I was born outside of the city and needed money to get by. I didn't know where to turn. I guess, in hindsight, I made a turn in the wrong direction, but for money, people will sell a lot of themselves," Brunick replied sadly. Ribus looked at the ground at Brunick's words, and Valdria turned her face so nobody could look upon her, but one thing was for sure—Brunick had struck a chord.

"Just for money?" CJ questioned like she couldn't relate.

"It's not always money. Sometimes, people compromise themselves for something else," Brunick shrugged.

"I don't think—" CJ was going to say that she didn't feel like she could relate, but then Saezyn gave her a glance. Suddenly, she remembered when she first met Xyles and how she knew he was married. It didn't stop her though, she used all her skills she had learned at the queen's palace as an exotic dancer to woo him and ultimately steal him from his wife. CJ had compromised just as much as the thugs and murderers walking in her midst. Tears came to her eyes—she too was like "them," people she used to compare herself to and feel good about herself, but no! That was a lie. She was just as monstrous as they were; her soul reeked of the same moral decay.

"I thought of it like that before," she finished weakly. Places she had once placed her self-worth and sense of decency crashed down all around her. Saezyn saw the pained expression on her face, and he too seemed sad. It was like he knew more about her than she had ever revealed to anyone. After that, she and many of the others walked in silence as they pondered things from a renewed perspective.

REPOSE

The motley group made it to the fringe of the great Dekdir forest as night began to fall. The Solbian moon called C'Yi shown silver as the last rays from Orgasoli receded behind quickly approaching rain clouds.

"We are close now!" Saezyn exclaimed joyously.

"Close to what? I was under the impression we didn't know where we were going," Cyra said somewhat irritably as she swatted a gnat.

"To my home! We can get some supplies and rest for our journey," Saezyn replied.

"That doesn't answer the young lady's question," Theban stated.

"No, it doesn't. That's because my directions are that we need to go in the opposite direction of Toria Vilorious. I have yet to be told what we are to find there," he answered.

"Fair enough. Where is your home?" the General asked.

"On the top of that cliff over there is a village: Drizda. It is the village of the Seldocs. Now, it is little more than a ghost town that many fear to enter, but we will find supplies and rest there," Saezyn replied.

"Why do people fear to enter it?" CJ asked curiously.

"Past the Dekdir forest, there are entities, dark and drear, specifically a tribe of savages called the Ridiculin; they practice dark arts. The Seldocs have raged war with them for many years. Our methods and weapons are not the usual weapons people are used to seeing, so rather than seeking understanding, people just turn to fear and dub both them and us quaint," Saezyn replied calmly.

"Like magic?" Brunick asked.

"You might call it magic, but if one explores the depths of the Seldoc methods, they realize that our power comes from Trilumina. The savages practice magic. Magic is a craft of Ordam and thus is vile in every way. Ordam is Trilumina's far weaker enemy, but that is not to say he is weak. Ordam is the one who crafted the defective Armada, and you guys saw what that can do last night," stated Saezyn.

Even in the heart of wretched Toria Vilorious, everybody knew that Ordam was the enemy of goodness in Ephesia and having just learned that Ordam was the origin of the Armada, many in the group shuddered.

It wasn't long before Saezyn lead them up a series of switchbacks leading to the top of a cliff. On top, the first thing to be beheld was a homely, little village built into a large cutout in the cliff side. The hovels of Drizda were small, but they were built into the cliffs which hid their true expanse. The village was placed in front of an ancient stone temple at the far end that also was built into the rock face. In between, all the structures were warm courtyards that were packed with fruit trees and other crops.

The second sight to enrapture the travelers was the view from the stone shelf that Drizda was built upon; below, they could look down on the Dekdir forest and the towering spires of the tigond trees. Past the forest, they could see the Myzex mountain range that they had nearly crashed into, and past this, they could see through a gap betwixt two mountains the city of Toria Vilorious. It was completely laid to waste. Fire ran rampant, and hundreds of large, grey ships hovered above raining fiery bombs down like rain drops in a fire storm.

"Look what the Armada has done!" Cyra murmured.

The General looked though the scope on his weapon and shook his head. "No, it isn't the Armada. Thankfully, they are gone!"

"Who is it then?" CJ asked.

"It is the Purge. Those are Purge ships. They are burning the city," Linia stated sadly.

"Why!? I thought the Purge was good!" Cyra was shocked.

Brunick knew the response because of what Saezyn did to his truck the night before, and he soon made it known: "They don't have any choice. They are containing the mechamites."

"That's right. I have seen entire planets fall to those metallic menaces. The ships you see now are the reinforcements I called in to help when we learned what the queen had done with the crystal. If we didn't purge the city, the Armada would have had a mighty hold on this world. It's either burn the city until it is glass now, or run a campaign that will last dozens of years against Solbia trying to get rid of them without any guarantees of success later. This is the only way. Whether you guys wanted to leave Toria or not, there is no going back," the General said grimly.

He soon looked away from the spectacle; he had seen this a dozen times before. Victory shouldn't look like this, but it was better than seeing a planet painted silver by the mechamites that would cover the world in their evil sheen if their plague wasn't contained. The others soon turned away as well; it was too melancholic to dwell upon for long.

Saezyn looked around suspiciously—something wasn't right. He quickly ushered the group away from the cliff and led them to a hovel and opened the door to let them in. It was his home. He quickly grabbed a long, complexly designed, metallic staff that was placed next to the door. It was clearly Saezyn's weapon of choice. With the weapon in hand, he motioned to a large round stone room just off the main entryway. "There should be enough couches and beds for you to sleep in there, and I have food stashed away in the kitchen. Help yourselves and rest up. I will stand guard tonight. You are well-protected." Saezyn pushed a button on his metallic staff that caused a long, sharp blade to extend out of the tip of the weapon as he said these words. It had an odd white crystal fixed in it as well. Saezyn wearing his robes now complimented by his futuristic halberd seemed rather menacing. He had also put on a hooded cloak to protect him from the rain that they could now hear cascading against the wood shackle roof; this hood further added intrigue to an already mysterious person. Everyone, including the Paladins, relaxed, and something about this humble abode was comforting and restful.

Saezyn showed the diverse group to the kitchen where they had a meal of mainly fruits and vegetables, but it seemed the best food in the world after their long trek. Saezyn partook of the vittles with them and set up places for them to sleep, but before they could thank him for his hospitality, he disappeared from their midst. From where they sat at couches in the main room, they barely turned in time to see the tails of his cloak blowing in the wind as he rushed out of the door. The wind and rain sounded louder for the moment the door was open, but the previous muffled, staccato fall of raindrops on the roof resumed upon the closing of the door. They all looked at one another, but nobody dared question their host.

"Where is he going? It's a terrible night to be out in the weather!" Cyra enquired.

"I would imagine he must be outside standing watch but also talking to Trilumina," the General thought out loud.

"He is certainly an interesting individual," Theban replied.

"Interesting is one word for it. Personally, I would go with eerie, peculiar, or strange," said Trigger. He was famous for his half-baked thoughts.

"You don't think he means us harm do you?" Valdria replied.

"Of course not! Trigger is just paranoid over there," the General responded and scowled at Trigger. Trigger grumbled quietly to himself.

"If you are going to grumble in private, I will order you to bed like a child. Do I make myself clear?!" the General bellowed in his signature voice for giving orders.

"Sir, yes, sir! Stopping grumbling now!" Trigger stood stone still at attention with his clenched fist crossed over his chest. It was the Paladin's method of saluting and stood for duty to the death with all of one's heart.

"That's better private! At ease. Go and help Linia prepare rations for tomorrow and then catch some well-deserved rest," the General smiled. Trigger gave a grin as he and Linia left the room. Theban and Cyra said something about helping too, and they strode from where they were in the main room. Ribus and Brunick had already found places to sleep, and they were comfortably snoozing, thus leaving the General, Valdria, and CJ sitting in the main room on couches.

"Do you trust easy, General?" CJ asked.

"Perhaps at times, but I found that I can read people pretty well. Usually," he replied.

"What do you mean by the 'usually?'" Valdria quizzed.

"In this group, I have a pretty solid perception on most of the people we have traveled with this past day. My team of Linia and Trigger are loyal to the Purge as I well know through past missions. Theban loves to make beautiful things and would prefer to be left alone but is a team player nonetheless, Brunick started life on the wrong foot but wants to go in a fresh direction. You, Valdria, are a fierce companion but loyal to your family."

"Except now they are dead, and now, I'm alone!" she said bitterly.

"Are you? I suppose only you can decide that," the General replied. Valdria seemed somewhat taken back.

"Why did you say 'usually?'" CJ asked noticing he didn't really say why in his first answer.

"The 'usually' in my judgments is actually provided by you CJ. You, I have some difficulty reading. For the most part, I know you don't mean any harm, but I feel you have more room to surprise me than, shall we say, some of our more decorated compatriots," the General smiled kindly.

"What about me and Ribus?" Valdria queried when she noticed he didn't finish his perception of them.

"I think you guys would make a good couple if *you* could get past your bitterness," he replied.

"Couple! What? That is not what I meant, and you know it!" she fumed.

"I know, but one person doesn't get so mad at another without killing them if deep down you don't have some reason for keeping them alive. Also, I think both of you are steadfast, not to one particular authority, but to your pursuit of freedom and to those who go with you in it," the General stated sagely as he finished his evaluations of Ribus and Valdria.

Valdria stared hard at him for a moment and then left the room to go to bed.

"You did that on purpose, didn't you?" CJ asked.

"I did. I do hope she can get past herself because they would make a good couple," he replied.

"Are you a matchmaker as well?" she smiled.

He just chuckled. "The other person I have trouble reading as you can probably easily guess by those who I have mentioned and those I have not, is Saezyn. I know he is fiercely devoted to Trilumina, but besides what he has chosen to share with us, we know very little about him," the General pondered out loud. At this thought, both sat quietly and mused about their circumstances. The rough torrent of rain on the roof occasionally broken by the flash of lightning lured them both to sleep where they sat in the comfort of the den.

THE TASK

Saezyn's cloak swirled about him, as the wind contorted it like an unskilled puppeteer. The torrential downpour did nothing to soften his resolve. He didn't need to go outside to protect his guests, but Saezyn had two intentions for going out into the tempest: first to pray to Trilumina and seek guidance for the mission he was to embark on and second, to dispose of rubbish. The rubbish was an entity of darkness that he had sensed when they made it to Drizda, nobody else sensed it, but Saezyn had raged war with the Ridiculin in the land for years on end, and this night, he sensed their darkness from miles off. They had a long-standing feud with Saezyn due to the fact that Seldocs killed the Ridiculin on sight as punishment to their allegiance to Ordam. They specifically hated Saezyn because he had killed more of them than any prior Seldoc. Hundreds of Ridiculin had died upon the edge of his blade.

Saezyn knelt down on a short stone plinth in front of the temple of Drizda. The platform had three steps leading to its top; upon this pedestal, Saezyn would meditate on Trilumina and seek guidance. Despite the wind and rain, nothing in his routine changed. The water pounded on his face, and Saezyn Seldoc lifted his hands to the sky. "My Father, Father of all creation and Craftsman of Ephesia, how I thank you for this life and for your mercy. Please grant me wisdom in the days to come and help me to guide these people you have spared. May I direct them to you so that they can receive the abundant mercies and gifts you want to bestow upon them. I also beg you with all that I am, all the heart you have put within me, all the breath in my lungs and the entirety of the soul you have placed in my frail form, please, please. Oh, my God, please help these people to pass from their way that ends in death unto new life. You have saved me from my wretched past, so I know that you, too, can reach the battered hearts of these people," Saezyn's tears that fell from his face as he pleaded with his God were masked by the rain that bespattered his face. The torrents continued and still without motion but with his soul racked with emotion, Saezyn waited for his God to reply.

"I will do everything in my power without denying them their free will. Your task is to go with them, and as you walk, I will show you what to do and what to say, and I shall reveal your path beneath your feet but now, rise from where you kneel and strike down your enemies for they have come seeking your blood. I have gathered them altogether so they might finally be put down," a voice whispered in the storm that fell around Saezyn: the voice of Trilumina.

Upon the hearing of these words, Saezyn was strengthened and rose to his feet with his staff in hand. He opened his eyes: All around him, the savages had him encircled. Saezyn slammed the staff onto the top of his place of prayer and yelled above the storm, "You would disrupt me while I pray! You shall not desecrate Trilumina's temple nor my place of prayer. Cursed be the air you breathe, you spawn of darkness!" Upon finishing the word "darkness," lightning cut through the sky and struck the blade of Saezyn's halberd. The energy didn't go into the ground or into Saezyn, it stayed in the crystal mounted on the staff, which in turn had glowed electric blue.

The chieftain of the savages began to chant strange incantations which the others began to repeat in a demonic frenzy. The chieftain lifted his weird incantation stick, yelled a word, and his rabble ran towards Saezyn. Saezyn didn't wait for them to attack; he was already running straight for the chieftain when the mob began to press in. The horde came from all angles. The savages being in Drizda was their first mistake, attacking a prophet of Trilumina was their final mistake. He didn't spare any in his Trilumina-bestowed fury. In Saezyn's first stroke of his ethereally charged weapon, he beheaded seven savages, and in his second, he cut the chieftain in two—from head to toe. The next four strokes cut down any within the range of his halberd, and for Saezyn's final strike, he drove the blade of his weapon into the ground. The lightning flashed from the weapon through the rain-drenched ground and flowed into the few remaining enemies. When the fierce vehemence of the lightning coursed through the dead and the savages yet to die, the power consumed the wicked with such fervency that only smoke soon to be blown away was all that was left of them.

Saezyn retracted the blade of his weapon and knelt once again in prayer. The rain was then reduced to a drizzle, as though the weather had sensed the now relaxed aura of Drizda. For another two hours, Saezyn knelt in deep communion with Trilumina and interceded with his God for the souls of his friends. After that, Saezyn rose up and went back into his home to prepare for the journey.

JOURNEY'S BEGINNING

The morning soon came, and nobody knew of Saezyn's exploits the night before, they just found him sharpening his weapon at the kitchen table. Around him, a large breakfast was set up for his guests. It was a platter complete with spards (a spicy, potato-like vegetable cut up hash brown style), gopla pastries (a delicious crimson fruit with soft skin and healing properties), buldalusia milk (a drink much like soy milk which came from the roots of the buldalusia plant), and excellently flavored, spit-roasted monarch crickets. It was a delicious breakfast—even the crickets because of their flavor that was not so different than roasted chicken. With his hood pulled back, Saezyn no longer looked so fierce, rather his wizened face and timeworn wrinkles lit up the room as he smiled at the sight of his guests.

"We have to eat up and get ready. Our journey continues today," he said warmly.

"Do you know where we are going?" CJ asked.

"It's doubtful," Cyra grinned.

"Actually, Cyra, I do. Sorta. We are continuing in the direction we were going yesterday," Saezyn replied while everyone sat down at the large beautifully carved kitchen table.

"I told you, he still doesn't know where exactly we are going," Cyra jovially jibed. Even the General smiled at her playful insults.

"Does anybody know exactly where they are going? Who can truly know where their path leads? Many a day with wisdom beyond that which most are gifted with, I have walked the face of Solbia and known only vaguely of my fate. Trilumina directs my path and indeed, many paths," Saezyn sagely replied and returned the grin. The comment silenced them on the topic, but few things could silence or restrain the friendly banter that was passed between the survivors of the tragedy of Toria. In a short while, certain individuals among the group had taken a shine to certain others. Still prejudices remained but not anywhere near to the degree as when the people had first boarded the *Double Edge* two nights before. When everyone realized that their survival out past the edge of the wild depended upon the others in the group, the previous qualms had to be pushed aside for the task at hand. An example of the banter that radiated throughout the room was currently about engines. It was being passed between Cyra and Brunick; both had knowledge of mechanical devices and other technologies.

"I'm telling you, Brunick, the type-37 engine is faster than the B9-454! It served me well on some of my more mischievous outings in Toria. I could reach speeds of 200 miles per hour on non-inhibited streets!" Cyra exclaimed.

"Two hundred? Is that all? Well, with a B9-454, by means of the proper mods, I could get *one-point-five* times that, and with some even better mods to my computer relay system, I could pass through all speed zones without being hit by the flak enforcement tanks!" Brunick exclaimed as he one upped Cyra.

"Have you ever hacked the core processor of one of the said flak tanks?" Cyra smirked. She knew she had just five upped Brunick. Brunick just shook his head and smiled—he knew she had him beat.

"Have you ever sniped a drone pilot through the view slit on one of said tanks from twenty blocks away?" Ribus asked wryly as he joined in the conversation.

"I can't say that I have," Cyra replied as she regarded him with a look of surprise on her face. The look of amazement came when her lightning-fast brain calculated that that was sniping a droid from over two miles and getting the shot threw a gap that was only an inch high.

"What weapon did you use?" Trigger asked excitedly. He was young, but his knowledge and passion of guns was unparalleled.

"A 7M XSS, better known as the specter rifle," Ribus said coolly. Trigger's mouth dropped open.

"The seven-mile extreme sniper system! That is a military-grade sniper rifle used in special ops; otherwise, it is a universally banned firearm! The specter rifle is the stuff of legends! How did you get one?" Trigger exclaimed.

"I built one with help from Theban. Sadly, it was destroyed in the destruction of Toria, but I have fond memories with it just the same." Ribus smiled.

"How did I help you? I don't recall seeing you before," Theban, startled by this revelation, coughed on the joko juice that he was sipping on.

"I ordered the metal of the proper strength and the precision tools from your shop. Under a phony name, of course, but the specter is, without a doubt, my favorite weapon. Being able to snipe a foe from seven miles is an experience like few in the galaxy of Ephesia." Ribus smiled smugly.

"If your ego was any bigger, we could board it and fly to wherever we need to go and we wouldn't have to walk," Valdria said dryly at Ribus's boasts. He looked at her and smiled faintly while everybody else laughed at her comment.

More smack talk and friendly banter of the same caliber ensued until the drinks were drained and plates were emptied. Soon, people pushed away from the table and prepared their packs with rations and clothes that Saezyn had had stashed away. They all found travelling cloaks to keep the rain out, and Ribus found a wide-brimmed, leather fedora that accentuated his gunslinger persona. He used his hat and leather trench instead of a cloak to keep the weather out.

"Ready to go?" Saezyn asked merrily. The group was in the main room where they were making final preparations to their gear.

"Indeed," replied the General as he hoisted up his bag on his shoulders

"What are we waiting for, gramps?" Cyra replied in her street urchin accent. She had a grandparent-like appreciation for Saezyn and thus loved to joke with him.

"You have to learn some manners, *Miss* Cyra!" he exclaimed and gave her a stern look, but she could see the sparkle in his eyes that revealed his disingenuous glare was a mask for the smile in his heart.

"I think we are all ready," CJ confirmed after a quick look around the room. Everybody had a bag of rations, clothes, and a weapon for protection.

"All right then, follow me," Saezyn replied with a mysterious grin. They all expected him to lead them out of the front door of the homey hovel, but he did not, he led them to the back of the food storage room. He pushed a stone button that blended into the wall, and the farthest wall from the entrance slid back to reveal a dark maw.

"Since you were so eager to go, after you, Cyra," Saezyn smirked.

"Now that it comes down to it, gramps, I think I am actually content to follow," she replied. The ominous opening had a way of discouraging.

The smile remained upon his face as Saezyn walked over to the opening and pushed another stone button inside the ingress. A brief, buzzing sound emanated from the darkness before lavender light erased the blackness and revealed a passageway.

THE HOLLOW

They walked for a few minutes down the passageway that descended below Drizda until they wandered into a large, high-ceilinged cave that must have taken up much of the center of the rock that Drizda was built upon. In the cave were large shelves of books and inscriptions carved in an ancient language.

"What is this place?" Linia asked.

"Some sort of cave," Trigger thought out loud.

"Duh!" Valdria exclaimed cynically. Trigger frowned at his own stupidity, and Valdria pointing it out.

"This is 'The Hollow.' It is a place where the Seldocs store food and record history and wise insights. As the years have passed, we have carved our knowledge upon the walls and wrote them into the ancient volumes that fill the shelves. Our entire history and many revelations bestowed upon us by Trilumina dwell in this place. Though I love to study in here, we have not the time, and we are merely passing through this great place. All I will take from this room is a tome of words from Trilumina bequeathed upon the Seldoc clan through the ages. It is my practice to meditate on such wondrous teachings. On the other side of this room, there is a cave that leads to Drilgon Prairie, and past that, I know not what we will find," Saezyn replied. They could tell that he loved this place by the way he looked around the room happily, and he occasionally touched an ancient, dust-covered volume as a smile spread across his face at his remembrance of the book's contents.

"Why don't you know what is past Drilgon Prairie?" Theban asked. He too was baffled by the size of the handsomely carved square pillars of the cavern.

"I have never gone that far in that direction. Usually, I have been bound for Toria, not the opposite bearing, so we should have an interesting next couple of days. I have heard rumors of what lies beyond, but whether they are true has yet to be seen," Saezyn elaborated.

"Such as?" CJ asked.

"What? The rumors? Oh, the usual: dragons, large insects of peaceful intentions, and spinderks of hostile motives." Saezyn smiled as the others looked on with expressions of discomfort upon their faces.

"Oh, don't you worry!" CJ said courageously out of nowhere. "Whatever of the rumors are false, those aren't real and therefore not worth our time and as for the others... We are a resourceful bunch."

"Well put! I personally look forward to an outdoor adventure!" the General exclaimed as they headed toward the dimly lit exit tunnel.

DRILGON PRAIRIE

A brief trek through another tunnel painted by lavender luminescence gave way to the wide open of Drilgon Prairie. Saezyn pushed aside the vines that veiled the exit as the others adjusted to the fresh light from the distant Orgasoli. Waist-high, yellow grass covered the lands before them. The grasses led up to the horizon where a dark sky in the distance masked the unknown they were to venture towards—the place where their fates would find them. The loud chirp of a nearby monarch cricket broke the silence that pervaded as they contemplated where they were to go.

"Is this Drilgon Prairie? It looks rather large," Trigger commented.

"Yes, and it actually is bigger than it looks. That's part of why I don't know what is past it. I got tired of the monotonous grasses and went home," Saezyn replied.

"Sounds lovely and boring," grumbled Trigger.

Saezyn laughed. "Boring! That's the funniest thing I have heard in a while! Drilgon Prairie is rather dull in color scape at times, but the creatures that live here keep it interesting while *trying* to pass through. I doubt it is possible to make it through without some sort of an adventure!"

"All right!" Trigger exclaimed enthusiastically as he cocked the bolt on his gun.

"Does your pet have an off switch?" Valdria asked the General in reference to Trigger.

"I have yet to find it," he replied.

"'Does her grumpy have an off switch?' is an even better question!" Trigger whispered to Ribus and Brunick. All three laughed in their sleeves until Valdria gave them a stern glare, at which point they acted like they were coughing.

"Should we start?" CJ asked.

"Absolutely! Let us!" Saezyn exclaimed. Thus they began traversing the endless grasses of the Drilgon.

"Hey, look! Another monarch cricket! Wow, this sure is exciting!" Trigger exclaimed sarcastically as he pointed out the large insect that jumped out of their way. "Where is the excitement you promised, Saezyn?"

"Perhaps you should be glad we haven't run into any trouble! If you want adventure, you could go back to Dekdir forest and play with a feldag hive," CJ suddenly burst out in Saezyn's defense. The group had endured Trigger's sneer comments for the past four hours, and she finally had enough. Trigger shut his mouth tight at the rebuke, but the damage was already done—his wish was granted.

"What is that noise?" Ribus asked suddenly. Alarm was in his voice.

"*That* is the sound of the adventure Trigger asked for," Saezyn stated grimly.

"What is it though?" Linia asked anxiously.

"A spinderk," Saezyn replied, "Come on, walk slowly, they *love* a good chase. If we walk slowly, they or it, hopefully it is just one, will think us too dull to trouble with. In any case, have your guns ready. Spinderks are sly and crafty."

"You're kinda freaking me out, gramps!" Cyra replied "What are they?". Her knuckles were white as she clenched her pistol.

"Take the most menacing rat you have ever beheld, cross it with the biggest spider you wish you didn't see, and cover the beast that is about the size of a large dog with black tines that rattle when the creature is hunting prey. In fact, that is the noise that you hear now," Brunick replied for Saezyn. Brunick had seen them before; he was nervous too. Everybody looked around and tried to see where these creatures might be hiding in the grass. Their efforts were in vain.

"Wait! What is that in the distance?" CJ exclaimed.

The General looked through the scope of his gun at the dark shape in the distance. "It looks to be some sort of abandoned hover truck! If we can get to it, we might have a shot at getting out of this field in one piece!" He began to move quicker, but Saezyn gently held him back. "No. The faster we move, the faster we die. I am going to tell you guys to do something, and you are not going to like it, but you must do what I say if you want to live." Saezyn stared his intense glare at all of them. They all stopped walking and looked at him.

"They sense body heat, and they like to play. If you move, they will come for you because they will think you are playing, but if you do not play, they will go after monarch crickets instead. They finish their games by eating their prey, so playing is not a good idea. Now comes the hard part, we must lie down perfectly still right where we are until we know they are gone," Saezyn said sternly.

"You want us to lie down?" Trigger exclaimed, but before he could rant on and become an even bigger pain in the butt, CJ laid down in the grass. Saezyn did likewise, and soon the others, even Trigger, were lying in the grass trying to relax. The sound of rattling spines grew nearer and nearer until CJ could see one of the menaces four feet to the left of where she lay. Its four snake-like eyes looked over them where they lay prostate; it grew nearer still until it was inches away from CJ's hand. Her heart felt like it was going to beat out of her chest, but she knew that Saezyn wouldn't lie, so she kept as still as she could. The fiend sniffed her hand. Its hot breath caressed her skin, and she cringed at the sight of its huge jagged jaws. After what seemed like an eternity of this, the fiend stopped, its tines ceased rattling, and it walked away dejectedly until a cricket chirped. At the sound of a more exciting prey, the spinderk ran through the grass. It did not go alone; the sound caused by the sudden rush of other spinderks joining the hunt for the monarch cricket announced that two dozen of the beasts were eager to play. At the creatures' flight, Saezyn still remained completely still. Nobody dared to move until he got up, so for the next hour, they lay there in wait for their chance to investigate the truck.

"Man, gramps! I thought you fell to sleep!" Cyra exclaimed when finally, the prophet stood up. Orgasoli had sunk lower in the sky, and evening was setting in.

"How did you know that would work?" Linia asked.

"I have had to do that many times, but the first time I did that, it was an act of Trilumina that spared my life. You see, a monarch cricket jumped into me and knocked me down. I was about to get up, but a still, small voice told me to lay still. Had I gotten to my feet, a dozen spinderks would have torn me up. Instead, they went after the monarch cricket that had knocked me down in the first place," Saezyn replied as the group walked toward the truck they spotted an hour before.

"You are one gutsy, old man!" Ribus stated in amazement and clapped Saezyn on the back. The others agreed to this sentiment.

It was only moments before they had made it to the large hover truck that sat in a small clearing. It was painted brown, green, and yellow in a camouflage pattern with a large laser turret mounted on top. It was big enough that it could comfortably carry six in the cab and another four in the bed of the truck. A few dead spinderks were scattered around the vehicle in combination with the one-time crew of the craft.

"If we ran, this is what would have happened to us, isn't it?" Theban asked sadly.

"More likely than not," Saezyn replied morbidly.

"Does it run?" Cyra asked. Suddenly, a wounded Spinderk jumped from where it had been lying. It hurtled toward Cyra as her question left her mouth. Nanoseconds before its jagged teeth would have been locked on her throat, Saezyn had run the beast through on his halberd.

"Whoa! I didn't think you could move that fast!" Brunick exclaimed. He was genuinely impressed at Saezyn's super human reflexes.

Cyra stood awestruck by the fact she almost died. Saezyn gently patted her on the back to break her out of the shock; she in turn gave him a hug. He returned the hug but quickly attended to the corpse that still occasionally twitched in death spasms upon his halberd. He jabbed his staff into the ground and held the dead spinderk in place with his foot as he pulled his weapon from it.

Brunick, Cyra, and Theban quickly began to look over the craft to see if it was functional. Cyra sat inside to recover further from her shock and to look over the computer system while those without technical know-how got into the bed of the truck to stand watch. From the bed of the truck, they could have a decent look of the surrounds.

Brunick tried the engine. "Curse of oblivion on you! You stupid bucket!" He yelled as he smacked the truck's steering console in rage.

"What's wrong? Won't start?" Cyra asked. She didn't wait for the curse word filled reply; she tried to turn on the computer so she could run a diagnostic. She shook her head when nothing came up on the main view screen.

"Will it run?" Linia asked.

"Perhaps with some TLC, but otherwise, we probably just have a place to set up camp for the night," Brunick said after a glance.

"No. "Saezyn said. "We should get this running if we can... Drilgon is not a place to spend the night. The viznaks that hunt the spinderks during the night are worse than the spinderks themselves. Also, the hunters that died here, yes, hunters. That is what they were. They came well prepared: a locker full of weapons, a heavy turret up top. Spinderks weren't what killed the majority of these people, they just came to pick the bones and take out the odd survivors," Saezyn thought out loud.

"In that case," Cyra said, "I need a large PPC (Power Processing Crystal) to get the power grid back online. I know we may need the main turret, but the only way we're going to get anywhere is if we get this bucket running. As is, the main core is fried beyond belief, these boys must have run her too hot and stranded themselves," she said with surprising mechanical know-how.

"On it," Brunick replied. He and Theban soon climbed into the bed of the truck, and in a few minutes, they had the core out of the central laser turret. Cyra, with some improvised components crafted by Theban on the fly, soon had the power grid online in another twenty minutes. At this point, she ran through the list of all that was wrong in the truck's self-diagnostic program. Brunick used his know-how of vehicles, and Theban used his tools that he always had on his person to repair all the essential functions of the truck. While they fixed the truck, Ribus, the General, and the other Paladins opened the weapon lockers and improved their armory. Much to Ribus's delight, he stumbled upon an M3-XSS. It wasn't as advanced as his M7 sniper rifle that was scrapped when Toria fell, but he was glad to be able to snipe from up to three miles. Valdria found some more explosive shells for her shotgun, so she was in a better mood than she had been in a while.

"Try the engine, Cyra," Brunick ordered as he and Theban made a final adjustment on the main engine of the craft.

She pushed the button. The craft grumbled for a moment and then roared to life as the turbines spun to full. It hovered a good foot off the ground, and everybody cheered. Soon, they piled into the cab or into the back. Those not as experienced with guns (Cyra, Linia, CJ, Saezyn, and Brunick) were in the cab while Ribus, Valdria, the General, and Trigger got in the bed with their guns primed.

"Are we all ready?" Cyra asked from where she gripped the steer stick of the truck.

"Let's roll!" Valdria exclaimed with gusto. She had used the same phrase when going on raids with her Zykor dragon biker buddies.

Cyra pushed forward on the steer stick, and the craft floated through the yellow grass like a ship on a sea of gold. A slight evening breeze picked up and caused the long shafts of prairie grass to bend in waves as the drafts touched the fields and further added to the image of the surf of the deep. The going from that point on was swift. None of the spinderks troubled the vessel, for it was too large to "play" with, and as Orgasoli bowed beneath the dark clouds on the edge of Drilgon Prairie, they spotted what looked like a line of trees.

DARK WOOD LODGE

The front lights on the truck cut crisply through the nighttime that now prevailed. The darkness had fallen like a curtain drawn on the play of daytime. Now, it was night and time for the second act: dark matters.

"What is a viznak exactly?" CJ asked Saezyn as they neared the edge of the prairie.

"They are creatures that dwell beneath the prairie and prey upon those that stay in one spot too long, like the spinderks when they sleep for example. Had we camped out overnight, they would have tried to consume us too," Saezyn replied sleepily. The movement of the truck made him drowsy.

"What do they look like?" Cyra asked.

"Ugly."

"Gramps, you know what I mean," she replied warmly at his tease.

"They are ten- to twenty-foot-long worms that impale and suck the life out of those who they come upon from underneath. They are a literal example of what happens to those who stagnate. Those who waste their life have it stolen from them by entities of the like of that, which is the viznak," Saezyn said dreamily. He was still in a sleepy phase due to the inertia of the vehicle. Cyra winced at his description of the worms.

"What do you mean about those who stagnate?" CJ asked.

Saezyn opened his eyes wider. "Toria Vilorious was a prime example of stagnation. The people sat in their city of wickedness all fat and happy while they ignored the poor, and they became viler within. People weren't designed to stay in any one place too long, or get too comfortable and lower their defenses. If we do, we forget our God, ignore those we should love, and become as vile as demons. It just so happened that the Armada saw that Toria was putrid from the inside out and almost had become completely defenseless in its high esteem of itself. It was a city prime for the plucking. That is what I mean when I say creatures like or worse than the viznak will take the life of those that stagnate."

"How does one avoid stagnating?" Linia asked. She had been listening to the conversation.

"Watch for it in one's self?" Brunick suggested.

"Exactly!" Saezyn exclaimed. "If one is on their guard against evil, and they are self-conscience of their actions, evil will have trouble getting the drop on you. Also, trusting in Trilumina to be with you—both when life is good and when it is terrible, this will help ensure that your trust is in the right place." Saezyn was now wide-awake. He was passionate about Trilumina and fighting all vile things. After that, few said anything. The brief conversation had given them a lot to think about.

"We are nearing the tree line. Once you go into Dark Wood there should be a hunting outpost called Dark Wood lodge due east a few miles. It's hard to miss," Saezyn said to Cyra as the dark blue boughs of the dred trees before them became more distinct.

"I thought you said you have never been past Drilgon Prairie?" Linia observed. She gave Saezyn a confused glance.

"Indeed I did, and I did not lie, but other Seldocs have passed this way, and they recorded their trips in the Hollow. I have read these records and therefore, know a small amount about the lands beyond the Prairie." He grinned a grin that said he knew even more but would not give it away until or unless the information became relevant. That was Saezyn's way.

The dred trees that spread eerily ahead of them revealed their mystery more fully as the craft grew nearer: they were mysterious dim trees even in the bright light of the truck. They had dark indigo bark with bloodred leaves. The branches stuck out at odd angles and, in many ways, mimicked pieces from an abstract art collection. After traversing the randomly dispersed trunks of these trees, they soon came upon the outpost mentioned in prior conversation. It was a largish, stout, circular hovel with a com tower protruding from the side farthest from where they approached.

"Cyra, turn off the lights and approach this place slowly," Saezyn whispered warily.

"Why? And why are you whispering?" Cyra asked as she too unconsciously started to whisper.

"Do you think something happened here?" CJ interjected.

Saezyn held a finger to his lips to silence their questions and waited until they had all gotten out of the vehicle and were together in a group before he responded to CJ's question.

"Yeah, the hunters we borrowed this truck from looked like they were fleeing from something— This was their home, so I have my reservations at spending the night in this place which may have been the site of an untimely and unfortunate event," Saezyn elaborated.

"I think you are right," Brunick muttered as he examined the building in the glow of the tactical light mounted on his gun. Scorch marks could be seen on the ground and building; also, several burned-down huts surrounding the main lodge and felled dred trees confirmed Saezyn's suspicion that something sinister occurred in this place.

"Regrettably, this probably is the best place we will find to spend the night in. We need to be quiet and make sure we don't do anything that would attract unwanted attention," Saezyn instructed to the group.

"All right, you heard the man. Linia, you stay with the vehicle while Trigger and I scout the place," the General ordered.

"I'm coming with you," Ribus stated calmly but with no room for discussion. The General gave him a look that said he would prefer not risking more lives than necessary, but the no nonsense expression on Ribus's face dispelled any doubts the General may have had. Ribus was a fighter and wouldn't be a liability when clearing any potential hostiles.

Linia did as she was bidden and stayed with the others. Brunick, Valdria, and Linia set up an improvised perimeter while Saezyn stayed with Theban, CJ, and Cyra. Everybody had their weapons at the ready, but all was quiet that night. A few minutes later, the General, Trigger, and Ribus came back and reported that the facility was clear and that they found a good place to set up camp for the night.

The others wordlessly followed them through the blackened front doors of the habitation. Saezyn held a small lamp, and the Paladins had tactical lights on their rifles that the group navigated the darkened halls of the lodge by. Furniture and supply barrels were placed randomly as barricades to give the people who died here a place of cover while they fought for their lives. Bullet holes, skeletons, and burnt fixtures littered the dwelling. Clearly, a long-finished battle had taken place in the building, but the communal ignorance of the origin of the disaster caused the group that now navigated the place to be on edge. Many heads and stuffed creatures were on the wall. These had died at the hands of the previous occupants of the place, but despite the skill of the hunters that once lived here, whatever had thought of them as prey clearly were more cunning than the hunters were.

"What happened here?" Theban muttered nervously.

"I have my suspicions, but I choose to keep them to myself until they are confirmed," Saezyn replied. Valdria seemed to jump to the same conclusion of what the cause of the mess was. She looked at Saezyn apprehensively and questioningly. He gave her a minute headshake that wordlessly told her to try not to think about it.

They rounded a corner and found themselves in the central room of the lodge. In the center of the room, a large plasma pot acted as a fireplace. Furniture made of varying hides and more stuffed trophies were placed around the heating unit. This room had showed signs of battle but not nearly as much as the rest of the camp; the hunters must have set up a perimeter around the edge of the building, but still, bodies could be seen here and there.

"They must have been attacked by a multitude of whatever it was. This dwelling shows all the signs of a place set up in a defensive pattern. The majority of the people were on the fringe of the building shooting out of the windows," observed the General.

"It didn't do them any good though, whatever the wretched fiends were that attacked, they were smart and came in through that hole in the roof and flanked them from behind." Trigger shook his head as he gestured towards a hole in the ceiling above them.

"I wonder when did it happen," Theban muttered again. His face was pale.

"Last night," Saezyn replied, "or the night before."

"How do you know it happened at night?" the General asked.

"Because he knows what did this!" Valdria exclaimed. She looked even more fearful than Theban did. She suspected what Saezyn knew.

"Do you?" Ribus asked Saezyn.

"I do."

"Would you like to share with the class?" Cyra tried lightly. But in a room where bullet casings and bodies littered the floor, humor didn't come or go successfully.

"I'd prefer not to, due to the fact you will be inclined to be afraid when I tell you, but I guess you are already afraid." Saezyn thought as he looked at the destruction in the room. "It was Zykor dragons. They only come out at night."

"Plural? More than one?" the General asked.

"Funny, now, what really did this?" Ribus scoffed.

"Yes, plural. Technically, it was the spawn of a Zykor dragon. The spawn are winged humanoid creatures that breathe plasma and serve the true Zykor dragon," Saezyn answered the General's question and then turned to Ribus: "You think they are myth, don't you?"

"I do. Nobody really knows what they look like, they are mythological in status, so I am going to be prone to think they are myths," Ribus replied.

"There is a reason my biker gang was named the Zykor dragons, they are rumored to be the fiercest creature on the planet of Solbia and one of the top seven deadliest creatures in Ephesia," Valdria exclaimed as she shot an icy glare toward Ribus that caused his mouth to shut as the temperature of the room seemed to drop at her severe distaste for his doubting comments.

"Well, tomorrow we will find out which of you is right," Saezyn replied as though he could care less at Ribus's doubts or Valdria's high esteem of the mythic beast. Valdria gave Ribus a death glare that said she thought him to be a fool.

"Come, let us forget about the doom-and-gloom and repair our spirits with some food and rest!" CJ said as merrily as she could. The others soon agreed to this, and they had fallen into quietly whispering over cold supper of leftover rations, but they never fully relaxed due to the threat of dragons coming suddenly in the night.

DESERTED LANDS

CJ woke with a start from a poor night's sleep. A quick look around revealed that the others looked as sleep-deprived, if not more so than she did. A room full of dead people was not a place to get restful sleep. All save for Saezyn looked tired and grumpy.

"How can you sleep in a place like this?" Trigger exclaimed.

"Sleep?" Saezyn laughed. "I didn't sleep last night. I spent the night in meditation and prayer for guidance. We are fortunate. Trilumina gave us directions."

"So you finally know where we are going, gramps?" Cyra asked happily.

"Yup, we are continuing in the same direction as yesterday. We are getting close to the end of this journey and the beginning of new one," Saezyn replied with a grin.

"Cryptic, old man, when will he give up his mystic speak," Brunick mumbled grumpily.

"Perhaps you should stop making cynical comments and try to understand his 'mystic speak.'" Theban glared at Brunick through his visor. Brunick just gave a dirty look in return.

"If you two were in my unit, I would have you do team exercise drills until your manners improved and you had a proper respect for one another," authoritatively stated the General.

"He is right, I'm sorry, I'm just tired from these past few days," Brunick offered an apology to Theban.

"Don't worry about it. I was out of place to tell you off," Theban replied. He extended a hand as a gesture of peace which Brunick accepted much to everyone's relief. Traveling when tired is miserable, but traveling where there is a grudge between the voyagers is far worse.

CJ walked around the room and looked at the statues and stuffed creatures that had survived the battle; they were stunning, especially a large spinderk that had been killed by a skilled hunter. She shuddered at the remembrance of its hot breath on her skin. In her walk around the room, CJ noticed that Valdria was looking at one head that was mounted upon the wall. It was very humanoid, too humanoid. The skin was silver with scales, and the eyes were that of a serpent's, and its tongue was forked like a lizard's, but otherwise, it looked almost exactly like a human head. Valdria seemed transfixed by its long dead stare.

"You okay?" CJ asked. Valdria shook her gaze from the statue and smiled slightly but said nothing. She knew more about that particular statue than she would let on. CJ glanced at a golden tag beneath the head. It said: "Zykor." Both CJ and Valdria gave a shudder and went to sit down for vittles.

A quick, cold breakfast was had before they all repacked their gear to continue on the quest. In the light of day that filtered through the broken windows and holes in the wall, they could see the damage was much worse than they had presumed the night before. No darkness was around to hide the extent of the devastated lodge or the number of the dead. It was worse than they had thought; when they reached the exterior of the building, this sentiment was further reinforced because it was realized that the main lodge had, at one time, two com towers, one of which had completely collapsed.

"They never stood a chance," Trigger said with a headshake.

"Are we headed towards wherever the Zykors came from?" Linia asked.

"I don't know currently, but by the end of the day, I suspect we will know," Saezyn replied.

"Why do we ask him any questions?" Trigger snickered.

"Because he has age, wisdom, experience, and knowledge. You don't exactly have an overabundance of any of those traits, so I'm astounded you haven't asked him even more questions," the General said in rebuttal. Everybody laughed including Trigger; he knew his superior was right and had him beat.

The group had soon made their way to the truck they had traveled in the day before. Everybody loaded into their previous positions and hovered off in the direction indicated by Saezyn.

The farther the truck traveled, the less that could be seen; plants, animals, and trees all grew sparse as the group went forth on their expedition to the unknown. The only things that became more prevalent in their path were blight and bare dirt. Soon, the plants that were visible at all were merely scorched sticks or burnt stumps of dred trees.

"Is anybody else thinking what I'm thinking?" Valdria asked through the back window.

"Not likely, we usually don't think about strangling puppies," Trigger whispered quietly to himself as he relaxed in the back of the truck. She heard his cynical comment but refused to dignify it with a response.

"What are you thinking, Valdria?" CJ asked from her seat inside the truck.

"That we are getting closer to the Zykor. I have never seen one alive, but the tales say that they have huge layers fraught with devastation," she replied.

"Yeah, I was thinking that too," CJ murmured.

"Don't wor"—Saezyn didn't get to finish his thought, for at that moment, the craft dropped into a crevasse that was disguised by an unusual, purple ground cover. Nobody was exactly taking the time to make observations, but if they had, they would have realized they had just fallen through a giant, purple fungus. The truck scrapped the sides of the narrow gorge and slid until it got wedged in between the two rock walls.

"Sorry about that. Is everybody okay?" Cyra asked kindly from her place at the driver's seat. The consensus among those in the cab was that they were okay. Linia quickly looked from person to person checking to make sure they were as healthy as they thought. In the back, Ribus, Valdria, Trigger, and the General had managed to stay in the bed, but they sustained some bruises for their efforts.

"Now, what do we do?" Theban asked.

"We continue on?" CJ ventured.

"That's right! You have a good head on your shoulders. In the future, that will serve this group well," Saezyn replied. CJ searchingly looked at Saezyn knowing that his comment was fraught with foresight and was a prophecy of her future, but he just smiled at her questioning glance and said no more.

"How do we get out, gramps?" Cyra asked. The doors were stuck shut against the side of the gorge.

Saezyn aimed a well-placed kick at the front glass. It popped out and slid across the hood until it fell from where the truck was stranded in the air. The glass landed about ten feet below with a crash.

"Follow the glass," Saezyn replied.

It didn't take long for them to jump from where the truck was stranded, and it took even less time to resume their expedition on foot.

From the first instant they fell into the crevasse, they were very conscious that they had entered what could best be described as another world. The ground was black, the sky gloomy, the plants ranged the color spectrum in gentle luminescence, and danger seemed to lurk in every bush. Linia was taking a keen interest in the plants she could see around her. The major ground cover consisted of blue grasses (literally blue) and large patches of purple fungi that emitted a sweet smell. Some of the plants included juniper-like bushes with black stems and deep red needles. Also, bright, aquamarine vines wrapped around the odd trees that had dark green boughs and white puffs for leaves or flowers—only Linia, and perhaps, Saezyn knew what they were seeing. In many ways, the contrast of the dark ground and dusky sky with the glowing plants resembled a light show, but it was not nearly as bright. While the others gasped at the murky beauty of this strange place, Linia was in raptures.

"Many of these plants are said to be incredibly rare or even mythical, with medicinal purposes spanning from sleep aids to pain killers all the way to energy boosters to aphrodisiacs," she said as she looked from plant to plant. Trigger's attention was caught when she mentioned aphrodisiacs.

"What plant was the aphrodisiac?" he asked attentively to Linia's horticulture lecture.

"When you are old and in need of one, perhaps I will let you know, but as is, it is doubtful you need any help," Linia responded with a gentle grin.

"What about this plant?" Theban asked in reference to a strange, hexagonal plant no bigger than a beach ball. It had a grey base that had a geometrically shaped, half-dome bunch of flowers placed right on top of it. The edges and outside of the flower were blue, but inside of the blossom, better described as blossoms because the dome was made up of dozens of flowers, it was bright orange. Inside each bud, a rather intimidating stamen protruded a half inch above the surface of the rest of the plant. These barb-like entities pointed out at all angles.

"Back away very slowly!" Linia exclaimed so suddenly that all eyes turned to Theban and the plant he had pointed to. He did as he was bidden instantly. Nothing happened. Everybody let a breath out.

"What was that about? You scared me!" Cyra said. She was clearly startled.

"Dart weed," Saezyn replied.

"What's so threatening about dart weed?" Brunick said smugly. He took a step toward the plant in his self-assuredness. In that moment, his question was answered. A dozen barbs shot out of the plant and stuck into his trench coat. He instantly backed away.

"That is what is threatening about dart weed. Now, look closer at the base of the plant that just shot at you," Linia ordered much like a doctor giving orders to their patients. He did as she said and soon backed even farther away from the plant. It was growing out of a human skeleton.

"Dart weed is a parasitic plant that injects barbs into the hapless passerby. If they do not remove the barbs quickly, the barbs will take root and use the creature's blood as water and nutrients in the blood as fertilizer. That doesn't seem so bad because it doesn't seem like one would forget to take the barbs out of themselves, but the weed has another trick up its sleeve: the barbs induce sleep. The more barbs one is hit with, the longer they sleep, the longer they sleep, the more time the barbs have a chance to take root. If too many take root without proper treatment, the infected will become consumed and die from the wretched plant," Linia explained. As she told of the dart weed's method of reproduction, Brunick was frantically pulling any of the devious shafts out of his coat. Fortunately, none had broken into his skin.

"Who knew plants could be so interesting." Theban made the mistake of saying out loud.

"Interesting? That's a spagging soul-sucker!" Trigger bellowed. Brunick just rolled his eyes at Theban.

"Don't get mad at Theban. I agree with him completely, it's part of why I have studied them so much, also, if I hadn't studied them, we might be in quite a fix right now," Linia defended.

"You are right, but can we talk about the wonders of nature at a safer distance from the demented vampire bush?" Ribus asked in his usual, cool cat tone. At his urging, the group started off once again being sure to keep their distance from any dart weed. As they walked, they kept their trigger fingers at the ready knowing now more than ever that danger was indeed closer than they expected.

ZYKOR

"This is just great! We are walking through some Trilumina-forsaken death trap full of exotic deadly plants looking for some random thing," Trigger began to complain.

"Trigger," the General said calmly but with an edge of agitation.

"Yes, sir," Trigger replied as he snapped to attention.

"Shut your face," the General ordered.

"Shutting face immediately, sir," Trigger replied before he grew quiet.

"He does have a point though. Saezyn, where are we going? I want a more solid answer this time." Valdria held her shotgun aggressively. Saezyn turned slowly and looked at both her and her weapon that she was brandishing.

He smiled. "Sweet miss, you cannot shoot answers out of me that I do not have. Also, I have messed with entities far more powerful than a moody woman with a shotgun. I do not doubt your ability to blow my head off my shoulders, but my question is: would you want to if I told you that we are about a hundred yards from a Zykor dragon?" Saezyn responded as though he was greeting a friend at a store.

"We are?" she replied in a much more civil tone. The dangerous edge that was in her eyes was replaced by fear.

"Indeed, but do not worry, we will be fine, and once we triumph over its scum, we will pass from these desolate lands to our destination," he continued.

"Do you finally know where we are going, gramps?" Cyra asked.

"Yes, I do. We are going to a ship, but that is all Trilumina has told me."

"Why didn't you just say that to me?" Valdria asked irritably.

"Maybe you should have said please," Ribus smiled. Much to his surprise, rather than Valdria shooting him a stern glare, she actually smiled back. Ribus grinned all the more in return.

"Come on, you love birds, let's see if these rumored dragons and ships are real," the General replied. Valdria blushed slightly, but it was impossible to tell if it was with embarrassment or rage.

A few dozen yards more revealed the truth in Saezyn's words. Before them lay an old quarry that at one time was used to mine dark stones called obsidasalt, but its current occupants had caused mining to halt. The facility and mining cars were left abandoned. In the middle of this black hole in the ground sat the glorious and beautiful Zykor dragon. It bore silver scales upon its snake-like body. The scales turned to a shimmering purple going up its neck toward both of its heads. The creature had heads much like a serpent's crossed with a lion's; they were even complimented by long, flowing, royal blue manes. Around this beast, creatures that looked oddly human gathered nearby in adoration for the beast. CJ recognized them as the same eerie humanoid creature that had its head mounted in the Dark Wood lodge.

Saezyn turned and looked at his group. "Stay here and watch what Trilumina can do." He walked to the edge of the crater and slid down the sloped walls of the quarry. He walked straight toward the serpent that haughtily looked upon its subjects. The servants of the beast parted to allow Saezyn passage to the creature. The Zykor looked down at Saezyn with scorn.

CJ and the others looked on in concern from their vantage point on the edge of the quarry. They all had their weapons at the ready in case something terrible happened to Saezyn. Valdria didn't say anything to Ribus about the Zykor being real, but she did give him a look that said those four small words: "I told you so." He just grinned and prepared to shoot the beast.

"Which head do you want?" the General asked Ribus as he looked through his scope. His rifle was going back and forth between the dragon's two heads. "Right or left?"

"I'm going to go with left. I'm pretty sure it gave me a dirty look," Ribus replied with a morbid grin as he zoomed his 3M XSS on the eye of the beast.

"What am I supposed to shoot?" Trigger asked. He felt left out.

"Anything that comes out of that hole that isn't Saezyn," CJ exclaimed.

"My pleasure," he smiled.

The Zykor then spoke so all could hear: "Saezyn Seldoc! Fah! What brings your filth out of your Hollow, what brings such a fool of Trilumina out of his hole!" It laughed wickedly. Its subjects laughed as well and flapped their wings in wicked jubilee. The spawn also breathed plumes of fire and smoke out of their nostrils as they chortled.

"Your time for retribution! Your lies and double speak from your twin heads have led these people astray and turned them into your vile spawn." Saezyn gestured towards the odd, silver creatures surrounding the beast before he continued. "It is time you go to the judgment in store for you!" Saezyn said with hatred painting his voice thick with rage.

"Retribution! Ha! You came to my fortress to do what? Poke me with a stick?!" It laughed, but its followers hissed with their forked tongues in hate of Saezyn. The beast then shot plasma from its mouth at a nearby mining car. The mining car melted into the ground under the barrage of heat. A glowing orange puddle of liquefied steel was all that remained.

"What can a mere prophet of Trilumina do against such might!" the Zykor boasted. The deceived that followed it, laughed in an uproar.

"I can do nothing, but Trilumina can do this!" Saezyn roared, and he jabbed his halberd into the ground. The sky split open, and light flooded the pit. From where CJ and the others watched, they recoiled when they now looked at the Zykor. It was the definition of hideous; the light showed it for what it really was—a lie. It was merely a large, two-headed snake with fiery eyes, protruding bones, decayed flesh, and a wicked heart. Other decaying Zykor snakes slithered around and through holes in the decrepit leading monster. These hissed in a demented and pained cacophony.

While the light streamed down, the Zykor screeched, and the people that had become its spawn crouched low to the ground and tried to hide their faces from the harsh rays.

"The truth of Trilumina reveals you for what you are! A two-faced and indeed, two-headed liar—but no more. Trilumina shall cast your heads upon the ground and halt your boastings." At these words, Saezyn's staff emitted a focused beam of light. He cut through the air with this luminescent weapon and severed both heads in one fell swipe. The decayed skulls fell smoldering upon the ground, and the rest of the body caught on fire and was consumed in hot, white flame.

The scales on the humanoid creatures in the hole also caught on fire, but they did not die; the fire simply seared off the scales that had coated the people. When the flames disappeared, it was plain to see that the Zykor's prior subjects were the miners that had, at one time, worked the quarry. They looked at one another in dazed confusion, as though waking from a dream and returned to mining as if nothing had happened. The exception to this was one woman who stepped forward to offer her thanks. She was clearly from the border lands of Bergda, a country of Solbia that was occupied by very distinct people. In true, border-lands form, she had dark skin, black hair, striking, light blue eyes, and strong, sharp features. She was middle-aged, looking barely past thirty, she was short in stature, but her time in mining had strengthened her frame. By the time she had reached Saezyn, the others had joined him in the quarry.

"Thank you so much! You saved us from that wretch! Who are you?" the woman asked of Saezyn.

"I am Saezyn Seldoc. Who might you be, and how did you fall into the trap of the Zykor?"

"I'm Mazzi. I took this mining job after fleeing Toria Vilorious because I refused to obey the queen's wicked plans, so I left for another life. I was born in Bergda, as it is plain to see, but I think that after what happened here, perhaps I should return to Toria. As for how we came into the wicked power of the Zykor, the creature came to this quarry a few rotations back and charismatically offered us a life of riches that was also free of labor. All we had to do was drink of its venom. One particularly discontent miner stepped forward and drank. He instantly became gleefully contented and said that the venom tasted like the best of fine wines. Upon hearing that the drink was not sour, soon, all the rest had stepped forward and partook of the venom. Once all had taken part, the deception of the beast was made known, for in an instant, we were morphed into part-dragon, part-human subjects. We had no free will of our own," she explained.

"The usual, unhappy story," Saezyn murmured.

"I have something to tell you," CJ interjected.

"What?" Mazzi asked.

"Toria is gone. In fact, the group you see here may be all that is left of the city," CJ replied solemnly.

"What should I do then? I can't go back, and I don't want to keep mining!" Mazzi exclaimed.

Saezyn looked at CJ and smiled. CJ knew what the smile implied. "You can come with us. We are just out rambling, looking for whatever Trilumina has for us, and to be honest, I'm not really sure what that is right now, but we are still alive, so if you want to join our sorry, ragtag band, you are more than welcome." CJ gave a weak smile. She didn't know if she was offering much, but Mazzi beamed.

"You mean it? Yes, yes, a thousand times yes!" Mazzi exclaimed.

"Do you have any weapons?" Ribus asked, "It can get a bit dangerous on the path we are going on."

Mazzi gave a grin and asked them to wait for one moment, and then she would be back with her gear. Mazzi disappeared into a nearby mining hut. She soon returned with a backpack and an intimidating disc launcher.

"What is that?" Trigger asked with eyes wide. He hadn't seen said weapon before. Ribus just laughed; he knew what it was and was glad to have somebody on the team equipped with one.

"It's a Dorva doom disc launcher outfitted with a mining laser. It fires discs into rock or metal, and then the user of the tool pushes a button to explode the discs. They are sometimes used in wars and conflicts, thus giving the 'doom' part of their name. The mining laser is pretty self-explanatory, it uses a laser to cut away rock with precision," Mazzi explained. Everybody could tell that she was very capable at mining and that she was a pro with demolitions.

Trigger looked at the General and asked in awe: "Can I have one?"

"Maybe for your birthday," the General replied with a smirk. The rest of the group just shook their heads at Trigger's love of all things lethal.

"It's good to have another member to the group, Mazzi," Saezyn said. "Somehow, I think you will fit in nicely, but we must make way," The group soon made it out of the quarry and began walking towards a nearby hill country. After the death of the Zykor, the land was now plain to see in the rays of Orgasoli that illuminate the once-darkened scape. The clouds had been chased away. From the new found light, it was easier to see that it was now high noon and time to move on to the next part of the journey.

SERENDIPITY

"How did Toria fall?" Mazzi asked as they traversed a gently sloping, blue-grassed hill.

"The defected Armada attacked it two days ago. It was gone within hours," Brunick answered.

"The defected Armada? So it is real," she thought out loud. After a few moments of processing the thought that a city as large as Toria Vilorious had fallen in a few hours, Mazzi asked her second question: "Do they occupy the planet currently? Are we in danger?"

"No, the Purge dealt with them," Trigger said gleefully.

"Yes, we are. Get down!" Saezyn said seriously. He was instantly on the ground, and the others knew that somebody who could defeat a Zykor dragon didn't spook easy, and thus, they followed his example. They had barely laid themselves flat in the grass when the alarmingly eerie whine of the approaching danger made clear the abundant peril they were in.

"What is it?" Cyra asked.

"Myriad, you can tell by the high-pitched drone of their dark energy generators. They are the fighter craft of the Armada. They have dual, dark static launchers and infection bullets," Linia explained.

"What are infection bullets?" CJ asked.

"They release mechamites into your system, which promptly try to wreck vital components, or they try to hijack your brain," Trigger explained in laymen's terms.

"Shhh!" Saezyn chided. It was now clear by the ruckus caused by the enemy ships that the myriad were closing. Mazzi stayed hidden in the grass, but she remained crouched with her weapon at the ready, so the second the craft had passed above them, she stood up and fired into the lead craft. There were three of the enemy ships. As soon as she fired at them, the ships began to turn back around to attack them.

"If you are going to fire at them, the least you can do is hit one!" Brunick hissed. He stood up with his repeater and began to pepper the sky with laser fire. Everybody went to follow his example, but Mazzi told them to stop. They looked at her in confusion, but she remained calm.

"I didn't miss," Mazzi smiled as she pushed a button on the disc launcher. Before the craft could complete their turn, the lead fighter blew into chunks. The explosion spread to the two following craft which, in turn, were destroyed.

"I said you would make a good addition to this team," Trigger stated smugly.

"That was Saezyn that said that!" Valdria corrected.

"He was right too," Theban cried as he looked at the falling debris in awe.

"I may have been right, but things just got more difficult," Saezyn sighed.

"They are gone, how did things get more difficult?" Mazzi asked somewhat dejectedly.

"Those ships are gone—yes, but the fact they were here at all means that the Armada hasn't been defeated on Solbia," Saezyn replied.

"I thought the Purge defeated the Armada?" Theban asked as he turned from watching the residing debris cloud.

"We did, but we must not have destroyed all the ships. A few must have scattered throughout the world, and they are doing what the Armada does best when they don't have complete control over the world—they are being a pest and spreading what devastation they can. They need to be hunted down, or eventually, they will be able to build up to a sizeable force once again, and the few stragglers will become a massive fleet, and they will take Solbia. Early in our campaigns against the Armada, we made the mistake of freeing a planet from their iron grip, but not terminating the entirety of their scum on the planet, and we in the end had to free the planet twice," the General explained. He had seen the Armada and their tactics time and time again. He knew how they played the game of war.

"So what do we do?" Mazzi asked.

"Isn't it obvious? We hunt them down," Saezyn said with a grin.

"With what? And why?" Valdria asked.

"With the ship we are going to find and because that is the task Trilumina has given us in his service," Saezyn replied.

"I don't even know if Trilumina is real. I think I am going to need some proof before I go on some mad vendetta hunting alien forces," she replied.

CJ shook her head at Valdria's stubbornness. She, along with the majority of the other group members, could clearly see Trilumina was real; it was so plain to see by the miracles Saezyn performed. Some of the others looked like they agreed with Valdria. The General, Linia, and Trigger did not agree with Valdria though, they, like all Paladins, had seen the evil of the Armada and knew that if it was real, then good must exist as well. The Paladin's trust in Trilumina was actually what had allowed them to live through some of the most intense battles in the history of Ephesia.

"Is that how you feel?" Saezyn asked the group with a stern eye.

Most of the group just looked uncomfortable, the Paladins said nothing, though the General had a look of rage on his face at Valdria's stubbornness. Valdria stepped forward. "If Trilumina is real, I want to see this so called ship we are supposed to find over the next hill!"

Saezyn stroked his chin before he tersely replied, "Fair enough."

The "next hill" as Valdria termed was a deuce of hill. It went up and up far longer than its appearance would have suggested it was capable of, and many swear words were used in its ascent, but Saezyn would not allow them to stop and take a break. It was the first time they had seen him seriously enraged. He was greatly angered by their lack of faith even after all they had survived through, but eventually, they reached the top of the hill. The group crested the summit, and to everyone's amazement, before them, in a slight valley, rested a ship. A beam from Orgasoli shown on it like a spotlight, but it was also like Trilumina was saying "Here is the ship. Now, don't you feel like a fool?"

Valdria and the others looked down at a large ship that had clearly been there a long time, but it was still in decent shape. Valdria was undone; she dropped to her knees and wept. Trilumina had finally broken through her hard heart, and she was, in that moment, finally aware of how rebellious she had been toward Trilumina, but yet here before her laid the ship she had asked for, and her miracle was complete with a beam of light highlighting it and saying: "Long have you hated me, but I love you and am faithful still, even when you are not."

Cyra, in that moment, realized that Trilumina had answered that prayer for salvation she had prayed several nights ago in Toria while she roamed the streets and sobbed in the elevator, but it now seemed so long ago. He had answered it though, and so, she too wept. The others realized in their own personal way the terrible lives that Trilumina had rescued them from, and so for a long time, they just stood and looked, or knelt in humility, realizing full well that they justly deserved to die in the city they had been saved from or remain cursed in the Zykor pit, but here they had been guided to and protected by Trilumina. Saezyn looked at them, shook his head, and suddenly turned and walked away.

"Where are you going, Saezyn?" CJ called after him.

"I'll be back, but I need to cool off. I'm baffled it took so long for you to finally admit Trilumina is real," he replied. At this, their hearts were smote all the more.

Ribus, who had long held Cyra in high esteem for her extreme abilities at such a young age, soon came to her side and asked her why she was crying.

"I... I... I just finally am able to let go... For the past few weeks, I have been angry at Trilumina for letting my mom die. It has been gnawing away at my insides whenever I allow myself to think about it. I was so mad that he allowed her to get run down in a high-speed chase. In seeing this ship, I realized that Trilumina had never abandoned me, and that he is more powerful than the bad that happened. He loves us too much to ever be anything but faithful," Cyra explained through sobs of joy.

"Wait! Your mom was run down where? And by what?" Ribus suddenly asked. A gnawing suspicion grew in his mind and seeds of guilt had taken root. He answered in unison with Cyra as she replied: "On the edge of Toria Vilorious in a gang chase."

She quickly noticed that Ribus seemed to know something about it. "Why do you ask?"

"No, no, no, no, why!" Ribus lost all composure. His previous cool was dissolved for the first time since they had become a group. "It was me Cyra! It was me! I hit your mother all those days ago! It was an accident. I was running for my life, and the streets were thick with cars, so I went on the sidewalk and ran into her among others! I killed them! I'm a monster!"

He sat down and wept. Everyone looked at him, not with judgment, but with sorrow, for this man who finally saw himself for who and what he was—a selfish man. Cyra, at first, looked at him with an expression of hurt, but as she saw that he was drowning in sorrow, guilt, and remorse, she could not hold it against him.

"What you did was wrong," she said as she sat down next to him. She then put her arm around him as she said these words, "but I forgive you."

"I believe you. I just don't know how to forgive myself." Ribus held his face in his hands.

CJ walked up and put her hand on Ribus's shoulder. "Ribus, look out at that ship lying before us with light shining down on it—placed there for us by Trilumina as a sign of hope of a future. Trilumina didn't spare you or me so we can dwell on what we were; he saved us for what we can be, for what we will be. I once stole a man from another woman and have stood idly by watching terrible things happen in the palace of the queen, or I have even aided in them, but I have turned from that path and begged the God of Ephesia to cleanse me of what I was. I... no, *we* are all just as wretched as you. If you ask Trilumina for forgiveness, he will not deny you it," CJ calmly explained. At her words the group rallied around her and listened carefully.

"You are right, but how can he forgive one such as me? I'm an assassin, a murderer, I've killed people just for kicks," Ribus vented his doubts.

"I've killed people too. I made the technology that hid the Vilkra sleepers from sensors. That allowed the Vilkra to do tremendous evil deeds. I alone enabled the single worst gang that plagued this planet. I profited from the deaths of hundreds, but Trilumina is merciful and loving beyond any wrong I can do... yes, I see that now... finally," Brunick interjected. A look of sorrow contorted his face.

"If Trilumina can forgive me, and her, and him, and us, he can forgive you Ribus. And if Trilumina forgives you, who are you to not forgive yourself?" CJ asked as she pointed to all those who had done so much wrong.

Ribus closed his eyes for a moment, took a deep breath, let it out, and then smiled with joy at having the weight of Ephesia removed from his shoulders. He, like Cyra, CJ, and the rest had let go of their past and put their trust in the grace of Trilumina. He stared down at the ship and muttered the phrase: "Serendipity, the finding of good things unexpectedly."

THE SHIP

It was evening before Saezyn came back to the group. They were still waiting for him on the crest of the hill. They had not left for two reasons: first, they knew they needed to apologize to him, and secondly, they knew he was the key to them getting this far. It wouldn't be right to go to the ship without him. CJ stepped forward as Saezyn approached.

"Saezyn Seldoc," she said firmly.

"Yes, CJ," he replied with sadness in his voice.

"I speak for the others when I say this: I'm sorry, we are sorry… you were right to be angry, and we were wrong to doubt you and Trilumina. Would you consider bearing with this stubborn lot of people still?" CJ's face showed all the signs that she was about to cry.

"I don't even have to think about it. Of course, I will remain with you still. I'll be with you guys for as long as you will have me. Trilumina had tasked me with guiding you days ago. When he gave the task, I thought of you as morally putrid people, but as I walked with you these days, Trilumina showed me that all people need to be loved. More than that, I gained friends. As for me walking away earlier, I am human too, and I get angry. I hope I didn't give the impression that I was abandoning you," Saezyn replied.

At Saezyn's words the group breathed a communal sigh of relief, grinned, and many hugs and slaps on the back were passed around.

"So now what?" Trigger asked.

Valdria rolled her eyes in true, Valdria fashion and replied, "Maybe go to the ship?" Then she gave a grin.

"Let's go! That's what it's there for!" Saezyn said excitedly.

It did not take them long to rush up to see the stately vessel. It was much larger than they originally thought; the distance they had been away from it masked that the ship was a little smaller than a Purge cruiser. The ship could hold a crew of anywhere from two hundred to three hundred men. The group walked around the vessel admiring the craft and looking for an entrance. It was shaped like a slightly deformed bowling pin lying on its side with one end larger than the other, narrow in the middle, and then the bridge section expanded out so it was moderately larger than the narrowest part in the middle of the ship. The narrower end faced toward the front. On the back, three engines were mounted. The middle one placed above the other two above the loading ramp. The ship was sleek, angular with vertical fins coming off the engines. All in all, the vessel was about a hundred yards long.

"What type of ship is it?" Cyra asked.

"I don't recognize the design," the General replied.

"It certainly isn't new," Ribus muttered as he looked at some age-worn spots that clearly indicated this ship had seen the far sides of the galaxy.

"It says I3 on the side. Does anybody know what that means?" Brunick quizzed.

"Intergalactic Intelligence Industries, called I3 for short. This was an exploration ship for the company. I3 was destroyed when the Armada first was unleashed on the galaxy three hundred years ago, but at one time, it was the single most powerful company in the history of Ephesia. This was one of their larger shuttles for scientific enquiry," Linia unexpectedly explained.

"Impressive, Miss Linia. How do you know?" the General asked.

"I have spent many hours studying the historical pieces in the silver halls of Zxe on Overlord. That museum has models and statistics on all kinds of ships," she replied.

Saezyn gave her a queer look, he sensed more was to this blonde bombshell than he may have originally suspected. She gave him a smile that told she guessed his mind.

"A shuttle, did you say? This is the size of a Purge cruiser!" Trigger exclaimed.

"The company would take no risks when it came to research. Their expeditions were massive. If I am right, this ship has everything from a large, cargo hold for specimens to a lab for studying and even a barracks for the security force that was used to protect the scientists on their outings. Some records list that they came unto some resistance from local organisms in their quests, thus making a well-armed security team a necessity," Linia explained.

"How do you know this when I don't? Where did you gain this knowledge? I have seen the silver halls of Zxe, and it doesn't say all that…" the General asked curiously.

"I have access to a rather large database on Overlord. I spent many years studying on that Purge base," she replied.

"What is Overlord? Is it a big Purge base?" Cyra asked.

The General chuckled. "Yes, Cyra, it is big, bigger than most moons. By the grace of Trilumina, it is and has remained a facility that can stand against the might of the Armada. I haven't been there in a while, but it is the pride and joy of the Purge."

"I'd like to see it!" Cyra exclaimed.

"Perhaps one day you will, Cyra, but first, we have to get this ship air-worthy once more," Saezyn stated warmly as he clapped Cyra on the back.

"What shall we name it?" Theban asked.

"It?" Brunick questioned.

"Her! All mechanical entities are females because they are temperamental and need to be treated right to reach their optimum," the General corrected.

"I just think women are just plain mental," Triggered grinned.

"And that is why you are still single," Valdria joked, but not unkindly.

"I think we shall call her 'Serendipity,'" CJ thought out loud.

Ribus remembered what he had said a few hours ago on the top of the hill and knew that was what she was referring to. "I think that is a good name," he said.

"Any objections?" Theban asked.

"Nope," Brunick replied.

"Serendipity, it is then!" Saezyn exclaimed.

RESTORATIONS

The next week was spent exploring and restoring *Serendipity*. It was soon discovered that, all in all, the ship contained a mess hall, kitchen, storage rooms, bridge, captain's room, crew living quarters, armory, main cargo hold, workshop, two hangars with a shuttle and two scout/light fighter craft a piece, a hydroponics station, and a lab. This was all fit into a space-efficient area. Some of the rooms were in lockdown after the time it had been dormant, but for being over three hundred years old, the ship was indeed one of the most advanced vessels in Ephesia, even still. It was one of the first vessels made by I3 to be equipped with the Universal Part Cohesion system which, by definition, meant that all the parts and power sources used by I3 could quickly and easily be transferred from one unit to another depending on the size of the unit and the part. This was used with power sources, weapons, building parts, and whatever was needed to be quickly transferable. In other words, the UPC system allowed simplicity in repairs and in swapping weapons and equipment from one craft to the other. The beauty of UPC was that it quickly caught on and was used by the Purge even after I3 fell, so the Paladins on board *Serendipity* were able to easily help repair and reprogram systems on the *Serendipity*. It did not take the new crew of the ship long to figure out how to work on the vessel. Theban had especially enjoyed working on the craft and using his craftsman abilities. They all had enjoyed restoring the ship, but more was repaired than just the vessel itself, relationships began to further be restored and cultivated. Ribus and Valdria had especially become fonder of one another. After Valdria saw Ribus break down a week ago, she had seen past his slick, gangster exterior, and she liked what she saw. He was human, and more than that, she saw that he cared about more than just himself. They spent every moment they could together, working on whatever project they found to do. There was a lot of work to get a three-hundred-year-old ship in working order, but after hours and days of hard labor, a momentous occasion was about to take place: they were going to power on the primary engines and see if *Serendipity* would fly.

The crew crowded into the bridge and waited to see if their efforts would be successful.

"Who should turn it on?" Linia asked.

"A better question is who should be captain of this beauty?" the General quizzed.

"I nominate CJ," Saezyn smiled. In the preceding week, she had been critical in maintaining cohesion between the crew and had a gentle, level-headed way about her. Also, when she helped Ribus get past his guilt for killing Cyra's mom, they heard what she said and saw how she acted and knew that she had all the qualities of a good captain. "Who agrees?" Saezyn polled.

Everybody besides CJ said, "I!"

She stood slightly flabbergasted and flattered, but Saezyn continued before she could object: "Well, that is settled. By popular demand, you, CJ Dreams, are Captain. So who do you nominate to turn on this craft?"

"I nominate Cyra to be our pilot from this point on. She is an excellent pilot and was critical in programming the control systems, so Cyra, you're the lady of the hour," CJ said with a smile.

Cyra sat down confidently with a grin and pushed several sequences into the main control station on the bridge. The screens all around them buzzed to life. They showed statistics on the ship and its subsystems. All eyes were bolted onto the little green number on the main view screen next to an outline of the ship's engines; the number represented the power level of the engines. As Cyra worked her magic, the number in the corner of the screen changed from 0 percent to 1 percent.

"Engines running at one percent power," she said with a grin.

"Will it fly?" Theban asked. Had his facial expression not been partially masked by his visor, they would have seen a scowl of frustration. He had put too much work into crafting parts from scratch for it to not work.

"Of course! The point is the engines are running!" Cyra exclaimed.

"Boosting power to twenty percent." Cyra pulled backward on the control stick, and immediately, the craft slowly hovered higher in the air. Once it reached a few hundred feet off the ground, she pushed forward on the stick; the craft skimmed smoothly through the air at great pace. The bridge erupted into cheers at their success.

"So captain, where to now?" Cyra asked CJ.

"Well, we have the ship flying, but we only have light weaponry on this vessel, and if our suspicions are correct about the Armada still having an occupation on this world, we need to get some bargaining tools so we can convince them to leave permanently. Does anybody have any ideas where we can increase our armament?" she asked of the group.

The General stepped forward. "Before this mess began with the queen and Toria Vilorious and the Armada, my team and I were stationed in Darknov in a small Purge base on the outskirts of Toria just outside the Bergda region. At this base, we didn't have an overabundance of weaponry, and after our raid on the city, our losses were severe, but the perimeter and base defense systems were left intact," the General explained.

"How does that help us though?" Brunick interrupted.

Before the General could make any utterance at Brunick's impatience, CJ simply lifted up a hand and told Brunick to give the General time to explain. Brunick was calmed, and the General was impressed at CJ's leadership abilities. She handled the situation with such ease.

"As I was saying, the perimeter is still intact—or should be and happens to contain some of the Purge's finest AA cannons. We could load these on with some heavy lifters at the base and hook them up to *Serendipity*'s grid."

"AA? Anti-air?" Theban asked.

"No, anti-anything!" Trigger grinned. They were talking about guns again, so his interest was piqued.

"I wish I knew earlier in my life that somebody manufactured anti-anything guns… Would have saved me a lot of trouble with less than savory women," Ribus muttered. Valdria gave him a playful shove.

"Can you plug in the coordinates?" Cyra asked.

"Absolutely," the General replied. He sat down at a nearby terminal and typed in the coordinates. The computer took a brief moment to calculate, and soon, the ship was going in that direction.

"ETA five minutes at only twenty percent power and that's going a distance of three hundred miles. This ship is fast!" Cyra mused as she briefly computed the speed of the ship and the distance left to travel. The velocity of the vessel was impressive indeed.

DARKNOV PURGE BASE

The *Serendipity* slowed to a halt above the small Purge base of Darknov. The sky was bitter black, and the rain streamed down in torrents which formed streams of water that flowed down the windows on the bridge. The lightless scene was an ominous blend of foreboding mixed with dread.

"Are you sure this is the place? I can't see much of anything, and our sensors aren't fully repaired yet," CJ asked of the General.

He looked out one of the windows with his hands clasped behind his back. He turned around. A concerned look was on his face. "This is Darknov. It's near the top of Solbia and gets less light from Orgasoli than most places on Solbia. It is also posted in one of the most intemperate places on this planet. You can thank Queen Odiria for that. We were only allowed to place a base in this region, otherwise, we would have had to have build while fighting the queen's armies, which, at the time, was not our goal. Nonetheless, I don't like this. Usually, we should be able to see the lights on the perimeter of the base, but I can't see anything in this storm," he said grimly.

"Maybe they went dark to avoid hostiles. Perhaps we could go in closer and turn on some lights and see what we find?" Linia ventured hopefully.

"That's if there is anything *to* find. Half the base staff was shot up when we went into Toria Vilorious to take out the amplifier,"

Trigger muttered glumly. Theban looked at the ground sadly. He built the amplifier, and because of it, countless people had died.

"Theban, the past is past. You can't go back, but you can go on," Saezyn told the craftsman kindly. "Besides, I gave the idea that brought the Armada, not you."

"True, but I just rolled over and built the accursed device that allowed ruination. I could have stood up to her," Theban replied.

"You could have, but you didn't. What's done is done. There is no sense holding on to mistakes if you have asked Trilumina for pardon from them. Also, something tells me that the next time you are in the presence of an evil dictator, you will make the right decision," CJ chimed in most judiciously.

"I'm sorry, Theban, I didn't mean to bring anything up," Trigger said apologetically as he saw the effects of his words.

"It's okay, Trigger. I'm just still working through the events of the last two weeks. Sometimes, I remember Toria, and though it wasn't morally attractive, the buildings were beautiful, and it makes me sad that it couldn't have been given another chance like us," he ruminated.

"It was given second and third and fourth and twentieth chances to repent, Theban. The Seldocs spent our lives trying to bring that city to repentance. *Toria's time had come.* Nobody is happy about it, but we must move on. The past is an unmovable burden that we cannot take with us if we are to have a future," Saezyn said firmly but kindly. Theban nodded solemnly in acknowledgement.

While they had discussed these things, Cyra had switched on the main lights on the hull of the *Serendipity* and lowered her closer to the ground. With the *Serendipity* on autopilot, Cyra climbed a service ladder to the floor below to the room containing the sensors. She then went to work getting the basic sensors online. A few minutes later, she came back and rapidly began programming the main computer.

"Done! Basic sensors back online!" she exclaimed proudly after a few minutes.

"It looks like they've located some sort of compound. Looks like it's the Purge base!" Mazzi exclaimed as she glanced at a panel displaying the sensor readings.

"It certainly is," The General murmured as he looked at the screens.

"Shall we land in the compound?" Cyra asked.

"I don't know. Shall we, Captain?" the General asked of CJ out of respect.

"Certainly! But we go in cautiously. We make our scan of this place quick to see if there is anything of use to us, and then, we clear out of here. This place is giving me all the wrong impressions," CJ responded.

"All right, Paladins, you heard the lady! Guns at the ready! Move! Move! Move!" The General ordered to Linia and Trigger. They were, in moments, jogging down the hall to the lift that would lead out into the stormy darkness. Saezyn, Ribus, and Mazzi kept pace with them while the rest of the crew stayed to protect the ship.

⸺◦/◦/◦⸺

The lift doors opened and revealed little but darkness. Cold rain mixed with hail pelted the faces of the party that volunteered to search Darknov.

"I don't see anyone," Mazzi whispered.

"I don't see anything at all," Trigger muttered.

"Turn on your night vision, soldiers," the General ordered. The three Paladins were equipped with glasses that allowed them to see in the dark, these glasses also allowed them to see where their bullets would hit based on wind speed, planet gravity, and a dozen other variables. Ribus didn't have these glasses, but the scope on his sniper rifle could see in the dark. Mazzi, on the other hand, had mining goggles that allowed her to see in utter blackness. Saezyn decided he would stay behind to guard the lift. He simply knelt in meditation in the middle of the elevator with the doors closed and halberd at the ready.

Upon the activation of their varying methods of night vision, the world was encompassed in green, and the picture of Darknov Purge base was made complete. This was what they beheld in their green died view: a base, they could plainly see they were in the base because of the varying com towers, fortifications, heavy turrets and cannons that surrounded them, but they could also tell something was wrong. The base was not in perfect health; no, not by any means. Several craters in the concrete, holes in the main wall, and several downed turrets showed that this place had been hit by some sort of attack. Besides ammo crates and three armadillo hover tanks, the compound was rather barren. What they couldn't see were any troops from any faction good or bad, but they couldn't see any bodies either. It appeared abandoned.

"What did this?" Trigger whispered.

"The Armada and the Purge," Linia replied. She gestured towards a downed myriad fighter craft.

"What do you mean the Purge did this too? They attacked themselves?" Ribus asked in a confused tone.

"What she means is that the Armada attacked, probably a small force, and the Purge fought them off, but the Armada hit some of our turrets with infectious munitions. The turrets began to transform into an enemy tool so the Purge here was forced to take out some of their own equipment. We can tell based on the ballistic damage on some of these walls. The damage also came from Purge weapons not only Armada devices," the General replied.

"Where are the Paladins that were left when we did our raid?" Linia asked.

"Are they dead?" Mazzi queried.

"There aren't any bodies," Ribus observed.

"They could have been taken over by mechamites and are waiting to ambush us," Trigger thought out loud. Everybody clenched their weapons tighter. At that moment, movement occurred in front of them and all around them. What appeared to be Paladins rushed forward from their hiding places with guns drawn. The soldiers surrounded them.

"Put the guns down! Guns down! Guns down!" one of the soldiers yelled at the General and the other crew members.

"No soldier! You put your guns down! I am General Drask, and if you don't do as commanded, I will put your butt on the ground faster than you can say 'insubordination charges!'" the General commanded.

Instantly, the Paladins that had come out of hiding snapped to attention knowing that their general had returned.

"What's your name, soldier?" the General looked fiercely at the one who had told him to put his gun down.

"Captain Belde', sir!" the Paladin replied.

"Captain Belde', I want a status report on Darknov two seconds ago," the General replied.

"Sir, yes, sir! We have endured several Armada attacks over the last week. At first, they were relatively small forces ranging from three to twenty myriads, but we took minimal casualties and were able to fend them off efficiently until two days ago—" Belde' had paused to gather his thoughts.

"What happened then soldier?" the General asked.

"We were attacked by an Armada cruiser. It took out our main power generator and left us in the dark, but we were able to use our armadillos to take it out. Of the fifty original base staff left when you went to take out the amplifier, we are now at thirty troops. Since we haven't had any orders from the Purge and our communications were taken out in earlier attacks, we have been following the standing orders of guarding Darknov," Belde' explained.

"What are the current logistics on this place? Specifically, what weapons and equipment are left intact?" the General asked.

"We have two ASP (Anti-Space Projectile) cannons, five shredder AA cannons, a dozen paragons, three armadillos, a cypher drop ship for air insertion of each armadillo, and some heavy lifters, plus thirty one primed Paladins. The turrets listed are useless without the generator working. We tried to get it back online, but the Armada cruiser tore it to ribbons. Why do you ask?" Belde' responded.

"Because you have new orders. I want all that you listed on the *Serendipity*," the General grinned.

"Sir?" Belde' didn't know what the *Serendipity* was.

"The *Serendipity*. The ship! Order your men to start getting the gear ready, and then you need to follow me," the General pointed to the large ship landed in the middle of the compound.

The captain gave the orders and then followed after the General.

CJ looked at Belde' as he stood before her on the bridge.

"The General tells me you want to join the crew of the *Serendipity*. Is this true?" She peered at him with a slight grin spreading across her face.

"He did? I do?" Belde' was flabbergasted. "I was just told to follow him on board the ship and load all our equipment on board."

"Well, would you rather stay at Darknov and try to defend a powerless base without weapons?" she asked.

"Of course not!" Belde' exclaimed.

"So would you and the other soldiers here like to join the crew?" she asked again.

"Of course! Anything is better than staying at Darknov!" he exclaimed.

"All right, Crewman Belde'! Go tell the men to get aboard so they can meet their new captain!" the General ordered.

"Sir, yes sir." Belde' snapped a crisp salute and hastily went to give the other Paladins the word.

It was only moments before the Paladins piled into the main cargo hold in ranks. CJ and the General came down to meet them while the other members of her crew busied themselves with getting the ship ready for the cargo it was about to take on.

"Paladins! Stand at attention while being addressed by your captain!" the General ordered.

The group stood rigid and looked at CJ as she walked towards them. Some of the younger men in the group gasped at CJ's beauty.

"Ladies and gentlemen, welcome to the *Serendipity*. The purpose of this craft is to hunt down the enemies of Trilumina and obliterate them. We are tasked with fighting for what is right, whatever the cost. Courage is a necessary, faith is a must, discipline will be had or enforced, and without trust in Trilumina, *we will* fail. If you lack any of these things you might as well get off at the first civilized place we find after we make way. We will be put up against the unknown, and I expect nothing less than your best. It is a fine ship, and with a fine ship, we need a fine crew. Are you up to the task? It will not be easy, but it will be rewarding," CJ orated in her finest form. Her speech was greeted by joyous cheers.

"All right then! Time to inspect the crew," she smiled warmly. She walked down the lines of the fresh additions to her crew and warmly greeted each one. Everyone instantly had great appreciation for their new captain. After she had greeted the last member of the crew, she walked back in front of them to give them their orders.

"My fine crew," she paused and said with smile, "it seems *Serendipity* is short on weapons at this time. Is it going to stay that way?"

"No, Captain!" They exclaimed and instantly rushed to get the weapons remaining at Darknov installed on the *Serendipity*.

"You are indeed a fine captain," the General whispered to CJ as the crew began to bustle about their business.

"Thank you," she smiled warmly in reply.

"Good news, Captain, the com system is now online, but I must request an audience with you and the command crew," Cyra said over the com. The command crew was, of course, those who had followed Saezyn and initially discovered the *Serendipity*.

PHYTIS

"What is the word, Cyra?" CJ asked as she walked back into the bridge from meeting the additions to the crew.

"Well, I have a… um… delay… problem… a something. I haven't a clue what the deal is," Cyra replied.

"What's wrong, Cyra?" CJ asked.

"We can't get into the hydroponics room and a couple of other rooms branching off of it," Brunick answered from a corner of the bridge. The others members of the command crew were piled into the room as well.

"Can't you basically do anything when it comes to computers?" Ribus asked Cyra.

"Usually, but someone or something is in the hydroponic station, and they countered all my attempts to open the door. The weird part is that the heat sensor readings of the room don't show anybody in the room—but rather that the room as a whole is warmer than the rest of the ship. Also, what we can get from other sensors is that an unusual humming noise is coming from the room," Cyra replied.

"What are we waiting for? Let's take a look!" Mazzi exclaimed.

"Sounds like a plan. Perhaps we can manually override the doors?" Theban suggested.

"You two can go, but first, let's consult Saezyn. What do you think, Saezyn?" CJ asked the mystic. He was sitting in a chair with a most thoughtful look on his face.

"I think I will go with the party that investigates the situation. It seems an intelligent entity resides within this ship," he replied. They asked him if he knew what was in the room, but he only would say: "Perhaps something I have long thought a myth."

Saezyn stood in front of the door with Mazzi behind him and Theban looking at an access panel beside the door. He gave it a brief scan with his visor before he popped the panel open with one of his many tools he had on his person at all times. Instantly, the hum that Cyra had described earlier became eminent.

"What is that?" Mazzi asked.

"I have no idea, but we are about to find out," Theban pulled down a yellow emergency override lever as he responded. The door clicked, but it did not open.

"You two stand back and stay quiet, I shall open this," Saezyn said. He pushed a button on his halberd which caused the blade to deploy with the sleek noise of metal gliding over metal. Saezyn carefully put the blade into the crack in the door and slowly pried it open to reveal an amazing sight. All three of them gasped in wonderment. The room was humming with large, purple, metallic bees that flew from plant to plant in the hydroponic facility. One hummed quickly over to the three people and landed on Theban's arm. From this closer vantage point, they could see the insect possessed large, shiny, oval, deep indigo eyes. Also, Theban could tell that they were tough creatures because the one on his arm weighed at least two pounds and measured six inches in length.

"What are they?" he mused as he observed the beautiful insect. It once again took flight and flew back into the hydroponic room.

"They are real! I thought they were a myth, but they are real" Saezyn said excitedly.

"That's not what he asked," Mazzi stated uncomfortably. She noticed that since the one bee had left, more of the bees were coming towards them.

"Oh, sorry. They are called Phytis. (Phytis is the name of their species while phytes is what they call themselves. Like humans are called Homo sapiens but are usually referred to as people). They are an intelligent race of bees. I believe they are capable of independent as well as group thought and are rumored to be capable of communication with humans," Saezyn replied. He then stepped forward slowly and spoke: "Esteemed phytes, we wish no ill will upon you and come with peaceful intentions. We would be honored if you would take time to tell us the tale of how you came to occupy this place."

The bees hummed louder for a brief moment as they flew at an increased pace as though they were spreading the news of what Saezyn had said. They then began to chirp to one another in communication as they debated what to do with the visitors. Soon, a bee far larger than the others came forth and chirped a command that all the other bees instantly obeyed. The large, cat-sized bee was clearly the leader of the hive. They began to climb onto one another, and before Saezyn and the others' eyes, the phytes quickly formed letters for Saezyn to read. This was what the bees had written using their bodies: "Our revered queen of the phytes wishes to speak to your queen."

"As you wish," Saezyn replied.

The command crew could scarcely believe their eyes when they came to evaluate this situation. CJ stepped forward into the room at the phytes beckoning while Saezyn and the others stood outside and watched. Nobody tried to disagree with CJ when she insisted on going alone. Everybody knew that if these creatures wished them dead they would not stand a chance, so all held their breath and hoped CJ could reach an agreement with the phytes.

"Honored ruler of the phytes, I am CJ Dreams, I come with intentions of friendship between our people," CJ began.

The queen of the phytes began chirping, and her followers formed themselves into words that CJ and the others could read.

"I Queen Izbiq, in the company of my hive, have occupied this ship for three hundred years. The previous crew of this ship tried to harm us when we refused to leave, so we removed their threat. If you try to get us to leave, we will destroy you as well. Why have you come?" were the words that rather quickly formed before their eyes.

"We were sent by Trilumina to use this ship to fight the evil Armada. We do not wish you to leave. In fact, we would be honored if you would ally with us and continue to pollinate the plants in this facility. I do not know what services we could offer a species such as you are, but we would be glad to render what services we can," CJ said warmly.

"We wish only to stay in the safety of our hive and that you treat us with the respect we deserve. We are colony of warriors and wish to be counted among your crew. We also wish to fight the long-hated Armada beside you, and I personally want to accompany you as one of your advisors so that I can help mediate between our peoples." Amazingly, Izbiq replied in an odd chirp dialect, but she did indeed respond in the language CJ spoke. She certainly had a steep learning curve to learn a new language so quickly.

"Sure! What do you mean by accompanying me though?" CJ smiled out of relief, but she was baffled by the Izbiq's last request. The queen phyte didn't respond by speaking or by telling her hive to spell out a response, instead, she flew from where she was perched on a large plant that was much like a giant, blue tiger lily and alighted on CJ shoulders.

"I guess that's settled then," Saezyn smiled.

The queen phyte made a pleasant, crooning chirrup, and the hive of phytes, in return, chirped in a joyous serenade. A peaceful resolution had been made much to both species jubilations and relief.

CJ looked down and smiled at the queen phyte that sat blissfully content on CJ's shoulder. Indeed, a beautiful friendship had been formed.

THE MISSION

It was two days before the *Serendipity* had all the gear from Darknov installed. In this time, the affection between the command crew, the Paladins, and the phytes grew significantly. The phytes had especially proven their usefulness by helping route power cables though tight places, and they unlocked any other rooms that they may have had locked down. Even the shields were restored in the few days of work, this, too, left CJ much in the debt of the phytes, for it was by their cunning and knowledge of the ship that the shields were restored. The weather had stayed dark and drear, allowing cover from any Armada forces that may occupy the planet, and soon, the work was finished without any hitches, but now, it was time for business. In the otherwise lackluster two days that the construction projects had taken place in, the General had been thinking about what Belde' had told him when they first arrived at Darknov, and deep down a shadow of forewarning had been growing in his mind, so finally he called a meeting. The command crew, captains among the newly taken Paladins, and captains among the phytes (called guardians) were present in this meeting. Of course, Izbiq was among the group along with her guardians; in fact, Izbiq had hardly left her perch on CJ's shoulders in the two days since their treaty. The two were best friends, and they were inseparable.

The General stood still and waited for all to be seated before he regally and seriously addressed his concerns. "I have engaged the Armada many times on many planets, on many fronts. I have fought in space, on ground, in zero-G, on the water, even beneath the water, and I know their sinister tactics better than any man would wish to know the thoughts of darkness incarnate. In this time and in these fights, I have learned that their first goal when they lose a battle is not to retreat. Their goal is to make the victorious force *think* that they have retreated. When the Armada was routed by the Purge after the fall of Toria, their main force left or was destroyed, but they didn't remove all their forces. They set up an abomination, a hive to spawn their treachery so that they can take back this planet slowly, gradually and most cunningly. I have long suspected that somewhere they were building an abomination, but coming here has confirmed my suspicions."

"Where is this hive?" Izbiq asked in her quaint dialect.

"How do you know? What caused you to become sure?" CJ asked.

"Belde' said that Darknov was attacked by an Armada cruiser. When the Purge countered the threat of the Armada in this system, I know enough of our own tactics to know that they would destroy anything as large and threatening as an Armada cruiser as soon as they found it, so the Armada cruiser couldn't have been in the force that attacked the city," the General replied.

"Couldn't it have come from off world?" Mazzi asked.

"The Purge barricades planets after securing them to protect from future Armada attacks. They would be able to detect and engage the craft before it made it in atmosphere," Linia explained.

"So the Armada must be building these ships. Where?" Ribus asked.

"And how big is this abomination?" Valdria questioned.

"The where is what we need to find out, and as for the size—the longer they go unopposed, the larger their factory will grow," the General stated solemnly.

"That's why we need to find it and give some opposition!" Trigger exclaimed with gusto as he cocked his rifle.

"For once, Trigger, I agree with you," the General smiled.

"Since the fall of Toria Vilorious, the communications network has been down, and the sensor grid is a mess. How are we supposed to locate this elusive hive?" Cyra asked from where she sat at her pilot's seat and rapidly looked on what was left of the Solbian network. There wasn't much to see.

"What are we supposed to do then? We can't just let the Armada tighten their clutches on this planet again! More people will die if they do!" Linia passionately exclaimed with a voice full of compassion for the souls at risk. It was one of the first times they had seen her say anything so zealously and full of feeling.

"Don't sweat it, Linia, I might know a guy," Ribus replied coolly.

"Where would we meet this guy?" CJ asked warily, knowing that Ribus had some questionable contacts in his past.

"The Eastern Expanse Space Platform," he replied grimly.

"The EE- SP! Are you serious? That is owned by the heartless Bandeesh Hemkil, and the entire place is steeped in corruption! He's the leader of the sex-trade operation and any other sick networks. I'm surprised its time of judgment didn't come when Toria's came!" Brunick exclaimed.

"The Eastern Expanse still has time yet to repent because few prophets have been sent its way," Saezyn interjected.

"Do we make to this port of brigands, Captain?" Cyra skeptically asked of CJ.

CJ looked at Ribus thoughtfully and asked, "Do you really think this contact can help?"

"Would I suggest it if I didn't?" he countered sagely.

"Very well, Ribus. I trust your judgment. Yes, Cyra, ready the ship. We make for the EE-SP."

Cyra flipped on the main engines and pushed forward on the main controls. The *Serendipity* glided out of the compound of Darknov and cut through the darkness and continual tempests of the region. Three luminescent blue streams of light emanating from the engines trailed the craft as it broke the cloud cover and then the Solbian atmosphere. The *Serendipity* was now fully equipped, crewed, and was now setting forth on her first mission as a fully functioning craft.

CONTACT

The *Serendipity* moved smoothly through space as it neared the Eastern Expanse Space Platform. It was a small city built in Solbia's orbit. The facility was complete with towers, warehouses, quays, factories, and an entertainment district. The whole place was painted grey scale from the metal it was fabricated out of, but neon signs and bright lights diverted one's gaze from that which was drear in the structural composition. The center of these neon lights was the entertainment district which was fraught with drugs, gambling, sex, filth, and lowlifes and it happened to be where Ribus said they needed to go to meet his contact.

The *Serendipity* cruised to a halt by a quay near the seedy district they were to visit. Ribus, CJ, and Saezyn were the party that left to investigate any potential leads while the rest of the crew continued working on the ship and restoring its systems. Izbiq and a dozen of her guardians stashed themselves in CJ's bag because they refused to be left out of the mission. CJ promptly agreed to take them because they would be handy in a pinch and would be an excellent distraction if worst came to worst.

"Keep a sharp eye and have your weapons where others can see them. A woman of your beauty would be a fine prize for any boss in the sex trade," Ribus whispered as they passed among the crowds of corrupt people.

"Where is this contact of yours?" CJ asked as she drew forth her pistol.

"In the Central Club. He is a gambler and spends his days swindling the people in the pub, but he has a surplus of information and a wide array of people report to him. Also, a lot of tidbits of information that get passed in between people in the pub are not lost upon his ears," Ribus explained.

"The Central Club is the black heart of this district though, isn't it?" Saezyn said almost rhetorically.

"Indeed, it is," Ribus replied darkly.

"Of course, that is where we would have to go," CJ sardonically muttered. As she said this, she noticed a group of thugs looking at her like she was a piece of meat. She gave them a stern look and cocked her pistol. The thugs looked away.

"Be ready. We will probably see those 'gentlemen' again. They are recruiters for the sex trade operation, and you, CJ, are a prime piece of real-estate in their eyes," Ribus said grimly.

"Don't worry, Carmine, we won't let anybody touch our captain," Saezyn said to her.

The Central Club was a huge building in the center of the entertainment district. It was gaudily decorated with vibrant, neon signs that showed all the seedy services it offered. The two large front doors slid to each side to allow access for CJ and her crew members. The opening of the doors gave way to show a dim-lit room with flashing, multicolor strobe lights, and a main dance floor covered with scantily clothed people dancing (more aptly described as grinding on one another or several others) to head-pounding, loud music with a hypnotic beat. The bar and gambling tables were on the far side of the room.

"Are we going to have to pass through that? It looks like just breathing that air would give one a disease." CJ winced.

"Yeah, keep your hands to yourself, and you should be fine… hopefully," Ribus replied. He muttered the last word quietly so the music drowned it out.

Saezyn and Ribus stood on either side of their captain. They were her bodyguards as they began to walk across the dance floor. Halfway across the room, a young man who was quite enamored by CJ's enchanting appearance tried to dance his way to CJ.

"Dance with me, my muse!" he exclaimed above the music.

Saezyn barred the way to CJ with his staff and bellowed: "Go dance with yourself. We're here on business."

"That will be the last mistake you ever make, old man!" the testosterone- and drug-pumped young adult exclaimed. The teen with a menacing look in his eye drew a knife. The crowd backed away, but the music only changed to a tune with a more intense beat. Saezyn acted in blinding speed as he deployed the blade from his staff in one motion, knocked the knife out of the punk's hand in the next, and came to rest his weapon with the tip of his blade just barely touching the youth's throat. Ribus had also pulled both his silenced pistols out in the same brief period of time and was scanning the room making sure that nobody else was approaching.

CJ stepped forward and spoke to the young man. "Had you touched this man, I would not have danced with you, I would have blown your stupid head off your body after Ribus over there shot out both you kneecaps."

Ribus gave a sinister grin that told he would love to permanently disable the hooligan. The youth swallowed hard. As his Adam's apple rose and fell, it put enough pressure on Saezyn's razor sharp blade so that a faint trickle of blood came from his throat. The youth turned and ran out of the room, leaving only the shards of his broken pride on the dance floor.

CJ and her body guards walked the rest of the floor unopposed, and the second they left the floor, the dancing resumed as though nothing had happened. Ribus led them over to a large gambling table where a man clothed in sleek, burgundy leather with lurid, chrome jewelry sipped on an expensive neon blue beverage and thoughtfully stroked his goatee as he looked at his hand. His matching burgundy fedora was tilted to one side further adding to the gambler's stylistic flare.

"Zekle! Still up to your games!" Ribus exclaimed as he approached the table.

"Ah, Ribus! Good to see you and nice to see you still know how to make an entrance!" (A comment obviously in reference to how they dealt with the punk on the dance floor.) "You brought friends!! Let me clear out these phonies, and then I will be right with you," the man exclaimed joyfully from where he sat. He was a shifty looking character, but one couldn't help but like him and his enamoring charms.

"Your contact, I presume?" CJ whispered in Ribus's ear.

"You presume correctly," Ribus replied.

"You sure this guy is trustworthy?" Saezyn asked. He didn't like the look of the swindler. Ribus just nodded.

The man was playing with six other players at a game called sulcus. Sulcus was Ephesia's equivalent to poker; each player would collect cards representing various facets of an army. The goal was to have the most powerful force or the most strategically superior force by the end of ten rotations of drawing cards and modifying what cards one had played on the board. Having the best force at the end of a rotation granted certain perks like drawing an extra card or taking one of your opponent's cards, but the one who had the best hand at the end of the tenth rotation won the pot. Like in poker, the game of sulcus was based on nerve, steel, and luck, Zekle had an overabundance of all these qualities measured in well-balanced proportions.

"Well, boys, it looks like we finally have a new victor at this table. What happened, Zekle? Did your luck finally run out? Look at your hand, its garbage!" one of the newer players at the board said as he laid down the best of his hand.

Zekle smiled the same grin that he always had plastered on his face, the same grin that made it impossible to read whether he had a good hand or poor hand, and then Zekle laid down his cards. Indeed they were low, terribly low, but it was also the hardest low hand in the game to get. Among the seasoned sulcus players, it was one of the few hands with a revered name—it was known as dissension. It was the one low hand that could overthrow all others because it represented division among the ranks; specifically, it represented division among the ranks of all the other players' hands. The young gambler who had been so boastful a minute ago sat aghast at the turn the game had just taken and the amount of his money they had also gone with it.

"You cheated!" the youngster exclaimed.

"I don't cheat, you best leave this table before I begin to get offended by your false accusations," Zekle retorted calmly. He still had his sly grin.

"You aren't the boss of me; I can go where I want!" the novice sulcus player spat back.

"That's where you're wrong. I own this table, literally. Leave it now or your brain matter will be used to redecorate the walls behind you," Zekle replied. His grin had left his face. The novice looked at Zekle's now forbidding face and realized that he was on thin ice indeed, but his wounded pride wouldn't let him walk away quietly. He slowly reached his hand under the table, but Ribus was watching this scene and knew the look upon the face of this man: it was the look of a man with hurt pride seeking to regain his name. The man was reaching to draw a weapon. Ribus beat the gambler to the draw, and by the time the novice had the pistol above the table, Ribus had blasted it from the man's hand. Two of Zekle's thugs then grabbed the loser, who was still rubbing his aching fingers and took him from the room.

"Thank you, Ribus, so what do you guys and the beautiful miss need?" he flashed a handsome grin in CJ's direction upon his mention of the "beautiful miss."

"We need information, but this probably isn't the best place to talk," CJ replied. As soon as she said this, the doors to the club slid open, and the thugs that had been eyeballing CJ earlier in the streets came into the club. Zekle noticed them instantly. Life on the EE-SP had sharpened his sense of trouble to the point it was a sixth sense.

"I see what you mean, miss— what is your name? And the name of your compatriot here, of course," Zekle queried for the names he did not know (of course, he knew his good friend Ribus). As he spoke, he ushered them into a side corridor to avoid the sex slave recruiters.

"CJ Dreams, I'm Captain of the *Serendipity*, and this is Saezyn. I hold few people in such regard as these two members of my command crew," she said as she motioned to both Saezyn and Ribus.

"You have a ship? Perhaps we should talk there. Things around here have become… unsavory lately. It's no longer fun and games like it used to be in the old days," Zekle whispered.

"Sure, it's on quay P119-105," CJ replied.

"Great, I know a shortcut. A couple back alleyways, a turn here and there, and we should be in your ship in a few minutes," Zekle replied as he took them out of the building. He took out a laser from his jacket pocket and sealed the door with a burst of concentrated heat that welded the lock shut.

"That's a nice welding job, Zekle, but do you really think you can deny Bandeesh his quarry?" coolly stated the leader of a group of a score of thugs that emerged from the shadows of the back alley behind the Central Club. The thug wore dark glasses even in the night and shady clothes to match his gloomy heart. Said impersonator of a black hole continued talking. "Our scouts saw this beauty over here, and they sent a communiqué to Bandeesh asking if we should pursue and take her in. He beheld this creature's beauty and wants her for his personal uses." The man gestured toward CJ and smiled a creepy grin.

Before anyone else could say anything, CJ held up her hand calmly and said: "Izbiq, do what you do best."

The thugs laughed, and one of them punched the arm of the other and said, "She must be crazy!"

The other thug scoffed, "Bandeesh likes them crazy!"

Before they could laugh too heartily, Izbiq and her guardians flew from CJ's bag and swarmed the guards. The phytes landed upon twelve of the thugs and drove their dual, glistening, fang-like stingers into their flesh and released a shock of electricity comparable to the best tasers on the market. Those stung fell to the ground as the electricity caused severe muscle spasms. As the phytes swarmed, Ribus, CJ, Saezyn, and Zekle took cover behind trash bins and opened fire on the guards that remained standing. Even though there were eight thugs still posing a threat after the Phytes attacked, Ribus and Zekle had them down in seconds. Both Ribus and Zekle were among the fastest gunslingers in Solbia, and they did not hesitate to drop the remaining thugs via a bullet to the frontal lobe. As the thugs fell to the ground, the muzzle flash of their guns momentarily lit up the back alley as the last nerve impulses spastically fired throughout their bodies to their trigger fingers as they feebly tried to defend against Ribus and Zekle. In moments, the criminals were neutralized, and their bodies lay still or twitching upon the cold streets.

CJ and her company came out from where they had taken cover to continue on their way, but they were halted when they found Izbiq taking care of one of her wounded guardians. In the brief crossfire, it had been hit by a bullet, but it still had had enough energy to land on one of the thugs and to sting him until he fell. Izbiq emitted a mournful hum as she looked over the phyte. The wounded soldier barely hummed as it spoke to his queen. She spoke something in an even, more low-pitched tone, and the blue indigo in the wounded phytes's eyes dulled to grey—it had died. Those who beheld this spectacle looked on sadly.

"What did you tell him before he passed?" CJ asked of Izbiq after witnessing the heart-wrenching sight.

"I said, 'Rest my child. You have lived and died valiantly,'" Izbiq replied. She then sadly went back into CJ's bag in the company of her eleven remaining guards. Though the thugs that had been stung were still alive, CJ didn't bother killing them because all they had energy to do after being stung was lie on the ground and moan.

"Come, let us leave this place. Bandeesh has many men in his service, and doubtlessly, he will send others to pick you up if we tarry in this place," Saezyn said seriously.

"He is right. If we aren't so rudely interrupted again, we should be to your ship in a timely manner," Zekle agreed.

FLIGHT FROM THE EE-SP

"Captain, you are needed on the bridge immediately," Cyra said anxiously over the com the second CJ, Ribus, Saezyn, and Zekle entered the *Serendipity*.

"I'm on my way," CJ replied as she quickened her pace.

In mere moments, they had made it to the bridge.

"Phew, you're here, there are half a dozen T10-C10 attack shuttles on an inbound vector, and we are now picking up three approaching hover tanks on our sensors. They will be on the quay in two minutes, and the shuttles will be here in half that time. What should we do?" Cyra asked for direction.

"Arm all weapons! All Paladins to their battle stations!" CJ ordered. People all over the ship rushed to man some weaponry or to help regulate a vital defense station.

"What happened out there? What did these people do to the captain?" Cyra asked. She was shocked at CJ's aggressive stance toward the approaching vessels.

"Maybe you should be asking what the captain is going to do to these people." Zekle grinned from where he watched from a window on the bridge. Cyra gave him a funny look but didn't have to ponder his words for long.

"General, tell the AA guns to fire a spread at the incoming shuttles the second they are in range and tell the men manning the paragons to shred the tanks. We are leaving this place," CJ calmly but sternly said to the General.

"They are in range now Captain," he replied.

"Well, make it rain then," she firmly replied. The death of Izbiq's guardian had provoked CJ to retribution.

"My pleasure," the General replied. He then spoke into his com to his men on fire control, "All batteries open fire!"

The AA canons fired two rounds a piece at the approaching shuttles, which were il-equipped to take the ghastly barrage. The AA munitions could best be described as oversized shotgun rounds that fired rods of heavy metal at destructive velocity. The shuttles were torn quickly and efficiently to flaming tatters, thus leaving just the approaching tanks.

Moments after the destruction of the shuttles, the enemy tanks rounded a street corner and hovered down the quay toward the *Serendipity*. The tanks opened fire, but the shields held fast. The paragon heavy machine guns unloaded hundreds of 20mm incendiary rounds upon the approaching tanks. The hot, white magnesium rounds viciously cut through the armor and killed the drivers of the tanks. The points of impact left glowing, bright orange holes in the armor from the extreme heat of the perforating bullets. The engines and fuel cells on the enemy tanks ruptured as the bullets pierced through, and chunks of hot metal were strewn over the quay.

"All right, Cyra, time to go," CJ said. Upon these words, Cyra gunned the engines and blasted into the vacuum of space, leaving smoldering piles of wreckage in the wake of the *Serendipity*. Soon, they were miles away from the city.

"What is that flashing light?" Valdria asked as she glanced at a nearby monitor. She was sitting next to Ribus holding his hand.

"We have another incoming ship," Cyra replied.

"From the city?" Ribus asked.

"No, from the planet. It's an Armada cruiser, and it's headed towards the city. Shall we turn around and engage it?" Cyra queried. A computer projection of a model of the enemy ship showed on the screen that had initially pronounced its presence.

It was twice the size of the *Serendipity* and covered in dark, sharp, battle armor; strange, glowing precipices; and several ports for deploying pods, energy blasts, and myriad.

"What do you think?" CJ turned to her command crew. She didn't exactly feel like the EE-SP necessarily deserved a rescue after her adventures there. She also wasn't thrilled at risking the lives of her crew for said corrupt city.

"If we don't do something, the city will most likely be destroyed. Could we summon Purge reinforcements from the blockade?" the General said.

"The Purge blockade is and has been occupied against a second Armada onslaught that came two weeks after the first failed. I don't think they can help anybody until they deal with their own foe. Personally, I would probably leave the EE-SP to their fate after what they tried to do to you," Zekle chimed in, though he wasn't a member of the command crew.

"It is not yet the Eastern Expanse's time of judgment. Also, any material the Armada gains from the EE-SP, they will use to build more ships," Saezyn stated solemnly.

"I say attack!" Izbiq exclaimed as she climbed from CJ's bag and perched on her shoulder.

"All right, that settles it. Turn the ship around, Cyra. We shall engage this craft. Shields up, weapons primed, and all crew to their stations," the captain commanded.

"What's the plan?" Mazzi and Theban said in unison.

"Don't know the details yet, but destroying the enemy comes to mind," she replied.

"General, where are the most weapons on the enemy ship concentrated?" Brunick asked.

"On the bottom of the ship so it can rain down its own ghastly version of the abyss onto its prey. Why do you ask?" the General replied.

"Our heavy weapons are stationed on top of the *Serendipity*, are they not?" Brunick further pressed.

"Indeed, what are you getting at Brunick?" the Captain replied.

"How about we fly over top of the Armada cruiser and turn upside down so we can hit them with all we have while they can retaliate with only minimal systems?" Brunick suggested.

"I like it," Trigger grinned.

"Me too!" Zekle exclaimed.

"Good enough for me. All right, General, order your men to rain fire upon the enemy as soon as we fly above it," CJ commanded. She then turned to Cyra. "Go as fast you can so they have little time to adjust for our approach and make sure we intercept them before they reach the city."

"All right! Strap yourselves in!" Cyra replied gleefully. She gunned the throttle and hurtled toward the cruiser. The enemy vessel was fixated on the city and didn't recognize the *Serendipity* as a Purge craft, so the Armada vessel did not alter its course to address the *Serendipity* as a threat. When the *Serendipity* showed no signs of altering course, the cruiser deployed a dozen myriad, but it was too little too late. The Paladins manning the paragon turrets cut through the enemy fighters like a plasma torch through tissue paper. The *Serendipity* then turned so its weapons were facing down at the cruiser and flew over the top while unleashing every caliber weapon they had on it. The crew of the *Serendipity* held on tightly to whatever they could get a hold of as they waited for the artificial gravity to counter the strenuous g-forces and to adjust to the orientation shift of the vessel. The enemy shields flashed into view as they absorbed the impact from the first volley of the AA canons, but the shields died completely as the first ASP canon fired. The second ASP canon blew a hole through and through the engines of the cruiser, and the second volley of the AA canons, ASP canons, and the perpetual pounding of the paragons obliterated the hull integrity of the Armada ship completely. The jagged, crystalline structure of the vessel shattered under the barrage and reduced the craft to chunks of glass-like pieces that drifted harmlessly through space like a window shattering in zero-g.

"Are all the crystal cores and mechamite facilities on the cruiser disabled?" the General asked perplexedly. He knew some of the debris would reach the city, and if functioning mechamites were among the shards, the city could still be consumed.

"Scanning now… reports are coming back—negative for any energy signatures. The only movement being picked up is from the drifting of the debris," Cyra replied.

"So can we leave this place now? In my opinion, that is more than enough action!" Theban exclaimed.

"We sure can," CJ replied somewhat breathlessly.

THE SEARCH

When the *Serendipity* was hundreds of miles away from the EE-SP, Cyra slowed the ship so it was leisurely drifting in space.

"Well, now that we have finally gotten away from that vile place, and we have what we came for, it is my pleasure to introduce, Zekle," CJ said warmly as she gestured toward the gambler. CJ also quickly introduced the other members of her command crew to Zekle as well.

"Thank you kindly," Zekle said with a slight bow, and he flirtatiously grinned in the direction of the ladies on the command crew. He continued with a smirk: "Why exactly did you kidnap me from the EE-SP? What information did you need?"

"We can return you any time so you can deal with Bandeesh and his thugs if you wish," Ribus retorted with a grin. He and Zekle had been friends for many years, and Ribus knew his sly humor.

"No, thank you. I think I like it here, but seriously, what information do you need?" Zekle pressed.

"We theorize that somewhere on Solbia," the General replied, "the Armada has a factory that is building ships like we just attacked. If we do not find it soon, the Armada may be able to mount another attack and this time, take the entire planet out from under the Purge. This is a definite possibility now that we learned the Purge is fighting the Armada as we speak and cannot focus their forces on planetary threats."

"I see. Well, that is a valuable bit of information, isn't it. I am happy to oblige you, but I have a request. You see, when we exited the EE-SP, I didn't leave it on good terms as you well know, and I need a place to live for a while, perhaps a long while. Would it be possible for me to stay here?" Zekle gave an innocent look in CJ's direction.

"You can stay as long as you like as long as you are willing to serve Trilumina and revoke your swindling ways," CJ replied sternly.

"I see. A ship full of holy rollers, gun totters, and intelligent bees. An interesting crew to say the least. I don't see how I can pass this up! I do have one other request though," Zekle pressed further.

"What would that be?" the General asked warily.

"Can I set up a sulcus table in the cafeteria or some room on the ship? Don't worry. I won't play for actual money but more as a way to give a place of relaxation to the crew." Zekle gave a charismatic grin and an innocent shrug.

"I guess, but if you are caught gambling. I will throw your butt out in the cold faster than a plasma strike, and you'll just be thankful I didn't shoot you out of the ASP canon. Also, you need to know if you are on this ship, you are part of the crew. Is that understood?" CJ gave a stern eye.

"Understood, Captain! And don't worry, I won't let you catch me gambling." Zekle gave a sly grin. CJ just shook her head at his unbelievable gall.

"He hasn't changed much in the time you two have known one another, has he?" Linia asked Ribus.

"Not a bit," Ribus smiled.

"I suspected as much," she responded with a hint of a grin. She couldn't help be a little taken in by Zekle's suave mannerisms.

"So about that Armada factory you guys are looking for. I have to say that I have no idea where it is," Zekle stated with a shrug.

"We just took on this hooligan for no reason then," the General muttered.

"Hey, sarge, don't sit on the wrong end of your rifle over there! I am certainly a hooligan at times, but I am not dead weight. I said I don't know where your factory is, but I didn't say that we couldn't find it," Zekle replied smoothly.

"Do you have an idea where we should start looking?" asked CJ.

"Not yet. Before I can give a good guess of the location of the factory, I need to know more about this foe. What drives them? What do they build with? What's there track record? It's just like tracking down somebody that owes you money: you gauge their habits and motives, you place a tracking device on their person, and once you have caught them in a secluded place, you beat the money they owe you out of them. I mean you persuade them nicely to repay their debts. Anyway, the point is the more you know your foe, the more likely it is you will know where to find them," Zekle replied.

"Allow me," Saezyn interjected. CJ gave him a nod to continue. "The Armada targets humanity because they are Trilumina's greatest treasure. The Armada was designed by Ordam to cause chaos in Trilumina's plans for Ephesia and humanity. They are driven by vengeance. Ordam desired to be equal to Trilumina and was cast from the great paradise for his pride. Ever since then, he does whatever he can to cause ruination and wreck lives. The Armada is the tool he uses to do this," Saezyn said in explanation of the Armada's motives.

"As for what they need to build their devices with, the mechamites in the Armada are made from varying metals, the ships are built from metal, and a dark crystal that they have managed to synthesize on every planet we face them on. At the beating heart of every Armada force is what we call a cursed crystal. It acts like the central processing for their dark forces," the General added.

"I see, I see." Zekle stroked his goatee. After thinking for a moment, he held up his hand and spoke, "Can we bring up a map of the hemisphere of Solbia the Armada attacked? Preferably a geological map that shows deposits of varying metals?"

"This is the best we have with the current, damaged intel grid," Cyra replied after several rapid keystrokes. On the monitor, a map of the upper hemisphere of Solbia showed on the screen. Next to any major city, they could see varying concentrated deposits of metals the Armada favored, but the picture was still full of holes, doubtlessly caused by damage to places hit by the Armada's guerilla tactics since invading the world.

"Perhaps I can help," Mazzi stated.

"How so?" CJ asked.

"I worked in mining for a few years, as you know, and my unit had some data on promising digs," Mazzi explained. She stepped forward and plugged a chip into the computer console. Many of the holes on the grid were filled in by this added data.

"We still have several blank places where there either isn't resources they can use, or the intel grid isn't registering that there are resources there. Hmmm... how can we narrow this down?" Zekle thought out loud.

"I've got an idea," Linia said. "The Armada doesn't have enough strength to defend against many attacks at this point, so they wouldn't put a factory in an open area. Cyra, how many locations on the map are resources-abundant, secluded, and easily defensible?"

Cyra plugged in commands into the computer, and soon, three locations circled in green rings showed on the map on the monitor. There was one next to a mountain, one in a valley, and one in the middle of a barren land.

"Well," Cyra said, "I would say that with the data we have available, we should look into these three locations. We have a location in the Myzex mountain range, the barren lands of Bergda, and Rubicon valley. Aka the place of skulls," she read off the names from the information available on the locations.

"The valley of skulls!" Theban exclaimed nervously.

"Sounds lovely," Ribus muttered in a sardonic tone.

"Where should we check first?" Mazzi asked.

"To Rubicon valley! So we can clear that drear-sounding place and get checking it out of the way," Saezyn exclaimed.

"An excellent idea, Saezyn. All right, crew! You heard the man, let us make way!" CJ ordered in a no-nonsense sort of manner.

The command crew hustled to various tasks that needed doing while Cyra steered the ship to the next destination: Rubicon Valley—the place of skulls.

THE PLACE OF SKULLS

"It doesn't look all that foreboding," Mazzi said as she looked out the window on the bridge of the *Serendipity*. The craft was hovering a few hundred feet above the valley, giving a great vantage point for looking down upon the river that had carved the deep gorge which comprised the Rubicon valley.

"The lavender leaves on the trees in combination with the deep green river at the bottom actually looks rather picturesque," Theban agreed with Mazzi.

"If it looks nice, then why is it called the place of skulls? You mean we aren't going to get to shoot anything?" Trigger expressed his exasperation.

"Well, so far, we aren't picking up any Armada activity, so we don't really have a reason to stop and figure out how the valley got its ominous moniker," CJ said somewhat apathetically.

"You mean we aren't going to explore this place?" Zekle exclaimed.

"I don't see any particular reason why we should. I mean we could send troops down and figure out why it is called the place of the skull and why it is called the Rubicon, which happens to mean 'a line that once one has crossed, they cannot come back from,' but I don't feel like it is good use of manpower to send people into a potentially dangerous place when the Armada is building ships as we speak in a location that is elsewhere. Do you?" CJ turned and looked hard at him.

"No, captain," he muttered and shut his mouth tightly.

"I do," the General interjected.

"You do what?" CJ replied somewhat tersely.

"I have a reason to look at this place up close. There are energy readings of some sort emanating from an inlet of the Rubicon river about two miles up. We can't get any significant detail. Besides, they don't appear to be Armada, but perhaps they have figured out a way to mask their operations," the General explained.

"All right, General. Assemble a team and scout the source out but come back quickly. And that is an order," CJ commanded with a faint smile.

"Yes, Captain!" the General threw a swift salute.

The General stood in the hangar bay 1 with Saezyn, Trigger, Belde', and a platoon of(ten to twelve) other Paladins. They stood in front of a cypher drop ship that had an armadillo tank attached in its back partition. It was to be the method of insertion into the Rubicon. CJ wasn't willing to try to land the *Serendipity* in the valley even though Cyra insisted she could land it successfully. The cyphers were going to drop off the troops.

"All right men, the captain wants us to search a suspicious energy signature in this valley, but if it has nothing to do with the Armada, we will be wasting precious time and will be wasting the captain's time, so we are going to make everything about this mission short, sweet, and to the point, including this pep talk," the General began.

A couple of the Paladins whispered something between themselves and snickered.

"Do you have something you would like to share, soldiers?" the General directed an intimidating stare at the Paladins that had been whispering.

"Sir, I was just thinking that you never give *brief* pep talks. That is all. sir," the soldier gave a swift salute and grinned. Several of the Paladins tried not to laugh but failed.

"There is a first time for everything soldier! I will make this quick. Gents, we go into the cave that this energy signature is coming from. We go in fast, we go in first, and if anything presents a target, we go in furious! Is that understood, gents!" he roared.

"Sir, yes sir!" they replied in a gusto filled chorus.

"All right then! The captain ordered me to come back quickly, so no slipshod behavior on this mission or any other mission for that matter. You are Paladins, act like it. Now, all aboard!"

The Paladins held a clenched fist to their chest and bowed their heads; a gesture that stood for the phrase "I serve with all of my heart," and then, they all piled into the armadillo.

The cypher's engines roared on, and the craft blasted out of the hangar and began its decent into the Rubicon. The broken reflection of the carrier shimmered in the rippling liquescent waters of the Rubicon river as the craft passed between stately trees with pale yellow bark and light lavender leaves. Ruby grasses bent under the force of the wind from the thrusters as the cypher set down a mile away from the location they were sent to investigate. The bank was too narrow for the cypher to touch down anywhere closer, so they were going to have to walk the rest of the way.

"All right, men, let's move! I want to be back before this evening fades too far into night," the General commanded. It was already getting dark.

"Also, tell them to be wary, I sense something ill is afoot," Saezyn said to the General.

"For those of you who didn't hear what the esteemed Saezyn told me, watch your back, something may be waiting to stab you in it," the General added. His warning was greeted with a unanimous 'Sir, yes sir!' They then quickly began traversing the inviting terrain of the Rubicon to the inlet that was the source of their inquiry.

It was deep into the evening when the task force made it to an ominous cave which was the inlet in question. To the surprise of everyone, the cave was carved to look like a large skull, complete with a gapping mouth and soulless, empty eyes. The mouth was the opening to the cave; this feature also doubled as the escape for the water that must have originated from some deep subterranean spring. The Paladins hadn't beheld the foreboding effigy for long when the dark eyes suddenly lit up with a spooky, lime green luminescence.

"I don't like the looks of that," muttered Trigger as he rammed the bolt on his rifle back. He let the bolt slide forward thus loading a cartridge into the chamber.

"Shhh… Let's see what happens," Saezyn held a finger to his mouth to silence the banter.

The evening fell into darkness as the group waited silently a few minutes longer, and the green luminescence increased tenfold. The General drew in a sharp breath as, suddenly, the cause of the light revealed itself. The light came from large, winged beetles whose posterior section emitted the brilliant light. The insects were the size of large bats.

"They are beautiful," the General stated in awe.

"And energy readings indicate they are the source of the power we detected earlier," Belde' stated after a glance at his portable scanner.

"Mystery solved, I guess. Let's get back to the *Serendipity*," Trigger grinned happily. He didn't like the look of the cave at all and was more than a little relieved to find the cause of their investigation was simply the byproduct of glowing beetles.

"Not so fast, Trigger. I think this cave deserves a closer look," the General stated bluntly.

"No. Respectfully, General, I disagree," Saezyn said. "The Paladins should go back to the ship. A great darkness dwells in this cave, and the weapons your Paladins are used to using are of no effect against such vileness, so return to the ship with your men. I will follow shortly. If you don't see me waiting for you where we were dropped off in an hour, destroy this cave, and continue your search for the Armada hive," Saezyn said calmly but seriously.

"Are you my superior?" the General retorted snappishly.

"No, I am not, but my orders come from Trilumina, and his word is above all, and right now, he is telling me that a great danger resides in this place. A great danger that I need to face," Saezyn responded.

"I don't doubt Trilumina, but I don't see why you have to face this danger alone," the General replied.

"It is a time of testing. Even prophets go through testing. Especially prophets," Saezyn answered. A distance from the moment was in his eyes revealing that deep thought was behind the words he had just uttered.

"If it must be so, I consent, but I will not leave you here. We shall remain outside and wait for your return, my dear friend," the General replied.

"It must be so. And thank you, General. I shall return shortly," Saezyn responded, and then he turned and walked to the cave. A faint green light shone from the mouth of the drear crevasse, which soon swallowed Saezyn as he strode in between the teeth of the massive jaws into the dim maw.

TEMPTATION

The large, olive green beetles swarmed lazily around the cave and perched on rocks or large deposits of metallic resources and paid no notice to Saezyn. He wasn't the first to pass into this cursed place. He glanced at the odd, glowing insects as he passed by. The creatures had six hemispherical eyes and long, flowing tendrils rooted in their heads that stretched back toward their abdomen, like long, black dreadlocks. They made no noise besides the hum of their wings, or the scrapping of their feet upon the crimson sandstone of the cave walls and stalagmites. It was not a long walk of observing these strange creatures until Saezyn came upon the main hall of the skull; it was a rather intimate setting (intimate is not at all an exaggeration). Luxurious, purple curtains were hung between ancient stalagmites and stalactites that had welded together over time and become pillars. The water that flowed down the pillars would join together and flow out of the cave; it was one of the sources of the Rubicon river. The pillars were on either side of an open floor that came up to a stage upon which a litter was set. On this litter, a woman of unsurpassable beauty lay upon her side with one hand supporting her head while the other hand rested upon her hips. She wore little else besides a coy but knowing smile and the garb of a seductress. Her lips were deep crimson, her eyes as beautiful as twinkling stars and as colorful as the nebula. Her hips and body were perfectly sculpted, and her voluptuous curves could be found in many impure fantasies.

"Saezyn Seldoc, it is a pleasure to see you. I do hope you can say the same for me, and I do hope you will stay the night—or perhaps longer," the woman said smoothly, and she let her ruby lips reveal her perfect, white teeth in a flirtatious grin.

"Indeed, it is a pleasure to behold you." Saezyn paused as he shook his head, and he focused his wandering eyes upon her face. It took a world of self-control to do this simple act. He continued with renewed determination not to be sucked into her game. "But who exactly are you?" he asked.

"An interesting question. I am desire. To some, I am love, to others I am lust, to most, I am a burning fire waiting to be released so that I can consume them as I steal them away to worlds of sensuality, to galaxies where wishes come true. I am the moment of ecstasy culminated with raptures of unparalleled pleasure, but to you, Saezyn—I am temptation. The gateway to this universe you have not yet feasted your eyes upon. Just reach out and touch it, feel it, Saezyn, and we will make way on a journey that is so glorious and so close, so close, if you just take hold and at the same time, let go," temptation grinned at Saezyn.

It was hard not to be drawn into her sensual imagery and charismatic tones. She was all *woman*, she was all there and offering what few willed to resist. Saezyn looked around to make sure that she didn't have any minions waiting to catch him off guard, but he saw little. Besides the curtains and the litter with this temptress posed suggestively upon it, the only other things to be beheld within the sandstone den of desire were statues of other racy figures and a tree that held the most ripe, delicious-looking, deep maroon fruit. The smell of the tree was intoxicating and seemed to beckon. Temptation held out her hand and gestured to partake of the fruit.

Saezyn looked at the tree and at the voluptuous woman on the stage and thought that if there were minions in the room, surely, he would know that her designs were foul, but it was just him and her as far as Saezyn could tell, and it made the moment all the more tempting. Had there been someone to fight, it would have been easy to kill all that was ill in the room, but little was ill looking about the woman, she was quite the contrary, and that made it all the worse. Also, they were alone together, and perhaps, nobody would know what took place in this den where hearts beat rapidly, and fantasies were limitless. Saezyn thought these things all in a moment, but quickly, he whispered in his head to Trilumina, "Oh my God, don't let me go… I feel like I am slipping."

Saezyn was then strengthened. He strode over to one of the curtains strung between two pillars and tore it down. He was expecting to see some minions or some deep dark secret the temptress had hidden, but all he saw were more statues.

"Expecting to see some skeletons in my closet? Why don't you have some fruit, it helps take the edge off. I know my residence is bit unnerving to look upon," she laughed.

Saezyn looked closer at one of the statues and was shocked by how realistic the effigy was, too realistic. Trilumina then whispered in Saezyn's mind: "Tainted fruit." It all added up in that moment—the fruit was cursed, it all was a trap, and the statues were all once people that had been tricked into eating from Temptation's hand.

"Shall I ask again? Would you like some fruit?" she tried once more.

"Only if you feed it to me," Saezyn answered with his most charismatic grin.

Temptation rose from where she lay on the litter and strode over to the tree. She gingerly picked one of the most succulent pods from the plant and slowly sauntered toward Saezyn. She looked even more luscious than the fruit, and the shine in her eyes told of all the plans she would have Saezyn believe she had for him, all her desires, but he knew he was simply to be another of her statues, another conquest—if she was allowed to have her way. She was now standing right in front of him, and both she and the fruit emitted the most wonderful aroma he had let waft through his nose.

She reached the fruit out for him to take a bite, but Saezyn held up his hand.

"Wait, before I partake of the fruit, I would like a kiss from those gorgeous lips of yours," he smiled.

She grinned and leaned in closer... closer... arm's length... closer still... she was now only three inches from his face and had an aura that tried to pull him in.

"That's close enough," he whispered. He then deployed the blade from his staff, and it went up into the bottom of her jaw and pierced through the top of her skull in one swift motion. Saezyn had coaxed her into where he wanted her. As she had leaned in, he had adjusted the angle of his staff so that once the blade was ejected, it would kill this hunter of men. He pulled the staff out from her skull and pushed her corpse back to where it collapsed on the ground and dissolved into dust. She wasn't a human at all, but merely a spirit in a seductress's form sent to destroy men of weak character. A creature from the depths of Ephesia's abysmal dark: she was a hellion.

"I'm not going to become restrained by my unrestraint, or become a servant to something besides Trilumina," Saezyn said softly as he watched a draft in the cave blow through the powder that represented all that was left of Temptation. The delectable fruit tree also wilted with the death of its owner, and its fruit fell upon the ground with a dull splat. Instantly, a terrible odor filled the cave.

"Tainted fruit, indeed!" Saezyn snorted as he held his nose shut and walked from the room.

"Saezyn! You're alive! What happened in there?" the General exclaimed upon the return of his friend.

"Oh, the usual— facing Temptation," he replied quietly.

"What temptation does a prophet have?" Trigger guffawed.

"You probably would have become a statue. I barely escaped with help from Trilumina," Saezyn murmured under his breath.

"What was that, gramps?" Trigger replied, having not heard what Saezyn had said.

"Show some respect! He clearly isn't in a talking kind of mood," the General ordered to Trigger.

Saezyn didn't answer the question ventured by Trigger because a loud, eerie screech coming from the cave halted all unnecessary conversation. At this sound, Saezyn simply said these words as calmly as he could: "We need to leave now!"

A hint of urgency and nervousness still was distinguishable in Saezyn's tone even though he tried to stay calm. The General instantly picked up on the uneasiness in Saezyn's voice. The General had seen Saezyn go against a Zykor dragon, so whatever caused him to be nervous was a cause for anxiety for him as well.

"All right, men! Let's move out! Double time, gents!" the General exclaimed.

The men turned to move, but the screech grew louder. They turned and looked back at the skull as they began to jog on the bank of the river. Everyone quickly noted to their dismay that the eyes on the skull had went from glowing bright green to blood red. The evil spirit that resided in the cave was gone, but Saezyn had failed to realize the beetles were her pets, and they had become very angry at the death of their master, thus causing the red color.

"How many of those bugs did you reckon you saw on the way in?" the General asked as they continued retreating.

"Too many to count," Saezyn replied.

"So how are we going to escape?" Belde' asked.

At the moment, hundreds of beetles burst out of the mouth of the skull—like bats disturbed from their slumber in the abyss.

"Shoot your way to the drop point!" the General yelled above the screeching.

Trigger gave a smile and opened fire along with the rest of his platoon. The beetles turned toward them in mass. In moments, they would have been overrun by the glowing menaces, but suddenly, a mass of blue light collided with the red and caused the beetles to stop their advance.

"What is that!" one of the Paladins exclaimed.

"They are phytes sent by CJ and Izbiq! They have our back. Let's get out of here!" the General yelled.

The mile and a half distance to the drop zone was covered in little time, and to their relief, a cypher drop ship was waiting to pick them up when they arrived. The task force piled into the craft and quickly departed the Rubicon valley. During the flight back to the *Serendipity*, they watched the blue glow of the phytes push the red glow of the "fearon" beetles (as they would learn them to be called later) back into their skull. The phytes quickly retreated from the scene, and the *Serendipity* fired an ASP canon into the skull once Izbiq's people were out of harm's way. The percussion of the blast echoed throughout the valley, and for a moment, the blast drowned out the engine noise of the drop ship. The cave was critically damaged and began to fall in upon itself. The red glow subsided as the rocks collapsed in upon the cave dwelling beetles.

BARREN LANDS
OF BERGDA

The captain and her command crew were waiting for the task force sent to investigate the Rubicon when the cypher drop ship returned. Saezyn was baffled as to how they knew to send in the phytes as reinforcements, so, of course, he asked.

CJ clarified, "When you went into the cave, the General gave me a situation report. In this report, he mentioned the fearon beetles. Izbiq had had dealings with said creatures in the past and had several thousand of her finest warriors sent to wait in case things went south with you in the cavern. Speaking of said event, I know Saezyn that you answer to Trilumina first and to me second, but next time you are summoned to go into a mysterious hollow, or need to do some other extraordinary feat, please give me an update."

"I am truly sorry, Carmine. In the future, count on me including you in the loop. Also…" Saezyn turned to Izbiq who was perched on CJ's shoulder. "Thank you for your help back there, Izbiq. We were in a tight spot, and you saved our skins."

Izbiq gave a hum of delight and gave a simple nod of her head in acknowledgment. Many of the Purge troops expressed their gratitude to Izbiq as well. From that time on, the phytes and the Purge troops followed CJ and Izbiq's example of pairing up in teams; in fact, the average Purge soldier on the *Serendipity* had at least four phytes that would accompany them everywhere. These same phytes proved invaluable in future missions and made getting the drop on CJ's men and women almost impossible. They were, in some regards, pets, in other regards, soldiers, but most of all, the quaint metallic wasps were friends to the people of the *Serendipity*.

"We've successfully investigated the Rubicon, so now, where are we off to?" the General asked.

"I looked at the data we had on the possible locations for the Armada hive and noticed the site in the barren lands of Bergda has significantly more resources than the site in the Zxyers mountain, so upon orders of the captain, we are making our way there as we speak," Linia replied to the question.

"How long until we get there?" Zekle asked.

"About an hour. Theban, and Brunick are currently working with some phytes to overhaul some of the ship's more timeworn systems, and Cyra wants to give them time to finish, so we are travelling at a slower pace for a while. Why do you ask?" CJ answered.

"I was going to invite some crew members to play some Sulcus—if that is acceptable to you?" Zekle replied.

"Sure, just remember not to gamble." The captain caused her voice to rise slightly.

"All right! Who wants to play some cards?" Zekle invited in his suave, gangster manner.

Ribus, Valdria, the General, and several of his Paladins followed Zekle out of the hangar to the cafeteria to go play cards.

"I think I will go to," Saezyn said suddenly.

"You play Sulcus!" Linia exclaimed.

"I do, I like the strategy. I even have my own deck. Care to join me?" Saezyn invited Linia with a smile.

"Sure," she replied.

"Wait, Saezyn, before you go I have a question," CJ stalled him.

"You want to know what was in the cave, don't you?" he replied.

CJ nodded.

Saezyn encouraged Linia to go on without him before he began his tale of the enchantress he met in the skull grotto. They sat down upon some chairs in the hangar, and Saezyn began telling the events that transpired. By the end of the account of the happenings, CJ had an uncomfortable look on her face.

"What is wrong?" Saezyn asked.

"First, I used to be something like the creature you came across today. When I was a dancer for the queen, I was not so different. It's uncanny to realize that, at one time, I was one that offered tainted fruit of another sort to the weak-willed. Secondly, and more importantly, I am curious if this entity you came across was from the Armada," CJ replied.

"Her cave was regrettably full of statues of those it had seduced, so I must think it had been there for a long time. It could have been from the Armada, but it would have been a defected spirit or hellion that landed on this planet a long time ago. I think now the Armada is more forceful in its tactics of destroying people," Saezyn replied.

"Well, that is a blessing and a curse, I suppose," CJ thought out loud.

The com blared and Cyra said, "ETA to the Barren Lands of Bergda fifteen minutes!"

CJ and Saezyn quickly made their way to the bridge.

The barren lands of Bergda stretched below the *Serendipity* and, in many ways, resembled a land of cakes decorated with white frosting. Huge mesas made of violet and purple stone were covered by the torrential snow that fell upon their summits and painted their cold tops white, giving the look of berry-flavored confections iced in vanilla frosting. Nobody was deceived though—the temperature was near subzero, and it was plain to see the rock monoliths of this land were not coated in vanilla frosting, but they were coated in cold, cruel ice.

"This looks like a place a force as cold and heartless as the Armada would go," CJ thought out loud.

Saezyn nodded grimly to her comment. These lands would make any assault on the Armada difficult, if indeed this was the location they had decided to set up shop.

"The inclement weather is making the sensors wig out, but it seems the sensors are picking up some energy readings. It could be nothing though," Cyra said as she piloted carefully in between the towering rock edifices.

"How long until we are able to verify if there is an Armada presence here?" CJ asked.

"Now!" Cyra pointed out the front glass. A strong gust of wind and a break in the snow revealed a huge construction built in between two large mesas.

"Put the ship down on the top of the nearest mesa. Let's hope they haven't detected us yet," CJ commanded. She then pushed the com button: "All command crew to the bridge immediately!"

"Is this an Arm…Ar…Armada facility?" Cyra stammered.

Saezyn stared wide-eyed at the monolith that reached two hundred feet above the tops of the towering mesas it was built between. He didn't even try to calculate how far underground the beast of a building extended into the depths of Solbia. To his amazement, it wasn't so much a single metal structure that was built piece by piece, it was millions of tiny robots mining resources and constantly building more robots and adding to the facility. The plant was growing.

"Yes. This is it." Saezyn gasped. As he looked at a sensor readout on a nearby terminal, he noted that it had twenty hangars, each large enough to manufacture Armada cruisers. From the look of it, he could see that all the hangars had cruisers inside under construction or waiting deployment.

"Yeah, let us hope this is the only facility on the world!" the General exclaimed as soon as he walked on the bridge and saw the monstrosity.

"What do we do?" Valdria asked.

"Shoot it?" Ribus ventured.

"We take as much data from where we are, and then we leave this place before we tempt luck too long so we can make a plan to get rid of this thing," CJ replied.

"We aren't going to engage it?" Trigger asked.

"Do you really want to engage *that* without a plan?" Theban exclaimed.

Trigger frowned. He was speaking without thinking again.

"Be sure to get a scan of the lay of the land around this place while the weather is decent," Mazzi interjected.

"What about calling for Purge help? They have the firepower to engage this," Linia ventured.

"I'll try to send a signal for help," Cyra replied. She typed rapidly in the controls. "We are being blocked. Probably by the structure. Wait—oh, no! Inbound contacts! They must have detected our outgoing signal."

"Do we have a visual?" the General asked.

"On screen in a moment. In the mean time, I am getting out of here," Cyra replied. She took off from where the ship had been resting on a mesa and began weaving through the other nearby rock formations.

Two dozen dots showed on the radar, and a diagram of one of the inbound hostiles displayed on the screen. It possessed five engines that rotated around its base and kept the vehicle in a state of levitation. The craft was complemented by various weapon systems, including a pod launcher.

"Blast! Armada hovies! All men to their battle stations," the General ordered.

"What are hovies?" Valdria asked pensively. CJ was eager for the explanation as well.

"Technically, they are called Armada deployers, but they are the smallest Armada unit that is equipped with shields, and they have a full array of weapons. They hover as their nickname suggests and fire infection pods from their main cannon while they fire lethal, dark energy and infectious bullets from their other turrets," Linia explained grimly.

"Can we fight them?" CJ queried for advice.

"Yes, but I think the sooner we get away, the better, so I would advise that we only destroy what we need to in our escape, the longer we stay without a plan, the longer we chance a fruitless self-destruction," replied the General. CJ looked at the other faces of her command crew: they all seemed to agree, even Izbiq, who enjoyed a good war now and again.

"All right, Cyra, get us out of here!" the captain ordered.

"There is communications outpost near Zxyers peak that we could try to contact the Purge by, should I make for it?" Cyra asked as the ship began to accelerate.

"Sounds good, but I really don't care where we go as long as you get us out of here," CJ replied.

"Yes, Captain!" Cyra retorted. A look of determination spread over her face. All her thoughts and efforts were now being focused on her daring escape. Cyra promptly dodged and weaved in and out of mesas and flew under hanging rocks of ancient stone formations. Pods were falling all around them or getting blown up by the Paladins posted on the paragon cannons. Cross fire blazed by the ship, impacted with the shields or scarcely missed by disturbingly small measurements. The hovies were quick but were unable to match the *Serendipity*'s speed once she made it to open air. Cyra knew this fact and so focused all her efforts into getting out of the maze of rock. Anybody that wasn't stationed on a gun was praying ceaselessly to Trilumina and holding on for all that they were worth to whatever was within arm's length. Zekle made sure that what was in arm's length happened to be an attractive female personal. After many near misses and heart-in-their-throat moments, CJ and her team watched thankfully as Cyra steered the craft into open air and rocketed the *Serendipity* out of the region to safety.

ZXYERS MOUNTAIN

"Sulcus!" Saezyn exclaimed. He laid down his hand victoriously. The ship had slowed for repairs after their escape, and there was once again time to play Sulcus, so Saezyn had finally been able to play against Zekle. They sat on the bridge and played a few hands while they awaited their next destination. CJ and Izbiq sat in the captain's chair thinking about what to do about the abomination in the barren lands of Bergda while they watched as Saezyn and Zekle strategized in Sulcus.

"The parliament!" Zekle exclaimed. He shook his head at Saezyn's hand, which happened to be one of the best hands in the game. It was complete with all the leader figures in the highest rank. Zekle couldn't believe the luck of Saezyn—it was the third hand that Zekle had lost to the prophet. "I can't believe your luck! Perhaps, it isn't luck… are you tapping into some divine aura for help, Saezyn?"

"Perhaps. Would that be considered cheating?" Saezyn smiled slyly.

"I'm thinking so. Are you?" Zekle retorted with a bit of a grin.

"I'll never tell," Saezyn laughed.

"So is this what you call being a productive member of the crew?" the General asked and glared slightly at Zekle. He had just walked onto the bridge. He grinned slightly when he saw that CJ was clearly amused by Saezyn's and Zekle's shenanigans.

"Don't blame Zekle," Saezyn answered, "this is my idea, I'm showing him that even those that are very lucky and indeed, skilled—eventually lose. Also, I am hoping that if we take a break from trying to figure out what to do about the Armada factory, Trilumina will bestow us with the insight of what we should do."

"Have you been successful?" the General asked.

Saezyn laid down another improbably good hand that trounced Zekle's; Zekle swore under his breath.

"I'll take that as a yes for teaching Zekle a lesson," the General said. "Zekle would you like to help Linia in the med bay, some of the crew were injured in our scuffle with the Armada and could use some entertainment to lighten their hearts and speed their healing," he asked kindly.

"Currently," Zekle said, "anything is better than getting the pants beat off me by a prophet of Trilumina. Let me tell you, if I had my doubts of Trilumina's existence before, I don't now. Playing with Saezyn is like playing against the God of Ephesia. For once, I am out of my league. Besides, Linia's company is the best I have had in this galaxy," he answered as he walked from the bridge to aid Linia in helping the injured.

"Care to take his place?" Saezyn asked the General.

"Sure, I love a good game of Sulcus as much as the next guy, and I have little idea of what to do about the situation in the barren lands. We still can't get through to Purge command, so we are going solo against the planetary Armada forces," the General replied. He sat down and began dealing the cards.

"Why did you come up here?" CJ asked.

"Oh, yes, I came here to inform you that repairs are going well and to ask what the situation is on the bridge," the General replied as he organized his cards. He stared hard at Saezyn in effort to gauge his opponent.

"Everything is going fairly well considering the circumstances. We will be making it to Zxyers mountain in about a half hour, so you have time for a few hands of Sulcus," Cyra answered from where she sat at the control station.

"Excellent!" the General smiled as he drew another card.

―――∞―――

Serendipity hovered lazily above the peak of Zxyers mountain as Orgasoli set in the distance and cast glorious rays of light ranging from crimson to cerulean in the backdrop of the stately ship. The snow on the highest precipices of the mountain was colored a dull blue in the light of the setting of Orgasoli.

"It's beautiful," Valdria murmured to Ribus as they stood together on the observation deck holding one another.

"It certainly is," Ribus replied softly, but he wasn't looking out the window, he was staring lovingly at Valdria. She looked at him and smiled. They had spent many hours together since the finding of *Serendipity*, but in their time together, they had not kissed. That was about to change. They moved closer to one another and gently pressed their lips together as a deep realization of the love they had for one another made its presence known. It was a simple act of affection, but it spoke volumes of the power of Trilumina. Less than a month ago, Ribus was a cold-hearted assassin that cared about only himself. Valdria in the past was so full of hate and rebelliousness she had little room in her heart to care for another, but here in the midst of chaos, they had found forgiveness, they had found purpose, and they had found each other—a hand greater than their own had been working all along.

Ribus and Valdria mused upon these things as they watched Orgasoli set. Ribus suddenly pulled away from Valdria. A concerned look was on his face.

"What is it?" she asked.

He pointed out the window at the remaining light in the evening sky. There were two large, dark shapes in the clouds.

"Do you think they are Armada ships?" she asked.

"It's not worth taking any chances. We have to tell the captain," Ribus replied.

They both ran to the bridge as the last few rays of Orgasoli receded behind the apex of the planet Solbia.

Ribus and Valdria ran into the bridge and began to simultaneously tell of what they had seen, but CJ held up a hand to silence them.

"We know that there are Armada cruisers inbound, but they aren't after us—yet. By the trajectory, they are headed toward Gu, a mining village at the base of the mountain. Whatever their intentions are, we are not going to allow innocent people to die. So first, we are going to destroy the ships, and then, we are going to figure out how to destroy their factory. Is that clear?" CJ stated authoritatively.

All crew on the bridge said in unison: "Yes. Captain!"

"Did we try contacting the communications post on the mountain?" Ribus asked.

"It's been abandoned for some time, we were debating taking a team to investigate it, but now, we have bigger fish to fry," the General explained.

"They have us out numbered," Trigger said as he stated the obvious.

"We know. How are we going to take out two birds with a stone?" Mazzi asked.

"I have an idea," Cyra grinned.

"What's the idea?" Brunick asked anxiously. His fiery, red hair seemed to burn brighter in his earnestness.

"We introduce some more *stones* in the equation: we deploy some fighters to flank the cruisers," she replied.

"We only have four light fighters. They are more for scouting than they are for fighting. We don't even know if they are functioning," Theban expressed his doubts.

"They are functioning, Theban!" Brunick replied. "You and I have spent the last few weeks restoring them to prime condition by adding power, armor, and weapons to them. They even each have a dozen missiles equipped too. We modified some of the missiles we got from Darknov so they will now lock onto coordinates. The fighters are not as weak as when we first got them."

"True, but we haven't given the fighters or the missiles a test run. There is no sense in sending soldiers out into the blue against ships a hundred times their size. They have limited shields, but what good is that if they fall like a stone?" Theban expounded his concerns.

"We don't have time to discuss this too in depth. Brunick, in your opinion as a mechanical wiz, are they air worthy?" CJ quizzed.

"Yes, Captain!" He replied.

"It's settled then, so what is the plan once we deploy our fighters? The enemy cruisers still have shields and are approaching the village at the base of the mountain as we speak," CJ reminded them of the pressure of the situation.

Saezyn quickly walked over to the computer terminal and began typing rapidly on the keypad until a diagram of the enemy craft that was farthest away showed on the screen. His eyes were in a trance, and he was moving as though he was possessed by a spirit (in fact, he was possessed by the spirit of Trilumina). Saezyn in his state of divine occupation soon had caused a specific point to show on the layout of the enemy ship.

"What is that?" asked Cyra who was flabbergasted at Saezyn's spastic behavior.

He suddenly snapped back to reality as he replied: "That is the weak point in the shields. A well-placed rocket will disable them."

"It can only be hit from the back though." Zekle said. "Looks like we don't have much choice but to deploy the fighters. So we flank the craft, take out their shields, and hit them with our main guns?" he thought out loud.

"That's the best plan we have time to make. Any volunteers to lead the strike team?" the captain asked.

Linia stepped forward. "Yes, Captain. I will pick out my other three pilots and make way at once."

"Good luck, Linia and may Trilumina be with you," CJ replied warmly.

Zekle frowned. In the short time he had been aboard the *Serendipity*, he had grown to love and respect Linia's quiet yet bold and beautiful ways.

She nodded and turned to leave the bridge, but as she walked past, Zekle gently grabbed her arm and said, "Kick some butt—but please get yours back in one piece."

She gave him a gentle kiss on the cheek and smiled. She then quickly strode from the room to pick the three pilots that would accompany her on the mission.

In moments, Linia and her chosen pilots had taken off into the night sky to get into position where they would await further orders from the captain.

CONFLICT OVER GU

"They are still approaching the village of Gu at the base of Zxyers mountain," Cyra gave the status report.

"Acknowledged. General, are all troops at their stations?" CJ asked.

"Yes, Captain!" he replied.

"All right, let's get their attention. Open fire with ASP 1 on the farthest ship and ASP 2 on the closer one," CJ commanded.

The *Serendipity* pitched slightly as the recoil from the ASP cannons spread through the hull of the ship. Shields flashed on the enemy vessels and sparks showered all around as the shot was absorbed by the cruiser's dark shields. Instantly, the enemy altered course, both ships.

"Both enemy cruisers are charging weapons and have altered course to intercept us," Cyra notified.

"Good, they took the bait. Time to execute step two of the plan: take them for a trip around the mountain," CJ plotted.

"Aye, Captain," Cyra said as she steered the ship around in effort to evade the approaching menaces. Streaks of dark amethyst energy arcs splashed across the night sky in waves of explosive color near the *Serendipity* as the cruisers closed in and fired at their provoker. The cruisers began to deploy dozens of myriad that joined the pursuit of their prey.

"Take us near the mountain. We need to get them close in order to draw the noose tighter about their necks. They think they have us outnumbered. Keep firing those paragons and other weapons to make them think we are putting up a fight," the General added to the captain's orders.

Serendipity flew near Zxyers peak, and the cruisers followed ever closer in her wake. Random bolts of energy that missed or arced off the shields of the *Serendipity* impacted with the rocks of the mountain and caused stone to cascade down the sheer face of the monolith. *Serendipity* soon cleared the mountain and coaxed the Armada vessels farther away from the village of Gu. The Paladins on board were putting up a good fight, and many of the myriad were being shot down, but the shields on the *Serendipity* wouldn't hold forever, and once they were gone, the only thing between the crew and ominous bolts of energy was the metal armor of the ship. CJ preferred not to test the structural integrity of her vessel.

"All right, Cyra, give Linia word to join us," said the captain.

Cyra pushed a key on her computer, and instantly, four energy signatures shone brightly on the radar screen: it was Linia and the other Paladins in the fighters, and they were behind the Armada craft! When the *Serendipity* enticed the Armada to follow them beyond the mountain, they had also drawn them past were Linia and the other fighters were docked on a cliff near the communications post built on Zxyers peak. Linia's task force instantly got down to business; they rocketed out of their hiding place, locked onto the glow of the enemy myriad engines in the darkness of the night and destroyed them. Any Armada fighters that moved to engage Linia's task force were met with heavy laser fire, or they were blown to oblivion by a tracking missile. Soon, Linia and her crew had a lock on the weak place on the enemy's shields. The modified missiles flew straight through the weak points in the shields—following the coordinates that were preloaded into the computers on the fighter craft. The missiles struck, causing the shields to overload and drop. The overworking of the shield's generators also caused substantial damage to the

Armada craft, which was plain to see by the sudden series of breaches in the hull of the ships. The spectacle of this firefight in the night was more magnificent to behold than the best firework shows.

"Shields down!" Cyra exclaimed.

She had scarcely uttered the two words when the *Serendipity* had lurched again under the recoil from the ASP cannons firing another volley. The first Armada cruiser called the *Pogonip* took both impacts to its back engine section. The engines promptly blew wide-open and caused the *Pogonip* to pull to one side. It happened to be hit on the side that would pull it into the second Armada cruiser. The ambush happened so fast that the other Armada cruiser named the *Hoarfrost* had little time to avoid its doomed coconspirator and thus took the full force of the impact. Hulls breached on dozens of levels, energy crystals overloaded, and gravity did the rest. Both ships pulled down toward the Solbian surface and soon painted a streak of shattered crystal and metal over a half mile of the Dekdir forest. Linia's squadron and the Paladins in the *Serendipity* on the paragon guns took out any remaining myriad fighters. The day was won, but still, the task of destroying the abomination in the barren lands of Bergda remained.

RESUPPLY

"I have bad news and worse news, Captain," Theban reported over the come link. He was working in the workshop portion of the ship on repairs to vital equipment. He was also taking inventory, which was the reason for his communique to the captain.

"I'd rather not hear either, but I doubt I have a choice, what is the word?" CJ replied.

"We are low on ammo for all our guns, and the communications station on the mountain was hit either on accident or on purpose by Armada munitions," Theban reported.

"Is there any good news?" Ribus interjected.

"We have several devices in the workshop that can fabricate ammo en masse, but we lack the resources to do so," Theban replied.

"I may be able to help with that," Mazzi stated calmly from where she sat eavesdropping nearby on the bridge.

"How so?" Saezyn quizzed.

"We just liberated a mining colony that has abundant materials, I have mining experience, and we have the manpower to pack up a good quantity of said material and feed it into our machines," she grinned.

"Excellent idea, Mazzi. Take Trigger and a team down and head up the operation to restock our ammo depot," CJ ordered. The captain then turned to the General and Ribus who were standing on the bridge. "Scans indicate that the cruisers are down, but there are still a few crystals that survived the crash. Not many by the looks of it, but enough that we can't afford to turn a blind eye. They are mobilizing a force that is headed towards the village of Gu. I want you two to head up a mission to take care of any stragglers. This is a sniper mission—I prefer to take them out from a distance. I don't think we currently have technology to deal with a crew member infected by mechamites. I don't want to lose anybody else to Armada." CJ finished almost in a whisper. From time to time, she still thought about Xyles who was consumed by the terrible mechamites.

Ribus went to ask CJ what she meant by "losing anybody else to the Armada," but the General gave a minute head shake that told Ribus he should let it lie. Instead, Ribus simply stated, "My pleasure. I'll pick out a nice sniper's nest on the top of the *Serendipity* and see what I can do."

Ribus, the General, and a half dozen Paladins armed with specter sniper rifles picked out sniping spots on the top of the *Serendipity* as Orgasoli rose once again into the sky and illuminated the Dekdir forest, which was soon to become a shooting gallery. Ribus had built the advanced rifles they were wielding in his free time using the advanced technology of the *Serendipity* and the layout of the M3-XSS he found in Drilgon prairie. CJ had positioned the *Serendipity* between where the Armada cruiser had crashed and the village of Gu. It gave the Paladins up top the perfect vantage point to snipe any twisted entities that rose from the rubble of the crash.

"I take it you like sniping don't you?" the General asked Ribus.

"Yeah, how could you tell?" Ribus replied.

"You haven't stopped grinning morbidly since we received orders that this would be a long-range mission," he replied.

Ribus then turned swiftly, pointed at the dark splotch in the forest that was the Armada crash site, sighted in his scope, and pulled the trigger. This all happened in less than four seconds. An invisible, hyper-concentrated beam of light noiselessly streaked into the wreckage. One of the Paladins who was acting as a spotter gasped: "He just bull's-eyed an enemy from over three thousand yards!"

"It's actually not that impressive. There is no bullet drop because the specter uses light to kill. It's simple—point and click," Ribus smiled. The other Paladins grinned as well; this mission was going to be fun.

Ribus, the General, and each Purgeist laid down behind their sniper rifles and scoped out a section of the debris field. Every time a bot built out of the debris reared its ugly head, it was promptly shot off. Of course, they made sure to shoot the creatures in the chest as well to disable the dark crystals that powered them. The Paladins cracked jokes as they laid waste to the enemy or kept track of how many kills they had racked up. They spent a good few hours making sure that nothing made it out of the wreckage.

"Looks like we've taken care of them," the General stated after they had gone a half hour without shooting anything. A couple of Paladins gave high-fives.

"You may want to look again, General," Ribus replied.

The General looked through his scope once more: a portion of the debris field that was nearly a hundred feet in length was moving. Instantly, Ribus and everyone on top of the *Serendipity* began taking shots at the mass of moving wreckage, but it didn't cease. Something was coming out of the crater of the ships—something huge. That something was a great metallic beast over a hundred feet long, coated in bent metal, dark crystals, and weapons that had been salvaged from the cruisers it was built from. It had many eyes upon its great dragonish head and glimmering scales that concealed countless weapons which would appear out of its body upon a dark whim. Its three tails were each equipped with a dark energy launcher apiece. This mass of bent metal and rage was headed straight for the village of Gu.

"Shoot out its eyes!" Ribus exclaimed.

The snipers fired relentlessly upon its head and hit many of its crystal eyes. This, of course, made the beast madder than ever. In return, it opened fire on the *Serendipity* with salvos of dark torpedoes and sinister, metallic barbs.

"Get back inside!" the General ordered. The snipers ran toward the service hatch they had come from, and they were almost all inside when a random barb struck one of the retreating Paladins in the head. The man was killed instantly, and his corpse soon fell off the *Serendipity* into the woods below. The General cursed his brethren's ill luck as the door closed behind the last of them.

"I think we are going to need tanks to deal with this!" the General exclaimed.

Mazzi had touched down in Gu three hours before the Armada scrap dragon had risen from the crash site of the two cruisers. Upon arrival, she explained the situation about their shortage of ammo and got permission from the lead miner in the village to take as much resources as they needed in payment of the defense *Serendipity* offered. And while the Paladins were racking up kills on their mental tally list, Mazzi, Trigger, and about two dozen other Paladins were busy using the shuttles to transport all kinds of raw materials to the *Serendipity*.

For the last three hours. Mazzi and the head miner stood talking in the middle of the mining compound and directing the operation. The lead miner in charge of the operation named Nevre' spoke to Mazzi in a thick Bergdian accent. "So what's cha gonna ta-do with these here materials?"

Mazzi smiled. She recognized the accent because many of her fellow miners had it in her last mining operation in the Zykor pit. "We have to take out the base that sent the cruisers to attack you. They have a base in the barren lands of Bergda."

"Cha, that's cha cursed place, last operation we had many chan accident. Lostcha collapses in our tunnels. Was sad taa cause we mined some good plunder from yonder land of the barren cold and abundant mesas." Nevre' motioned in the direction of the barren lands of Bergda.

"You used to have an operation there?" Mazzi asked.

"Cha, you could say that, don't know what's left of her though," he replied. Mazzi and Nevre' stepped out of the way as a large mining tank rolled into the tunnel to draw out more resources. It was a tank that would dig, place supports, harvest materials, and keep its crew safe, the pinnacle of mining technology—that was until the advent of the Armada on Solbia.

"Can you give me a layout of the tunnels as you left them?" Mazzi asked.

Nevre' pulled a computer chip out of his pocket and handed it to her. "Thank you, Nevre'. You may have just saved this planet." Mazzi shook his hand warmly in expression of her gratitude.

At that moment, three cypher drop ships from the *Serendipity* came down and dropped off three armadillos. The General in the company of Ribus and Saezyn stepped out of the lead Purge tank while the other two drove away to set up a perimeter.

Trigger walked over to talk to the General. "All clear here, General, no need for the tanks though I appreciate the thought—so far, this mining operation has gone off without a hitch. It's actually rather boring," he reported.

"Well, soon Trigger you are going to have more stuff to shoot than you may be able to deal with. We have an Armada scrap dragon inbound," the General informed his trigger-happy subordinate. Saezyn stepped forward and handed a rocket launcher to Trigger.

"A scrap dragon!" Trigger, at first, had a disturbed look on his face. He had seen the fact files about scrap dragons in basic, but as soon as the rocket launcher was in his hands, he gave a grin.

"Keep this mining operation safe!" the General ordered.

"Sir, yes sir!" Trigger saluted. He then went with a platoon of other Paladins to take up defensive positions on the roofs of the buildings around the edge of the compound.

"What is the plan? What should me and Nevre' do?" Mazzi asked.

A roar from the approaching beast and the sound of the main guns on the armadillos firing at it gave further urgency to Mazzi's words.

"Mazzi, you use your disc launcher to rig that rock arch over there," the General gestured toward a huge rock structure that was the entry point to Gu. It was enormous and had been set up as a monument to when mining first began at the site. "And then go with Nevre' and wait in that mining tank for the beast to walk under the arch, then you blow the arch, and drop the debris on the wretch."

Mazzi gave a serious nod and quickly launched five discs into strategic places on the arch. They stuck fast with a dull *ching*. Nevre' showed her the way into the front part of a nearby mining tank. It wasn't currently being used because it was in the middle of going through repairs and being retrofitted with more advance technology.

"So what are we to do in the mean time?" Ribus asked.

"We shoot it until it collapses back into the pile of debris it came from. And hope that our weapons can penetrate its thick armor enough that we can hit its crystal core, if we don't, it will just keep repairing itself," the General replied.

"Sir, should I provide support for the other tanks?" Belde' asked over the com. He was in the tank that was still hovering by the General, Ribus, and Saezyn as they strategized.

"Yes, go and do what you can to hit it in the belly, that is where the Armada usually put the crystals in their mechanical menaces," the General answered.

Belde' promptly moved out and joined the other armadillos that were already engaging the dragon.

"What should I do?" Saezyn asked.

"Pray to Trilumina and see if you can do something like what you did with the Zykor dragon," the General smiled.

The beast gave another roar and showed its ugly head uncomfortably near to the village, it was launching dark energy from its three tails and showering bullets from its many other guns. The armadillos backed up through the arch while they continued pelting the monster with high velocity rounds. The beast had already sustained heavy damage, but its core remained intact, so it kept repairing itself, and it kept coming. The General and Ribus took up defensive positions behind piles of excavated stone and began sniping at some of its open wounds sustained from the armadillos.

The beast gave another roar and opened its mouth wide; Belde' took the opportunity to blast the monster in the throat with the armadillo's main gun. Debris blew out of the back of the monster's neck, and its head was left tilting to one side, but it still kept coming; but this time, with renewed speed, and it launched waves of bullets all over the compound causing all the Paladins in the compound to duck for cover. At the last possible second, Trigger peered around his place of cover and fired his rocket launcher at the front leg it was putting its weight on. The blast caused the beast to trip and fall forward. This momentary pause in its assault gave Mazzi time to blow the arch. Huge stones dropped onto the back side of the scrap dragon and destroyed two of its three tails, which was fortunate, but regrettably, the main body sustained little damage. The two disabled tails scrapped noisily upon the ground as the dragon continued its advance. The beast was livid at this turn of events and quickly regained its footing and opened up with a fresh barrage of energy. The remaining tail fired a bolt of dark energy that hit Belde's armadillo in the front and damaged its controls—it was disabled. In a moment, the behemoth was upon the craft and took it in its jaws. The dragon shook the Armadillo like a dog shakes a tennis ball and then swallowed it whole.

Everyone watching was horrified at the sight of the massive beast consuming a tank like a mere morsel. Belde' and the gunner in the armadillo were surely killed in the creature's jaws. Moral began to drop at the seemingly invincible beast, but just as hope began to sink lowest, a massive explosion emanating from the monstrosity's gut tore the dragon into two pieces. Somehow, Belde' miraculously survived the shaking long enough to overcharge the main core of the Armadillo and blow both himself and the dragon's ghastly innards into oblivion. The back legs and tail were disconnected from its head and front legs; both parts flailed in the beast's duress. It tried to once again regain its feet in its new and unexpectedly weak position, but Izbiq had given the word for her phytes to attack. The scrap dragon never stood a chance; thousands of phytes flooded into its wounds and massive openings from where it was blown in two. They jabbed their jagged stingers into the conductive surfaces of the dragon and unleashed a relentless barrage of electricity that engulfed the flailing form of the monster. The electricity disabled the mechamites that were trying tirelessly to perform repairs. With the threat of the mechamites disabled, Izbiq's people borrowed through the metal until they found any crystals that were the driving force behind the scrap dragon. The phytes quickly and efficiently found all remaining crystals and destroyed them. Once again, the scrap dragon fell to the ground in a lifeless pile of scraps. It was finally beaten.

BOMB

"We lost three in the battle with the scrap dragon: Belde', Rew, and Derv. All were valiant Paladins that followed the Purge motto until their dying breaths. Mazzi and several other Paladins took some barbs in the fighting, but since the crystals were destroyed, the infection didn't spread. Linia is patching them up as we speak," the General gave the situation report to CJ on the bridge of the *Serendipity*.

"I am truly sorry about the loss of the crew members, General." CJ said. "Their names will be scribed upon the hull of *Serendipity* above where we scribe the names of the Armada cruisers they helped destroy." CJ patted the General's arm in consolation. He gave a smile that tried to mask the sadness in his eyes. He had lost many men in his long service in the Purge, but he had never gotten used to losing his brothers and sisters. Part of him wished that the pain wasn't so acute, but the rest of him knew that the ability to feel both sorrow and joy was part of what separated him from being like the heartless robots that he hunted.

"I have some good news for once, Captain," Theban interjected.

"I could use some good news, Theban. What is the good word?" CJ answered.

"Two things, Captain. First, we are fully supplied with all kinds of ammo for all guns, including some incendiary rounds for the paragons. Second, Mazzi and the other Paladins are reported to be making an excellent recovery thanks to Linia's skill and Zekle's diverting shenanigans."

"That is excellent news what-" CJ paused in midsentence, for at that moment, Mazzi came onto the bridge with both Linia and Zekle in tow. Mazzi had her arm in a sling and a very determined look on her face.

"I need to speak with you, Captain!" Mazzi exclaimed.

"You need to get back to the med bay so your wounds have time to heal!" Linia interjected, she was quite annoyed at Mazzi for leaving the med bay while still in the process of being healed.

"Hold on, Linia. Let Mazzi speak," CJ cut in. "What is it, Mazzi?"

"It's this!" Mazzi held up the data that was given to her by Nevre'. She plugged the chip into the main computer outlet. A diagram of the barren lands of Bergda showed on a projector.

"What exactly are we looking at?" Brunick asked. He too had been standing on the bridge with the rest of the command crew listening to the situation report.

"These are tunnels that Nevre' and his people worked on before they began the site here at Zxyers peak. I was thinking that we could potentially send a team into this tunnel here and plant a bomb." Mazzi pointed to a tunnel that led deep under the abomination.

"A bomb?" Valdria exclaimed.

"Do we have any bombs lying around?" Brunick cracked.

"I might have one or two under my bunk," Trigger chuckled. Valdria just shook her head in response to Triggers immaturity.

"Seriously though, we need a large scale explosive to do any serious damage to the abomination. How are we supposed to get a hold of that kind of power?" Linia thought out loud.

"I might have something that can help," Saezyn stated calmly.

"You? A bomb? You walk around with a stick, and I have never seen you use a gun!" Trigger laughed.

Saezyn pushed a button on his staff, and the two-foot-long, razor sharp blade came into full view.

Trigger swallowed hard. "I mean a very intimidating stick, sir." He averted his eyes from the glare Saezyn was giving him.

"That's because I don't need a gun, as you well know. Anyway, in the Hollow near my house in the varying books and records, I, at one time, stumbled across an ancient design for a bomb found by my great-great-great-great-grandfather Cephus Seldoc. He found it in some place where only he, a few others, and Trilumina know, but it traces back to the time of Pleothiria and Millidiram. I wasn't a scientist, and I still am not, so I couldn't and didn't have need to build the device, but perhaps, if we put our heads together now, we can assemble it," Saezyn explained.

"Pleothiria and Millidiram? They are the start of humanity in Ephesia!" Linia exclaimed.

"They were given designs for weapons by Trilumina himself to combat the evil of the Armada! You have designs for one such weapon!" the General replied ecstatically.

"I do," Saezyn replied, "but we must be swift, for every second we delay is another moment that the forces of Ordam have time to press their advantage. Also, what little I do know is we are going to need some obsidasalt for the construction of the bomb."

"We have some obsidasalt from among the other resources we gathered here at Zxyers peak," Mazzi informed.

CJ put her fingers through her gorgeous, red blonde hair as she thought of what to do. She remained silent for a time before she spoke: "Saezyn, you go to the Hollow in a shuttle and find the plans to the bomb. Trigger and Linia will go with you and make sure the shuttle makes it there and stays secure. Do what you need to do and get back here as soon as possible. A pair of fighters will escort your shuttle, and you are to report back here once you have completed your mission. In the meantime, the *Serendipity* will maintain defense of Gu."

Saezyn saluted and made way to the hangar bay where his shuttle awaited his departure.

THE DEEPEST HOLLOW

"Incoming!" Linia yelled. The cockpit's scanners suddenly came alive with activity. The shuttle soared though the night sky with a luminescent, blue trail of light coming off the engines. Suddenly, streaks of sinister purple passed uncomfortably close to the shuttle, breaking the serenity of the nighttime vista. They were halfway to the Hollow, and they had thought, perhaps, they were going to seamlessly make it there and back without trouble. The words that Linia just uttered destroyed that hope.

"What are we up against, and where is our fighter escort?" Trigger asked. An air of concern was easily distinguishable in his tone. Two flashes of fire below in the forest lit up the night and confirmed that the escort was no longer with them.

"From the scans, we have three Armada deployers on our tail, and the fire we just saw below us in the forest was our escort," Linia replied.

"Three hovies, and we have no air support!" Trigger walked over to a weapons storage unit and popped the lid. Inside was a rocket launcher with two rockets. "We only have two shots on the launcher, and those spag dish hovies are packing shields. We are done!" Trigger despaired.

"Pull yourself together. We are not done because we are not alone. Trilumina himself is our protection and our strength. Trigger, you must learn to trust not just in the guns in your hands and the bullets in your clip—you must learn to trust in the God the Purge serves," Saezyn replied to Trigger's doubts in a tone full of faith.

Another burst of energy streaked by. It was so close that the temperature of the shuttle went up noticeably, and the hull integrity was decreased as part of the roof melted away so that the darkness of the sky above was visible through several unnerving holes.

"Your talk of trust is inspiring, Saezyn, it really is," Linia expressed, "but we could use some of the strength of Trilumina right now! You better have a plan of action to back your words!"

It was plain to see that she was struggling with the controls after the last near miss, and that evasive maneuvers were now significantly more difficult to do without potentially crashing the shuttle.

"Open the back cargo doors," Saezyn replied.

Linia pushed the button, and the doors to the back of the shuttle opened wide. A stream of infectious bullets from one of the deployers cut into the hinges of the left door. The door flapped open wider than originally intended, wobbled awkwardly for a moment in the rush of air going around the shuttle, and then it was ripped off its hinges.

"What are we doing?" Trigger exclaimed.

"I'm going to drop their shields. Then I need you to fire one rocket at each of the closest two deployers," Saezyn ordered. Trigger nodded in affirmation as he hefted the semi-automatic rocket launcher on his shoulder and lined up the scope with the enemies.

Saezyn pointed his staff in the center of the three Armada crafts that were gaining ground by the second. The end of Saezyn's staff shone a bright white for a moment until a burst of what can best be described as chain lightning blasted from his staff into the first enemy. The luminous bolt spread instantly from the first enemy to the second and to the third in the blink of an eye. Their shields flickered and failed before they could even try to dodge

Saezyn's bolt. Trigger didn't hesitate to do as Saezyn had ordered; immediately following the loss of their shields, two rockets shrieked through the night air and hit the axle upon which the entire levitation system of the deployers rotated. The axles of the first two hovies disintegrated immediately, sending the now free-flying engines to go wherever physics would take them. Several of these randomly dispersed projectiles slammed into the only still functioning deployer and mercilessly tore it to pieces.

"I can't believe that worked! Those hovies are now nothing but scrap!" Trigger exclaimed excitedly as he stood bracing himself against the wall of the shuttle with his mouth open in awe. He watched the fiery debris splash into the ground below.

"Your biggest foes are not hovies, or cruisers, or even the dreaded Armada abomination," Saezyn said, "Trigger, your biggest foe that you ever will face is your fear, your unbelief. Know this, if you can master your fears and have faith in Trilumina, no foe will be too great for you, and if ever you are in a situation where your death seems nigh, it does not matter whether you live or die because whoever has defeated their fears and is faithful, they will be eternally victorious," said Saezyn sagely as the shuttle neared its destination.

The scorched shuttle set down outside of the back entrance of the Hollow. The shuttle was positioned in the shadow of the cliffs of Drizda. Saezyn quickly jumped from the shuttle and strode into the secret back entrance of the Hollow. Linia and Trigger stayed behind to guard the ship. Saezyn quickly walked to a shelf full of ancient manuscripts and carvings, but upon the completion of his fruitless search of the shelves, he remembered that the most ancient manuscripts were stored in the "Deep" of the Hollow. The Deep was a secluded cavern that could only be reached by going down a secret winding passageway. In the Deep, the most precious and secret records and artifacts of the Seldocs were stored. Saezyn walked over to a wall to the right of the door he had come in. On this wall was a bookshelf made out of ancient architecture from a bygone age. It contained many diaries, journals, and records upon its shelves. Saezyn scanned the tomes until he came to a book called the *Dangers of War in Space*. It was the only book that didn't fit in with the other works. Saezyn pulled it off the shelf and pushed a button that was concealed behind the book. The bookshelf groaned for a moment, and the sound of mechanical devices moving beyond could be heard as the shelf slid to one side, allowing Saezyn access to the depths of the Hollow.

He stepped through the opening but turned suddenly to look behind him (a sudden feeling of uneasiness found him). As he looked around, he saw nothing, so he quickly hurried on. Saezyn grabbed a crystal from a shelf. Next to the crystal, there was also a lantern that was designed to contain the stone. Once the rock was placed in the olden-looking fixture, it emitted a relaxing, blue aura that illuminated the dark, but Saezyn was far from relaxed. He sensed that something else was in his Hollow, and he was far from okay with it.

The winding passageway that went gradually down in a spiral soon came to a straight tunnel that Saezyn knew would lead into the Deep. He jogged to the doors that would allow him access to the most clandestine knowledge of the Seldoc clan, and he took the crystal from his lantern and fitted it into a groove in the doors; the crystal glowed brighter for a moment before the doors slid to either side and granted Saezyn access to the large grotto that was the Deep. He stood on a small platform with a sheer drop on either side of him. In fact, the room was, in many regards, just a great, big hole in the ground with a cavernous ceiling, but it did have a lone island in the exact middle that stood on a pillar which rose out of the darkness. Here on this island was a podium that had a few shelves for varying works and a slab that had the ancient tome Saezyn sought laid upon it. The only way to this island in the dimly lit chamber was a narrow, stone bridge. Both the ceiling and floor of this mysterious place was masked by the darkness that encompassed all.

Saezyn then threw the light crystal he had used to open the door into the abysmal darkness below. The crystal emitted enough light that it soon disturbed the occupants of this subterranean realm. Bats of disturbing sizes came rushing out of the gloom in search of a way of escape, but the awakening of the bats awoke the other creatures of the Deep: the dark mountain creepers.

Soon, light shown all around as hundreds of large spiders known as dark mountain creepers came to life. The creepers were bulky spiders that filled their bodies with gas and floated in caverns. They would work together in teams and build webs between five or six themselves as they levitated. Creepers used their webs as nets to catch swarming bats. The room became light because when these quaint spiders opened their eyes, they emitted a hypnotic, lavender luminescence.

"How are you doing my beauties!" Saezyn exclaimed as he walked along the bridge and looked at the spiders as they began to spin webs to catch any flittering bats that remained. He even reached out his hand to pet the occasional spider that was within reach. These creatures were his pets, but he had no time to pay too much attention to his colony of creepers. Saezyn reached the podium and scanned the work on top of the stone slab: it was the ancient set of glyphs that contained the plan for the bomb and various other ancient devices, including his staff, but the tale of how Saezyn's staff came to be belongs to another legend from years and years before his time.

Upon grabbing the ancient work from the podium, Saezyn turned to leave the Deep, but his previous anxieties were confirmed as he looked towards the exit—he wasn't alone. With a pistol leveled with Saezyn's head, Queen Odiria stood scoping out what would be a kill shot should she pull the trigger. Her left half was covered with a metallic coating, a sign she had been infected by mechamites when Toria fell.

"Queen Odiria, this is an unexpected pleasure. I see you have had some work done." Saezyn tried to sound confident, but he was really caught off guard. Queen Odiria was an intimidating sight to behold when she looked normal, but with the metallic sheen that covered part of her visage, she was all the more menacing.

"Yeah, I have you to thank for that. Allow me to explain in detail what you caused to happen to me. Delduna tower was soon overrun by mechamites when the Armada invaded my city of Toria Vilorious. Pods crashed into the building en masse, and many of my brave bodyguards gave their all defending me, but their efforts were in vain. My chambers were among the first to be flooded, and the spawn of Ordam quickly and painfully set upon me after coating my guards in metallic shells of death. It was the most excruciating agony I have ever felt in my life. They cut away at my flesh and replaced what was me with more of themselves. In the assault, crystals from the pods were imbedded in me as well, making it impossible for me to escape the mechamites. The room was full of my guards that had been turned to statues. I thought I was going to meet the same fate, but just as the pain was the most unbearable, suddenly, it ceased. The mechamites weren't trying to kill me—they were trying to equip me to deal with scum like you. They saw me as a potential help, so they kept me alive. Specifically, they kept me alive to hunt you. The Armada is a powerful ally, and I should thank you for introducing me to them, but I still am going to kill you for causing my city to be destroyed," said Odiria as she recounted the tale of what happened to her.

She focused her pistol on Saezyn's head intently, but before she pulled the trigger, she hesitated. "Perhaps, I shouldn't kill you so easily. Maybe I should stun you and allow the mechamites to have their way with you. Seems like poetic justice to me, you wrecked my city and left me to die at the hands of the infectious whims of the Armada, it seems fitting I do the same to you."

"How did you find me?" Saezyn asked in an effort to buy some time to think of a way out of this dilemma.

"When I was joined to the Armada, I soon found others like me who had been converted by the mechamites, and from among their ranks, I dispatched spies to find you. One such spy tracked you to this place. Then we just waited until you returned. Now, my vengeance shall be complete." As soon as Odiria had elaborated on her methods of finding Saezyn, she aimed for his right knee cap, but he was ready: Saezyn did a backflip and landed on the other side of the podium. Odiria followed him with the pistol and kept firing as she tracked his movement, but her efforts were in vain. Saezyn landed unscathed. Debris showered over his head as Odiria continued firing at the plinth he took cover behind. Soon, a reassuring click stemming from her pistol sounded that she was out of ammo, and it gave Saezyn time look over the bullet-perforated stone.

"Fine you want to play it that way!" Odiria bellowed in a warped voice. Suddenly, her left arm (the one covered by mechamites) began to disfigure slightly into something like a hand but different. Then it dawned on Saezyn—it was becoming a dark energy launcher! The crystals inside Odiria acted as a power source for this newly constructed launcher, and the hateful darkness in her hard heart powered the crystals so that her weapon was the equivalent to a rocket launcher.

Saezyn barely had enough time to jump out of the way as the bolt of darkness slammed into the podium. Chunks of debris flew in every which way, and pages from other ancient works fluttered down into the darkness of the Deep. Saezyn coughed in the dust and slowly regained his feet with the book he had come for in one hand and his staff in the other. Blood trickled from varying lacerations caused by the debris that cut into him.

"And now, Saezyn Seldoc, you will pass from the land of the living." Odiria smiled cruelly and pointed her weapon at his heart, but Saezyn wasn't about to give her the satisfaction. He jumped off the island into the abysmal darkness just as her bolt streaked towards him.

LEAP OF FAITH

Odiria screamed in rage having been robbed of her sport while Saezyn fell into the blackness below. He knew that if he were to have stayed on the island, he would maybe have been able to beat Odiria, but he couldn't guarantee the safety of the designs for the bomb, and so he jumped off the edge. He didn't like the sound of jumping, but Trilumina whispered that he would protect Saezyn. Truly, this was a leap of faith; perhaps, he would fall into some water at the bottom. These things passed through Saezyn's mind as he fell. Unpredictably, Saezyn sensed his descent slowing, and he felt that he was passing through some sort of dense thread mesh. As Saezyn suddenly and gently came to a halt, he looked around but couldn't discover the cause of his cessation until the cause found him. Light of a relaxing, lavender hue shown all around him; he had fallen into a den of sleeping mountain creepers and had woken them up thus causing them to open their eyes and light his surrounds. He was stuck in the webbing of his very own dark mountain creepers. He looked around and saw dozens of the large spiders floating around him. Saezyn had fallen into and through several of their nets that they used for trapping bats. Fortunately, the one he was in had acted as a safety net and prevented him from meeting a grizzly end far below.

The creepers, observing that the entity in their net was none other than their master, filled their bodies with more gas and began to gently float Saezyn out of the Deep. Trilumina had used the most unlikely of creatures to spare his servant, Saezyn. It took several minutes for the spiders to make up the distance that Saezyn had fallen, and it took a few minutes more for Saezyn to cut away the web once they had delivered him once again near the door of the Deep. Fortunately, Odiria assumed Saezyn was dead; Saezyn looked forward to their second encounter and proving that assertion wrong.

Odiria met up with three of her bodyguards in the main room of the Hollow. They were all covered partially with mechamites as well and were just as wretched as she was.

"We can now report back to our master Ordam that the mission was successful. Saezyn is dead," Odiria reported with a frown.

"Why do you look so depressed? Didn't you want to kill him?" a guard by the name of Dro asked. His face was completely untouched by the mechamites, but the rest of his body was entirely consumed.

"I didn't kill him! He jumped off the cliff!" she shrieked.

"Shouldn't we search the floor of the Deep to make sure he is dead?" another guard asked.

"Yeah! Shouldn't you make sure I am dead?" Saezyn exclaimed from where he now stood in doorway that led down to the Deep.

Before any of Odiria's guards could fire at him, he used his staff to cut the two guards nearest to him in half with a beam from his ancient weapon. Odiria quickly ducked for cover; her guard named Dro went to follow suit, but Saezyn was quicker and cut off his unspoiled head with another beam of light.

"Curse you, Saezyn Seldoc!" Odiria screeched. She then put all her hate and darkness into a bolt of energy and came out from her cover and blasted the huge stream of darkness at her foe, but Saezyn refused to die. He didn't fall into oblivion and crawl back out again just to be killed by Odiria for good. The bolt careened straight at where Saezyn stood at a speed greater than could be avoided, so Saezyn did the only thing he could do: he leveled his staff with the projectile to block the incoming rocket. Much to his pleasure and Odiria's shock, the staff not only acted as a lightning rod that absorbed the bolt of energy, but it also sent it back in the direction that it had come from at tenfold the speed. Odiria's own bolt of hate festering energy drilled straight into her and kept going. For a moment, she stood completely bewildered with a six-inch-wide hole in her chest that went from her front to her now charred back. It was a hole which Saezyn could see clear through. She blinked twice, still glaring at Saezyn, and then she collapsed backwards to the floor.

Saezyn ran past her body to the secret exit and quickly hopped into the back of the shuttle he had come in.

"What took you so long?" Trigger asked.

"I ran into some uninvited guests, but I have the pages," he replied as he drew the ancient works from a pack.

"Who did you run into?" Linia asked.

"Queen Odiria."

"Is she dead now?" Trigger asked in surprise.

"When last I left her, she had a gaping wound in her chest, but she has recently joined the ranks of the Armada, so I didn't exactly stop to feel her pulse. In any case, whether she be alive or dead, this place is not safe, and I think it would be prudent to leave," Saezyn gave a nod to Linia to usher her out of the area.

"I agree!" Linia exclaimed as she cranked the throttle of the shuttle and soared into the night sky of Solbia.

DEVIOUS DEVICE

The return of Saezyn, Trigger, and Linia was greeted with great joy, and once Saezyn produced the ancient manuscript from his pack, Brunick, Ribus, Zekle, and Cyra took a keen interest in the olden glyphs upon its pages. Brunick made special note of the diagrams that were printed on the leaves. CJ pensively looked on as her command crew looked at the designs.

"Can you build it?" she finally asked.

"I think so! These diagrams are pretty plain to read," Brunick exclaimed joyfully.

"It shouldn't take too long to decipher this ancient language. If I can find what each of the symbols mean in modern letters, we should be able to plug the data into the computer and make a translated version of the pages," Cyra said as she looked intently at the patterns she already was observing.

"All right then, that's what I want to hear! Let's build this bomb!" CJ proclaimed with gusto.

By Cyra's divinely imparted knack for hacking, solving problems, and just being smart above and beyond what people expected or imagined, she had deciphered the ancient Ephesian language on the plans to the bomb—in two hours. And fifteen minutes after Brunick and Theban looked at these newly deciphered plans, they had already started laying out parts for the building of the said destructive device. In fact, after the plans passed to Brunick and Theban (who in their service together on the *Serendipity* had become so accustomed to working with one another that it was like one was the right hand and the other was the left on the same body), nobody hardly saw them unless they requested help. They had become so engrossed in their work for two reasons: first, their lives and the lives of all on Solbia depended upon it, and second, it was rather fun to build something from thousands of years ago.

For three days after the retrieval of the plans, *Serendipity* still hovered serenely over the mining village of Gu. Besides a run in with the odd Myriad fighter, or perhaps a skirmish with an Armada deployer, they saw little of the Armada. Upon the bridge of the *Serendipity*, CJ expressed her concerns about the latest turn of events, or rather lack thereof:

"We have gone a full twenty-four hours without facing off against any Armada reinforcements. I would expect their attacks to increase, not decrease, as their base grows in size. It may sound cliché', but it is quiet, too quiet. I bet they are getting ready for something terrible."

"You are probably right. My past experience battling the Armada confirms your suspicions," the General agreed. Linia nodded in agreement as well, both she and the General had been in a few too many sinister battles that had resulted in the deaths of many of their fellow soldiers.

"How are we coming on that bomb?" Trigger asked from where he slouched in a chair on the bridge. Since joining the *Serendipity*, his former military discipline had begun to lack.

"I haven't talked to Theban or Brunick at all today," CJ replied, "but word has it that they haven't slept since they got the plans, and much to the crew's dismay, they have recently confiscated all joko Juice on board in their quest to stay awake," she said with a slight grin at the humor of the joko juice situation. Valdria sat and sulked when the captain mentioned the confiscation of the joko Juice. Ribus tried to comfort Valdria, but it was early in the morning, and she refused to let her frustrations so easily subside.

"We have it! It is complete!" Brunick and Theban burst suddenly onto the bridge to exclaim elatedly. Both were covered in all the dirt, grease, and grime that one would expect to see on craftsmen that had worked three days straight without bathing or sleeping.

"The bomb is done! Already?!" the General expressed his surprise.

"Yes, sir," Brunick smiled.

"It's a miracle," Saezyn laughed happily.

"It certainly is," Trigger muttered sarcastically.

CJ gave him a scowl before she further addressed the situation: "So we know that this bomb will work?"

"Yep, it sure will, even if we didn't get all the ratios right (which we did), we have enough elements that will hyper-combust in combination with each other to blow a dozen Armada cruisers from the sky. I can't even theorize what would happen if we put this underground in a confined area, but I can't wait to find out," Brunick chuckled insidiously.

"Yes, Captain," said Theban, "you have my word as a craftsman that this bomb will do the trick. Also, we were able to replicate the bomb's technology on a miniature scale, and we built a score of rounds for the ASP cannon using said technology—they should pack quite the punch," he encouraged.

"Well, in that case, Cyra, take us to the barren lands of Bergda immediately. We have an abomination to scrap!" CJ ordered.

"Yes, Captain!" Cyra exclaimed enthusiastically.

DARK MIND

The *Serendipity* neared its destination, perhaps its final one, but nobody wanted to think about the odds of one ship versus a foe that seemed to be made of near-limitless resources. The cold wind blew through the empty barren lands, and a gentle snow drifted through the air; a solemn reminder and foretaste of what the planet would look like should they fail to destroy the abomination. Cyra took the ship in a more roundabout course as she piloted the craft toward the mining tunnel that led deep under the abomination they purposed to destroy. The plan was simple: fly the bomb under the base using the *Serendipity*'s drop ships, unload the bomb, set the timer, and then get out of the place before the bomb blew and scrapped the abomination along with anything in an estimated three mile radius.

The General walked into the hangar bay containing three cypher drop ships that were being prepared by a dozen Paladins who were to accompany the General and Saezyn on this perilous mission. He walked around an armadillo that was getting outfitted with the top of the line weapons available when then the General saw it (the bomb) and caught his breath. It was the size of an armadillo tank, and oddly enough, it was beautiful, very beautiful. Brunick and Theban followed the designs exactly, and this meant they even decorated it with the ancient symbols and imagery that the plans included. The bomb was in the shape of a great geometric eye that was elevated off the floor upon seven struts. In the pupil of this eye, faded light came forth. It was the spark that would be released and explosively combine all the elements contained behind its intimidating stare once the countdown reached zero. Around the edge of the eye, intricate carvings of spiritual entities added an extra touch of reverence to this object that already commanded much respect. Fortunately, Brunick and Theban realized that they were building a design that was imparted to man by Trilumina, and though the artistic work on this weapon wouldn't affect how it functioned, they knew that the artwork included in the designs was there to pay respect to the Giver of the plans.

"It is said the gaze of Trilumina pierces flesh and bone and measures the heart and motives of a person," Saezyn commented. The General didn't even notice that his friend was there because he was so absorbed by this work of art.

"Let us hope that this does the same to the Armada and destroys the black heart of the enemy. Let us make way, We have given our foe too much time to prepare for our arrival as it is," the General replied.

The General, Saezyn, and two other Paladins piled into the cypher with the bomb in its back holding area while the two remaining armadillos were loaded onto the other two cypher drop ships. These were outfitted with five Paladins a piece. The armadillos were set backwards in the clamps that held them in place behind the cyphers so that the main gun was facing behind the drop ship in case any Armada crafts tried to flank them while they flew into the mining tunnels. The lead ship was outfitted with heavy machine guns complete with incendiary rounds to guard their approach and passage down the tunnel. The rest of the command crew and the other Paladins were to stay on board the *Serendipity* and cover the exit of the teams sent to destroy the abomination.

The *Serendipity* soared near to their target, and a break in the weather gave the crew a glimpse of their foe. The abomination had grown from a mere factory to a great metallic tower speckled with the occasional large splotch of dark indigo crystal. At the very highest point on this tower, it split into two twisted and sinister hands reaching toward the sky with their fingers spread wide, as though they were reaching for something or waiting to catch something. Nobody on board the *Serendipity* wanted to find out what that was. They knew it couldn't be good.

The General sat in the cockpit of the shuttle with Saezyn and was able to see this daunting sight as the hangar bay doors opened to allow them departure from the *Serendipity*. The General looked at the great hands and knew exactly what they were: a gateway to oblivion. He had seen this before; the hands were one end of a portal that connected to another Armada-occupied world. The two portals would link and grant mass quantities of Armada reinforcements unopposed access to Solbia. The General had fought the campaign where this lugubrious fact was learned and lost many men as the hard lesson sank in.

"Captain, you must fire on that tower with all that you have right now! It is a portal that allows the Armada to transport ships from another world they occupy! It must be destroyed immediately!" the General exclaimed into a com link.

CJ didn't immediately reply, instead, she gave the order for the *Serendipity* to open fire with its ASP cannons. The General watched in horror as the two shells fired at the dreadful tower were absorbed by a massive energy shield.

"Sorry, General, the shields are too strong," CJ said, "and I think that our attack has attracted some attention. Now is your chance to go into the tunnel as we keep them busy up here. Go now and may Trilumina be with you," the captain ordered.

The General, who knew that now the fate of the world rested upon whether or not they could get this bomb into position, needed no second bidding. He rocketed out of the hangar with two cypher drop ships as his escort. As he flew down toward his destination, which was a large hole in the side of a mesa, he glanced back at the *Serendipity*. Cyra was taking the large ship through tight evasive maneuvers as five Armada cruisers closed in on its position. It seemed this time, the Armada didn't want to take any chances—they intended to destroy the *Serendipity*. Dark bolts aimed at her stately prow streaked by. Some of these projectiles barely missed the General and his escort. The opening to the mining tunnel soon approached, and rapidly, the General and his team veered quickly into the gap but not before he took one last look at the battle raging above. The *Serendipity* was returning fire, and one of the cruisers suddenly vaporized in a flash of blinding light.

"Five Armada cruisers converging on our position! What is our plan of attack?" Cyra asked the captain.

"Take the *Serendipity* through the ravines of these badlands in effort to evade fire, and maybe, we can cause our foes to collide with some misfortune. Also—" CJ turned to Linia who was acting in the stead of the General. "Order all batteries to open fire on the nearest cruiser."

"My pleasure, Captain," Linia replied with a slight smirk. "All batteries open fire and introduce our guest to some of our newly replenished incendiary rounds."

Instantly, the staccato report of the paragons could be heard echoing down the corridors of the *Serendipity*, and the brain-rattling vibrations of the shredder AA guns rattled the bridge. Hot white fire spread across the shields of the nearest enemy cruiser in the middle of the approaching five. The fire sat on the shields and burned. Soon, the shields flashed off.

"All right, Linia, take it out," the captain ordered.

"ASP fire control, fire an experimental round at the center cruiser!" Linia ordered.

The *Serendipity* shook as the report of the ASP roared. The experimental shell hurled into the enemy craft and detonated. It wasn't a fiery explosion that came from this miniaturized ancient weapon, it was far more terrible than that: the entire sky around the craft flashed silver, and the hit cruiser shattered into dust as a huge shockwave ripped outward from the core of the disintegrated vessel. The shields on the other four ships flashed off, and it was plain to tell that their hull integrity was reduced to nil. The next rounds from the *Serendipity* mopped up the cruisers like shooting nesting birds. The abomination suddenly roared to life at the realization that they were going up against a ship with ancient technology granted by Trilumina—the *Serendipity* was now a threat. Huge doors opened on the abomination allowing dozens of cruisers, hundreds of deployers, and thousands of myriad opportunity to join the fray. CJ just kicked Solbia's biggest wasp nest, and now, her only option was to try to evade the peeved menaces that swarmed out seeking vengeance. Then the worst part of the latest turn of events was realized: energy was streaming into the sky from the hands on the top of the enemy tower. The portal was opened, and soon, countless Armada reinforcements might stream through the abysmal portal.

"Captain, I think we have a problem," Cyra murmured as she headed away from the now very active abomination.

"I think you are right," CJ replied nervously.

The rock walls and occasional, metallic support of the tunnel streaked by in the light of the cypher drop ships which cruised swiftly down towards the bowels of the abomination. Above, rumblings and explosions could be heard stemming from the raging battle between *Serendipity* and her many foes. Upon some of the nearer shockwaves, rocks fell from the ceiling. Fortunately, the loosened debris fell short, or was small enough that it bounced off the taskforce's vehicles. The route to the basement of the abomination was miles in length, but it took little time to complete with the speed of the cypher drop ships and the adrenaline of the moment.

Unexpectedly, the tunnel stopped and gave way to a huge room; not just any huge room—but the control room of the abomination. They had entered the place that contained the crystals in charge of all Armada operations in the barren lands of Bergda. The place was lit with dim blues and purples, and in the middle of the room, there stood what looked to be a gnarled forest of jagged, crystalline formations and towering, dark precipices. Random bolts of dark energy would flow up its crooked growths, much like a tesla coil conducting electricity, and occasionally, these energy spikes would reach out to other growths on the walls. This was the central brain where all the Armada's thoughts of darkness on Solbia stemmed from, and it looked just as twisted as the sick imaginings that it birthed.

The General quickly flew as near to this dark creation as he dared and released the bomb, which fell heavily to the ground with a dull thud of metal upon rock. He landed the drop ship nearby so they could get out and arm the bomb.

"All right, boys. I can't send out a transmission here due to interference from this monstrosity, so book it on out of here and wait for us at the entrance to the tunnel but make sure you tell the captain that we have made it to the control room and will have the bomb blown shortly," the General ordered to drop ship beta. The craft that was ordered circled around the strange entity and flew back up the tunnel they had come in.

"Drop ship alpha, drop your tank so that I can pick her up and have some cover for my hide in case it gets hot on the way out. You go now and follow beta. We won't be here long," the General ordered to his Paladins in the other ship. Alpha team dropped their armadillo and went to follow beta out of the tunnel, but as it was in the middle of flying around the Dark Mind, a random spike of baleful energy went to flow to one of the growths on the far wall and hit the cypher instead. The cypher was blown to bits instantly, and the five Paladins aboard comprised some of the pieces. The General swore under his breath and a sad look spread across his face when he thought of the fates of his men.

"Come, General, let us blow this wretch to the abyss," Saezyn put his hand on the General's shoulder in consolation.

"Let's!" the General replied with a look of stone-cold determination.

They walked over to the bomb and pushed the button to engage; the countdown of five minutes began to tick down. It gave enough time for the party to get out of the tunnels and hopefully, get out of the blast radius. Saezyn and the General and the two Paladins by the names of Vab and Srim who were with them walked back toward their vehicle, but before they could get to it, another energy spike impacted with it, destroying it as well. The armadillo was now the only way out of the cave in the four minutes left on the countdown—if only that was the extent of their problems; it seemed that when the first cypher was destroyed, the Dark Mind noticed the explosion and noticed a prophet of Trilumina was in the room. Upon this realization, it dawned on the Dark Mind that it was in grave danger, so naturally, it called for reinforcements. Rapidly, the walls of the chamber began to move as mechamites poured into the control room and began to form larger more devious entities. These entities were eight-foot-tall, metallic bots equipped with four arms and swords in each hand. They all had their many eyes glued on Saezyn and the bomb that he stood guard over.

"Get out of here!" Saezyn yelled to the General and his two Paladins.

"I'm not leaving you here!" the General rebutted.

"You will die if you stay here, and it is not your time, I must defend this bomb, and if I pass in its defense, then I will pass on to paradise where I will meet my family. Long I have missed them, but you still have many years to have your own family and enjoy this life. Do not dishonor me by refusing to listen," Saezyn yelled. His staff was beginning to glow horrifically, and his appearance was morphing as the spirit of Trilumina came upon him to aid him in the battle he was about to face.

The General knew that it was unwise to cross a prophet of Trilumina, but he was not pleased at the concept of losing a friend. Still, the General relented. "Fine, Saezyn Seldoc, but you cannot deny me a parting shot!" The General jumped into the armadillo and boosted the engines to max. He cruised around the large control room at top speed with guns blazing and rockets firing. He ran down any Armada bots in his way. Vab and Srim manned large turrets hanging out the side, and they too aided in the slaughter as the armadillo cruised around the room and then out of the tunnel at top speed.

The timer was now down to two minutes and thirty seconds, and Saezyn stood next to the bomb waiting for his foes to approach. The General had nearly cleared out the room when he left, but the Armada cascaded down in large waves of mechamites, and soon, Saezyn's hostile company of sword-toting bots had increased tenfold. All at once, they rushed forward to take on this lone prophet of Trilumina, but it was not Saezyn who was nervous. Five hundred bots, two thousand swords set against him, and still, the Armada knew they were outnumbered going against this mystic who had the full force of Trilumina protecting him.

The Armada moved to strike, but Saezyn struck first. He let loose a bright beam of light from the end of his staff and cut down a hundred bots in front of him with a single movement of his staff, and after that point, his kill count only rose by leaps and bounds. The more enemies he killed, the more they poured into the control room, the Dark Mind of this abomination knew that if it couldn't stop the bomb from going off, then the Armada would lose its foothold on Solbia, so hundreds and thousands of menaces moved to assail Saezyn, but he was the quicker. He cut them down wave by wave as he screamed in a zealous rage.

Thirty seconds left on the countdown when out of the side entrance of the room, a myriad flew into the chamber at top speed and purposely crashed into the ground right next to Saezyn. In the spray of twisted metal and rocky debris, Saezyn was blasted against the far wall. His staff landed quivering, sticking out of a large rock ten feet from where he lay. His foes surrounded him and scowled down at this prophet.

"Good effort. You almost managed to defend the bomb long enough for it to blow, but your efforts were fruitless, and in your failure, you shall die with the rest of this pitiful world!" the Dark Mind in the middle of the room laughed. Several bots walked over to the bomb and picked it up to put it onto a craft that would take it out of the control room.

Twenty seconds on the timer. Saezyn laughed hysterically as he breathed heavily. His wounded chest had shrapnel poking out of it. He coughed up blood as he spoke his last: "It has a remote!" He then held up his hand and pushed the button on the remote detonator. The room flashed silver.

The *Serendipity* flew through the rocky formations, dodging countless foes as she unleashed a relentless barrage of fire upon the Armada scum hunting her. The ASP canons had already gone through all the experimental shells that had replicated the technology of the bomb that everyone was waiting to blow. The results of the ASP shells were most pleasing to CJ: the shields on all cruisers and deployers in the initial blast radius of any of the shells were instantly and irreparably downed, making the crafts that once had them—easy targets. The second that the experimental rounds had been dispensed, Izbiq ordered her phytes to join the fray. Over three thousand warrior wasps streamed out of the *Serendipity* and latched onto whatever Armada craft they could find, and then they shocked until they had died, or until they had brought down that which they had landed upon. Many an Armada vessel that day was wrecked unforeseeably by Izbiq's kamikaze phytes. The *Serendipity* and her crew had already done the impossible that day: dropping over twenty cruisers without Purge reinforcements in ship-to-ship combat, but as the *Serendipity* avoided fire by dodging and weaving in the mesas, she had taken a beating. Shields were low, and structural integrity was falling with each enemy impact.

"Two cruisers converging in front of us," Cyra said, "and at least twenty cruisers lying in wait above the trench, we have no escape from this gully we are in. What are your orders?" she asked frantically.

"Keep going straight and keep firing! We need to give Saezyn and the General more time to blow the bomb. Our lives mean nothing if we don't give all that we are to stop the spread of evil," CJ passionately commanded.

Cyra flew straight on, and soon, the command crew could see the cruisers lying in wait, but just as they thought that the enemies would unleash a terrible barrage of fire, the cruisers unexpectedly left their post and began to fly back towards the abomination.

"Looks like luck is finally on my side again," Zekle grinned as the *Serendipity* pulled out of the trench and found that the entire Armada force was retreating back to the abomination.

"No," said CJ, "it looks like they finally got wind that there is a bomb in the heart of their precious abomination. We still need to make sure that they don't stop the detonation, if they do then, they will get hundreds of more ships through their portal, and we can't go through another onslaught like that, so Cyra, follow those ships!" the captain ordered.

"We have thirty cruisers in front of us, not to mention hundreds of deployers and myriads, what should I target?" Linia asked.

"Target whatever is closest to the abomination and rendering aid against our friends," CJ replied.

Linia spoke into her headset. Moments later, a quick succession of blasts from the ASP canons tore into the cruiser that was farthest away. The first shot dropped the shields, and the other two tore the cruiser into chunks. These chunks flew back and impacted with the ships following in its wake. Many of the ships that were hit sustained heavy damage or were ripped apart also and thus added to the chain reaction and spread further wreckage. A full quarter of the enemies' forces were disabled by this clever ploy devised by Linia, but the rest of the force made it to the abomination and were also safe inside its shields from *Serendipity*'s attacks.

"What do we do now?" Valdria asked; an apprehensive look was on her face. Ribus held her close as they watched to see what fate had in store for them.

"We hope that Saezyn and the General were able to complete their mission," Ribus thought out loud.

"Incoming transmission!" Cyra exclaimed.

"Is it Armada?" Theban asked.

"No, it's a cypher drop ship, and they are hailing us," Cyra replied, but it was plain for anyone to see the words "incoming transmission" on the main view screen.

"Put them through and open the hangar bay to allow them aboard," CJ ordered.

The General appeared on screen as his ship touched down in the *Serendipity*, and he relayed the urgent news: "This is cypher ship beta. The other two ships were destroyed in the drop off of the bomb. I was able to use the one remaining armadillo to catch up and get aboard cypher ship beta and make our escape."

"By our escape, you mean your escape and Saezyn's?" CJ asked.

"Negative." The General's eyes watered as he replied. "Saezyn stayed behind to defend the bomb against the onslaught of Armada that rushed in to counter our attempts."

CJ shook her head sadly before she asked, "Was he successful?"

A flash of blinding silver illuminated the entirety of the barren lands of Bergda, and just as quickly as the flash erupted, it disappeared to reveal that all the land within a radius of ten miles around the abomination was collapsing in upon itself. As for the abomination and its sinister tower and even darker mind, the blast completely disintegrated these evil entities and left only a cloud of dust where they once occupied.

They crew of the *Serendipity* looked on happily that they were successful in their attempt to stop the Armada, but saddened by the price that was paid by their dear friend Saezyn and the other five Paladins that gave their all.

After watching this emotional spectacle, the General quickly made his way to the bridge.

"We need to leave this place now!" the General bellowed.

IN THE CRATER

Cyra didn't need any second bidding, she knew the General wasn't the type to get up in a fuss for nothing, so she put all power to engines and limped away as best the *Serendipity* could manage after the battle. In a few moments, she was miles away from the blast site. In the site, there remained some Armada reinforcements, but they were disorganized with the death of the Dark Mind and thus hovered confusedly over where the abomination used to be.

"Why did we need to get away so quickly? They don't seem to be much of a threat with their control center down." Brunick noticed. He was watching the Armada ships that were still left from the bridge window.

"Because when we took out the abomination we destroyed the portal on top," the General replied.

"I don't understand. Why does that make any difference?" Brunick replied.

"Because the portal was active when we destroyed it, and that means that hundreds of Armada big ships were in transit, and now, the portal which would have slowed their arrival is not there to do so. In other words, pretty soon, hundreds of Armada crafts are going to impact with the barren lands of Bergda, going well over several thousands of miles per hour," the General had scarce said the words when one of said ships rammed straight into the main group of remnant cruisers. The colossal impact devastated the witless fleet, but it was just the beginning. Soon, the hundreds of ships that the General had foretold came crashing down into the already waylaid barren lands of Bergda like a rain shower of meteorites. After the first dozen ships, the disturbed dusts and flaming wreckage dispersed throughout the land had caused such a cloud that it was impossible for the crew of the *Serendipity* to see the destruction being caused. It was another two hours before the relentless barrage of ships crashing down stopped, and it was four days before the smoke, dust and debris had settled again allowing them to see what remained of the one-time, bitter, cold Bergdian wildlands.

FOUR DAYS AFTER ABOMINATION'S DESTRUCTION

The *Serendipity* hovered over the barren lands of Bergda in the company of a Purge fleet that had come three days prior. The fleet had witnessed from space the destruction wrought by the collapse of the Armada portal and came to investigate. Finally, the dust had settled, and to everyone's amazement, the scannings of the region indicated that something had survived the destruction. The energy readings were not Armada in origin though. The only thing left in this region that was Armada in origin were the shattered hulls of the ships that had been decimated upon their impact with this now heart-chilling graveyard of vessels. But somewhere in this desolate place, an energy reading was coming through loud and clear.

"Coming up on the source. It seems to be in the crater of the Armada abomination," Cyra announced to the command crew of the *Serendipity*.

"Put it on screen, Cyra," CJ replied kindly but grimly. Being aboard the *Serendipity* had taught those that occupied her stately form some difficult lessons about right and wrong and fighting and dying.

Cyra pushed a button to display what the scanners were seeing. Everybody on the bridge gasped.

"It's not possible!" the General exclaimed.

To be continued…

LEXICON OF SERENDIPITY

abomination: Armada factories that make mass quantities of cruisers, Deployers, Mechamites and all things devastating to humanity

Armada pod: A sinister bomb used to spread mechamites. They are dropped from Armada cruisers, deployers, abominations, etc.

barren lands of Bergda: a land full of tall mesas, cold snow, and long-forgotten secrets.

Bergda (Burg-da): the region in Solbia that neighbors Toria.

buldalusia (Bull-dah-lou-she-ah): a large bulbous plant.

creeb: Mystical sheep-like animals with crimson and silver fur.

cruisers (Purge/ Armada): The main space ships of both the Purge and Armada; they hold many soldiers and fighter crafts.

C'Yi (See-I): The mysterious, rocky moon of Solbia.

dark mountain creepers: Large spiders resembling hot air balloons that have luminous eyes, gas-filled bodies, and they hunt bats.

Darknov (Dark-nov): A shadowy, murky region of Solbia that gets a lot of rain and little light.

dart weed: A weed that shoots sinister barbs.

defected Armada: The sins of humanity revisited upon them in robotic form.

deployers: The smallest Armada craft equipped with shields, they hover upon five engines that rotate around the base; they are equipped with pod launchers, infectious bullets and dark energy canons.

dred trees: Oddly shaped trees with red bark and blue leaves.

Drilgon prairie (Drill-gone): A great sea of grass in the Drilgon region.

Drizda: The village that Saezyn lives in.

drones: Robots that comprise much of the queen's security forces.

fearon beetles (Fear-on): Large beetles that emit a glow from their back abdomen depending upon their mood. They are beetles that are drawn to damp caves.

feldag pouncers: A sinister wolf-like pest that resembles an excessively large, furry flea.

Gu (Goo): A mining village in the Myzex mountains.

guardians: The protectors of the queen phyte

hellions: Dark entities from Ephesia's dark side. They are the opposite of prophets of Trilumina. Hellions are powerful, and they use dark magic to destroy people. They are wielders of fire, tempters, deceivers, and are vile to the core.

hovies; Nickname for deployers

I3 (Intergalactic Intelligence Industries): An exploration company that one time was debatably second only to the Purge in power.

infiltrator: A Purge strike craft

Paladins: Those who fight for the Purge.

mechamites: Near-microscopic robots that make up the core of the Armada.

Millidiram (Mill-ah-der-am): The first man made by Trilumina

monarch cricket: A delectable tasting cricket that is about two feet in total length ranging up to fifteen depending upon the species.

Mussolb nebula: A large nebula in Ephesia. Its colors range the full spectrum, and its beauty can only be fully grasped if one actually beholds said space anomaly.

myriad: An Armada fighter craft

Myzex (My-zex): A mountain range on Solbia that divides the land of Toria from the lands of Bergda.

Nevre' (Neev-ray): The owner of the mining village of Gu

obsidasalt (Ob-sid-ah-salt): An obsidian black stone that will combust under the appropriate circumstances.

Ordam: Trilumina's much weaker rival; the one who directs the Armada to cause mass destruction.

Orgasoli (Ore-gah-sole-ee): The star that gives life to the galaxy of Ephesia.

phytes: A race of metallic intelligent wasps

phytis (Fie-tus): The technical name for "phytes"

Pleothiria (Plee-ther-ee-ah): The first woman made by Trilumina

PPC (power processing crystal): The main power source of vehicles and weapons in Ephesia.

pyrian falcon (Pie-re-an): A large fire breathing bird that eats corpses

Ridiculin (Re-dick-you-lin): A tribe of savages on Solbia that worship Ordam and wage war against all goodness and reason

Seldoc (Cell-dock): The clan from which Saezyn is from

Serendipity: The name of the I3 shuttle Saezyn, CJ, and the others find

sleeper: Hover cars

Solbia (Sole-bee-ah): A planet that had evaded the grasp of the Armada for three hundred years.

spinderks (Spin-derk(s)): Large, spine-covered beasts that dwell in Drilgon prairie and hunt whatever moves.

the Deep: A part of the Hollow that is deeper down than all the rest of the Hollow; the Deep contains many ancient secrets.

The Hollow: A cave below Drizda that contains many secrets and words of wisdom.

the Purge: The only force in Ephesia that has technology and numbers sufficient enough to square off against the Armada.

the nebula: A reference to the Mussolb nebula

thorns of Ordam: A highly addictive drug of the Torian shady side.

tigond (Tie-gond): A large tree with triangular leaves

Toria (Tor-ee-ah): The most prominent region of Solbia

Toria Bondervous (Tor-ee-ah Bon-der-vuus): The slums of Toria Vilorious

Toria Vilorious (Tor-ee-ah Vill-lore-ee-ous): A large vibrant city in the Toria region of Solbia

Trilumina (Tri-lume-in-ah): The God of Ephesia

Viznak (Viz-nack): Subterranean worms that spring upon their pray suddenly and impale and suck the life out of them

Zxyers (Zye-ers): a peak in the Myzex Mountain range

Zykor dragon (Zye-core): a sinister, two-headed beast that will trick hapless people into becoming its minions.

CPSIA information can be obtained at www.ICGtesting.com
Printed in the USA
LVOW04s1103230315

431632LV00001B/68/P